Like a Single River

Like a Single River

Sid Gardner

iUniverse, Inc.
New York Lincoln Shanghai

Like a Single River

iUniverse, Inc.

For information address:
iUniverse, Inc.
2021 Pine Lake Road, Suite 100
Lincoln, NE 68512
www.iuniverse.com

ISBN: 0-595-31544-5

Printed in the United States of America

CONTENTS

▼

PART I

▼

PREPARING

CHAPTER 1

They called Maria Dolores Chavez many things. They called her the Mexican Gandhi, and somebody even called her the Mexican Joan of Arc, which made no sense at all. But whatever she was, what she *did* changed California forever.

For a journalist, it had been a hell of a story. I had written about it for a year, moving from deep in Mexico up to Southern California, with many side trips to Sacramento and LA. It had been a very tough year, and had taken a lot out of me. But at the end, I had gotten too far inside the story, and may even have lost my bearings for a time. So I was through with the story, and I hoped it was through with me.

As part of winding down, I was having dinner in Oakland with an old college friend, Sophia Stockton. A brilliant English major, she had settled into editing for a small West Coast publishing house. She had aged wonderfully, carrying her half-century plus with graying grace and deep blue eyes wearing the wisdom she had won from life after good battles.

Of all my friends, she had proved over the years to have the best judgment about my work—and me. It worked very simply: I asked her a question, and she answered it truthfully, without any filters. It meant she sometimes said things that stung, or came at me off-angle. But time after time, she had helped me see other facets of ideas that I had at first only seen as flat. Down through four decades, she challenged me in a way I let few people ever do, drawing on a deep source of honesty that had never run dry.

We had decided somewhere along the line that we were going to work at a first-class friendship and ignore the roller coaster romance we had in college. It mostly worked.

After we ordered, Sophia started by asking what everyone wanted to know about—Maria Chavez. "So what kind of a person was she, Sam? You knew her, you did all those stories from down there and along the way. What was she really like?"

It was the same question my friends outside the press and media had been asking for the last year, since the whole thing ended. I didn't blame them for asking. The story had been in the headlines and on TV for months, and people wanted to know what was behind all that.

"She was a very complicated person. Most people who write about her either sanctify her or see her as Satan incarnate. There still isn't much middle ground about Maria Chavez."

"So why don't you tell your story? You were there—paint the whole picture. Do a book, weave all those articles together." She was, as always, cutting close to the heart of things, sensing that I was uneasy with the story for some reason.

"I'm not sure I can. I was too close." I paused in my doodling on the napkin. "I don't trust my judgment on it yet."

She laughed and poked me with her hand, gently. "Sam Leonard, you mean you're going to give back the Pulitzer you won?"

I shook my head. "No, that was different. That happened because she let me inside. She said they trusted me to write it straight. And I did, mostly." I was getting irritated all over again just talking about it, remembering all the judgment calls at the end. "But I just don't know if I can get it right in a book."

She frowned, then changed direction. "Do you really think it's going to happen again? Isn't that what she said—that this is just the first of the big marches north?"

"That's what she said. We don't get to choose if they're coming, we only get to hope that they choose Gandhi as their model instead of Bin Laden. But I just don't know if anyone could ever put it together again the way she did. It was such a complex set of events, with a lot that never got written, by me or anyone else. What didn't get written mattered a lot."

"Tell me, then. How did it begin?" Sophia leaned closer, watching me almost hungrily. When she was listening like this, she made me want to talk for hours.

CHAPTER 2

I had been working in Mexico City, sending audio feeds to National Public Radio and writing for magazines, doing feature pieces for the big news syndicates. Late one afternoon, I got a call to go check out a lead the NPR people in Washington had picked up from some little town nobody could find on a map, somewhere southeast of Mexico City.

Mexico had been home base for the past three years, with my time taken up filing stories, trying to write a play, and decompressing from working on a film in Peru. The film had gone badly, proving once again that journalism and the movies were lousy bedfellows.

I lived in an apartment I loved, the site of a far more celibate life than I wanted, a few minutes walk from the Zócalo in the Colonia Condesa. My Spanish had always been good, since I had spent most of my career working all over California, covering California politics and U.S.-Mexico relations. I had eased into a routine, filing a tape for NPR over the Internet once or twice a week, writing a feature piece at least once a month, working on the play, and earning enough to pay for the apartment and send my daughter her tuition at USC.

The lead from Washington told me next to nothing. The call came from one of the self-important assistant producers, Rochelle somebody, who left a message that simply said, "Some woman is gathering an army of peasants to invade Texas. She's in some village twenty kilometers southwest of Puebla. Could be a good feature for next Sunday. Go check it out and call us."

Even though the details were sketchy, it sounded like a good four-or five-minute clip, so I tossed my sound equipment in a hard-side briefcase, loaded up my Highlander, and headed out toward Puebla on the 190.

The Highlander was a compromise between the greener instincts of my environmental conscience and my fundamental American lust for mechanical power. Toyota had come out in 2005 with the first decent-sized SUV anyone sold in the U.S. that had a hybrid engine and 4-wheel drive. I needed both, to save the gas and to get through some of the worst of the back road mudslides. So I kept it and cherished it. It had an extra-large gas tank, and I could drive it for weeks without paying Mexican gas prices.

I headed out of the City at 5 a.m. Always an early riser, I got a bonus that morning: a spectacular view of the sentinels of the east, Popocatepetl—the Warrior and Ixtaccihuatl—the Sleeping Lady, both volcanic peaks over 17,000 feet high. The sunrise off the two volcanoes was one of the great landmarks of the morning drive southeast from the District. Though often invisible from the City, they emerged off to the east out of the brown haze of pollution as I headed out on the 190.

Soon, the second bonus appeared. There is a moment on the 190, just after the road bisects the village of Rio Frio, when Popo disappears completely behind Ixtacc and then reappears. It is a magical piece of the journey, and I never tired of it.

You could judge expatriates in Mexico who traveled a lot by the roads they took. Route 190 was the old, "free road," and was far more picturesque than the newer toll road, the 150. The 150 was just like an interstate in the U.S., although at spots, it reminded me of the best of them along the few uncrowded stretches as they climb through the Sierras or the Rockies.

But the 190 was my choice, with its wide curves through many miles of pine forests and rocky slopes all the way up to the Continental Divide at 10,480 feet a few miles outside Rio Frio. After nearly two hours, with the Highlander scoring about 30 miles to the gallon on the dashboard gauge, I came to the turnoff to Cholula. Cholula, once the sacred city of the Aztec confederation, is five miles west of Puebla.

I drove through Cholula, my morning brightened by the profusion of colorful tiles on walls and the sides of buildings. I came to the village, which was located in a small valley on the edge of the volcanic rise about fifteen kilometers outside Cholula. The valley walls were dotted with pine trees—it was about 6,000 feet above sea level. The village itself was small, with only a few dozen houses.

I saw what looked like two or three hundred tents in a wash just outside the village. As I drove up, I could see that a crude barricade of brush was blocking the road. Four men stood up from a game of cards and planted themselves in front of the barricade, having seen the dust from my car rising from the dirt road that led up to the village. They were wearing the universal cotton white pants and shirts, with sashes around their waist embroidered in intricate multi-colored patterns. I slowed down and carefully got out of the car, letting them see my hands and hoping that this was a peaceful movement.

"I'm with National Public Radio in the U.S." I said, with as much of a smile as I could muster, once I saw they were carrying pistols. "I want to interview your leader."

The biggest of the four guys stepped out in front and looked at me for a long time. Finally, he said, "Wait here and I will see if you can go further. What is your name?"

I told him and then went back to my car to wait. As I sat down, I heard the low chopping sound of helicopters coming over the ridge. There were three of them, with Mexican army markings, and they slowed and circled the area once and then flew north slowly. The guards, if that was what they were, looked at them once, idly, and went back to their card game.

The top guy came back after ten minutes or so and said "Follow me. She will see you."

I got in his '58 Ford, wishing that I could get it to San Diego and restore it. Mexico is full of these wonderful 50's models, some junk heaps and some in pretty good shape. This one was pretty beat up, but had this incongruous steering knob on the steering wheel that looked as good as the one I had on my high school roadster nearly fifty years ago. He never used it, but kept his hands carefully at the 10 and 2 position. He told me his name was Eduardo, but that was about all I was able to get out of him on the drive.

As we got closer to the center of what I realized was a fairly large camp, I spotted a large tent with a painting on the outside of The Eagle and the Serpent—the Mexican equivalent of the Stars and Stripes. Off to the north, about a hundred yards away, just outside a large white tent, up on a platform, there was a white statue of a woman in robes. From a distance, it looked like a version of the statue of the Virgin of Guadalupe I had seen in churches all over Mexico.

We pulled up and he got out, motioning me to wait on a large hemp rug that was just outside the tent.

"Wait here." He went inside the tent. As I looked around, I noticed a bank of satellite dishes set up on top of an RV parked on the other side of the tent.

After a minute or so, Eduardo ducked back out from under the tent opening and waved me in.

CHAPTER 3

She was small, but not more so than most women of this part of Mexico. She had on a bright yellow peasant's dress, and as she came forward her face was smiling slightly. Her face was a little longer than round, with cheekbones marking her descent from people who crossed the Bering Strait tens of thousands of years ago. I guessed she was in her late thirties, but with an agelessness that made her seem older. Her dark, straight hair was gathered up by two silver ornaments shaped like arrows, then fell straight to her shoulder blades.

There was no one else in the tent. She had been working at a desk made out of a door placed flat on top of two plywood filing cabinets. Pinned to the wall of the tent were three things: a painting of the Virgin, a photograph of the Teotihuacán Pyramids, and a map boldly labeled "Spanish Land Grants in California del Norte." There was also what looked like a well-equipped late-model Dell desktop on the table with cords that ran to a generator over by the tent wall. On top of the desktop was a voice recognition microphone.

She motioned me to two chairs set up around a small, hand carved wooden table. When she spoke, I almost had to lean forward to hear her. "Welcome," she said in a soft, low voice. "I am Maria Chavez. Please sit down. Would you like some coffee?" Her English was very slightly accented.

"I will answer your questions, but first let me tell you something about who we are and what we are going to do." She spoke as if she were telling me about what she had bought for dinner at the market that morning. "You are the first media person to come from the U.S. and we want to be clear about our mission."

I started a tape and placed the recorder on the carved table between us.

She began, looking at the recorder for a moment and then looking me full in the eyes. She sat back in her chair, totally at ease.

"We are assembling a group that will walk from here to Tijuana and then cross into California. We are going to Los Angeles to present our..." she paused for a moment, "our *requests* to the Governor of California and other officials of your country. We will carry enough food for six weeks in our trucks and our backpacks. The rest of our food we will get along the way. We will carry no weapons, and anyone carrying or using drugs or excessive amounts of alcohol will be sent back."

She paused, making sure I was getting it. "We are asking peacefully for a restoration of a portion of the lands taken from our ancestors by your country."

"How many people do you think will come with you?"

"We *know* that a million will come with us."

For a moment I thought she might have had a problem translating her answer into English. "A million?"

She smiled. "It is a nice, round number, don't you think? And it will fit into your newspapers' headlines so easily."

At that point I realized this was not some vision-clouded peasant woman, but a very shrewd operator. "And you want me to broadcast a story that will let them know you are coming? Don't you think they will stop you at the border?

Her answer, of course, became the slogan that described the whole thing. She smiled again and said softly, but with an edge, "How do you stop a million people, when they all come at once?" She paused, folded her hands, and went on. "We hope to show the people of the North just how many people of the South there are. We will ask for justice," and then she stopped smiling, "with the force of our numbers."

"Do you think you will frighten people when they see what you are trying to do?"

"Yes, some will be frightened. But some will rejoice that their countrymen, their *compadres*, have come to join them in *El Norte*. And some will help us with food and shelter because they are good people, and because they agree with us."

She was so small that she continued to look up at me, even while sitting. It made her tilt her chin up slightly, in a way that looked almost pugnacious, but when you heard her soft voice, it took the edge off a little.

"But some will try to lock you up."

She smiled again with that angelic face. "It seems they only have enough cells in all of Southern California for 80,000 of us—and they would have to let out some very bad people to lock us up."

She bent forward a little, intensity growing in her voice. But the smile was still there, and it was not a politician's forced smile, feigning ease, meaning *I have to look like this because otherwise you will see that this matters to me*. It was real, and even promised a small laugh.

"You know the saying, of course. "Poor Mexico, so far from God and so near the United States." We have been thinking about this for a long time. But only recently have we realized what the second part really means. It means many of us could walk north *together* to reclaim what is ours. For years, we have come, one by one, secretly, hiding, seeking jobs. Now we will come in great numbers, seeking justice."

As she talked, her hands were moving, then stopped as she folded them in her lap. I was completely off balance, trying to catch the full meaning of what she was saying, even though I was taping it, while watching these small hands making graceful curves in the air as she described her mission and the inevitability of their cause.

Her face in repose almost always had a half smile, but when it became full—when something amused her, or she liked something you said—it was like somebody turned the lights up three notches. With the full smile on, she could have modeled anywhere in the world. With the half smile, she was merely alluring, but not in a sexy way, far more mature, more charismatic, a grown-up woman. She made you want to hear anything she said. Later, for a million or so people, it turned out they wanted to *do* anything she said.

Over time, I developed a resistance to her extraordinary presence. But the first time, I felt my journalist self stealing out of the tent and leaving an entranced boy behind.

"What do you think is yours?" I asked her.

"We are claiming ten percent of the land grants taken from our ancestors in California."

The land grants, I remembered from my college history courses at Occidental, included huge expanses of some of the highest land values in Southern California. "You mean, the San Gabriel Valley, most of Orange County, the West Side of LA—all that?"

She smiled again, "Only ten percent of all that."

Somehow I suspected she knew the present assessed and actual value to the nearest hundred million dollars.

She went on. "We are only coming to reclaim what is ours. It is ours by history, it was taken from us illegally, and today it is ours by need. What other basis do we require?"

"How many people are here now?"

"More arrive every day. Our count two days ago was 35,000. We expect to pick up most of our members along the way."

One of the men who had been outside the door of the tent stuck his head in. She softened her voice as she asked for more coffee, "Please, José, could I have a refill?" She asked it as if it were a huge favor she was asking. He nodded quickly, seeming gratified that she had asked him to do something for her.

I asked, "Won't your own government stop you?"

She looked up angrily at the sound of the helicopters, which had returned, and said, bitterly, "Do you think they are sad to see us go? The worst government in the Western Hemisphere? They are watching us to *make sure* that we go!"

"Are you saying they support your movement?"

"Not at all. But they believe they will win something from your government by letting our movement build. They have not yet decided when or how they will try to negotiate for that gain."

"Ms. Chavez, you know that sometimes Mexico is a violent country. Do you fear that someone will try to stop your movement by eliminating you?"

She looked quickly at me and showed, for a moment, the hardest look I saw from her that day. "It is sometimes the way of our country—and yours—to use the assassin to do what politics cannot. We have taken precautions, but we know that it is impossible to stop a determined killer."

Then she smiled again, but sadly. "We also believe that the so-called leaders in our country will think twice about having a female martyr in a nation which reveres the Virgin." She paused, "But we are not as sure about yours."

She ended the interview at that point, glancing at the flap of the tent where three men were waiting. I noticed that all of them were carrying portable computers and cell phones. It seemed that this was not exactly a peasant movement.

> Broadcast #1:
> *In a dusty valley about fifty miles from Mexico City, a remarkable woman is assembling a vast group of people she intends to lead all the way to California. I met with her today and heard her plans for what she is calling "the March." Maria Chavez told me that she believes she can raise more than one million people as she begins a walk of about 1800 miles north to California.*
>
> *What she intends to do when she gets there is as remarkable as the number of people she plans to take with her. She is renewing, to use her word, the claims of Mexicans to one-tenth of the land values of the areas their ancestors originally owned in Southern California. No one knows yet whether she will make good on these promises, whether she will raise the million people or win her claims to billions of dollars of land values. But she is going to try, and she already has thirty thousand people gathering at her campsite outside Puebla.*
>
> *When I asked her what she thought would happen at the border, she answered with a question: "How do you stop a million people?" It's a good question, and it looks like it'll be one that a lot of California politicians will be asking themselves in the weeks to come.*
>
> *This is Sam Leonard reporting from Puebla, Mexico, for National Public Radio.*

CHAPTER 4

I left, drove back to Mexico City, and filed my story. It got good play, with a lead quoting her about the impossibility of stopping a million people. The print media picked it up the next day, and it quickly went national. Within days, California politicians were denouncing the "invasion" and demanding that both the federal government and California authorities stop, as one state senator from Anaheim put it, "this blackmail invasion of our borders."

The governor of California made a fairly innocuous statement about "efforts to resolve the issue peacefully." The President said nothing and his press secretary only said, "We are in touch with the California and Mexican authorities on this matter." Meanwhile reports from the dozens of media people who had flocked to the scene made clear that the encampment had grown, with one estimate putting it at 100,000.

Once I had returned to Mexico City, I tried for a few days to work on some other stories, but NPR and several other outlets were after me to go back to the staging area and begin continuous coverage of what everyone was now calling "The March." My first interview had made me an instant expert on the movement, since no one else had covered it at that point.

It wasn't clear, but it also seemed that I was going back because Maria and the other leaders of the March had refused interviews with all other reporters who had requested to see her. The other media people were down there covering the obvious growth of the numbers of the March, but she had not yet talked with any of them. No one at NPR had any idea what that was about, but I figured I would go and if I got turned down, I would still be able to interview some of her followers.

So late one afternoon a week after my first interview with Maria, I headed back down Route 190. When I got to the site, I could see that the camp was much bigger. The local papers had been saying that the count was up to more than 125,000, all living in the staging area for the March, with 10,000 more coming in every day, according to "official" estimates from the Mexican authorities. People were walking from their villages or getting off the buses in Puebla and walking the rest of the way to the camp.

Once the word got out that she could feed them, along with what she was saying about Mexico and its claims to parts of Southern California, the bus stations all over central and northern Mexico began to fill up with families who decided they were going to be part of this. Apparently they figured they would get fed, and the attitude seemed to be, according to reporters who had interviewed the crowds, "who knows—we might get something else, too." After all, for several million Mexicans, taking a chance and going up to El Norte was not exactly a new experience. The bus companies had added special routes to get to Maria's base camp.

The inner area where Maria and her lieutenants were based was at the center of a huge area of tents and blue tarps. Those blue tarps had somehow become the worldwide weather covering of choice, and Mexico was no exception. They added a new color to the greens and browns in this section of Puebla.

To see 125,000 people camped out in the open was to begin to understand what these numbers meant. The tents and lean-tos were close together, but it was all much neater than the shantyvilles I had seen all over Latin America and Asia. There was a campfire for every ten tents or so, and firewood was piled up beside each campfire pit, which had been made of overlapping slabs of the grey stones that covered the hillsides. Trash was covered with boards, and somebody had obviously cornered the market on green trash bags in central Mexico, because they were everywhere.

I had been in a lot of slums covering stories, both in Mexico and California, and as I drove through the camp, I realized what was missing: it wasn't a slum, and it didn't smell bad. Whatever was going on here, the garbage and mess of that many people living together without plumbing had been handled with some solid advance planning, and some discipline.

There were about twenty old trucks that I could see, some with faded markings of both the Mexican and U.S. armies. Later, I learned that this was how they were transporting their supplies.

I was taken in to see her, after driving through the staging area and checking in at an informal screening area that had been set up since my last trip. Seeing the numbers of tents and trucks, I believed the number 125,000 was probably low.

She was in the same tent with the same furniture. I began by thanking her for seeing me. "I understand you have turned down other interviews."

She nodded and said "We want to make you an offer. You will be allowed to come with us and have full access to all that we are doing."

This caught me off guard. The journalist in me started looking for the hook. "If I do what in return?"

"If you listen and write what you see and hear. That is all."

"Why me?"

She leaned forward. "Because we have read what you have written and heard your broadcasts—and you are fair. Because you have written about Mexicans in

California with real insight. Because you grew up in Southern California. And because you were once a Franciscan."

That shut me up for a minute. I never thought of myself in that way any more, not since 1968 when I walked out of a seminary three months before taking final orders. "But why? What does that have to do with it?"

"Because we think you are one of the Anglos who may understand some part of what we are doing and may write about it in a way that tells our story honestly. We know that the whole world will be watching this, and CNN and all the rest will do what they do. But we need one honest journalist from California who is inside the March with us and who can tell the truth about it. And we think you will tell the truth."

I realized that she—or somebody—had researched dozens of reporters and had made this judgment very deliberately. I wasn't sure what I thought about this, but I decided to get the interview off me and back to her and the March.

"When will you begin?"

"We leave in two weeks. By then, at the rate they are coming in, we will be at 200,000. Any more would be too many to move from here."

"How are you feeding them?"

"We have worked very hard on that. We are not taking these people on a long, hard, dangerous walk to starve."

At that point, I learned later that week, she was feeding them by shipments that were coming in on a fleet of trucks from all over Mexico. The government was letting them through, realizing that they would suffer a public relations disaster if they let so large and so visible a group go hungry.

I also learned that she had recruited a group of about twenty MBAs and public administration students, mostly native Mexicans who had gotten their degrees at Harvard, Stanford, Princeton, and other business and public policy schools in the U.S.. Some of them were the guys I had seen with the portable computers and cell phones outside her tent. This brain trust had planned the logistics of the food and the travel down to the last liter of milk and bag of corn meal. This group was joined by an equal number of Mexican-American U.S. citizens who had worked closely with Mexico and had similar credentials.

But she had a third group of lieutenants, and they were in some ways a much more interesting group. There were about fifty of them, and they had all graduated from Mexican universities—from Universidad Nacional Autonoma de Mexico, UNAM, the oldest university in the hemisphere, and the largest one in the world with 300,000 students. There were dozens of other recent graduates from the state universities as well.

Later, I met with some of them, and they turned out to be very different from the U.S.-educated ones. The groups had very different assignments, I learned. The U.S.-educated group helped with the media, land grant research, technical logistics, and other issues that related to the U.S. side of the March. The Mexican group helped with the March itself and relations among all the groups that were part of the March.

I looked around her tent, which seemed much more crowded with file cabinets and phone equipment than when I had first visited her. A new passageway now connected the tent to another, larger tent where several people were working.

I started the questioning. "How sure are you that this is going to succeed?"

She leaned back in her chair and said, "I once read a wonderful play by the Danish playwright Ibsen. It is about a leader whose followers are very excited about their quest, and as they rush along one of them cries out 'Will victory be ours by Tuesday?'" She looked out the door of the tent at the hillside, now full of campfires in the twilight. "We must be very careful not to give our people the sense that it will be that easy."

"What do you think will happen at the border?"

"They have already begun calling it an invasion. They will have troops and police there. We have spent a great deal of time thinking about what we will do." She paused, and called to one of her aides who was working in the other room. "José, please bring me one of the cards." He came in and handed her a small laminated card, which she passed over to me.

"We are not sure what will happen. But we know this—everyone who walks with us will carry this card, and on that card, as you can see, are the words, 'If we come in peace, we will find justice.' I believe that, and we will carry ourselves so that all will see that we all believe that."

"It sounds like Gandhi."

She shook her head, the full smile in view this time. "It sounds to us like good old-fashioned Anglo-Saxon parliamentary procedure, right out of Robert's Rules of Order. We're calling the question. And the question is very simple: who gets to live in the U.S.? And the next question after that is how anyone gets the right to pull up the drawbridge after the first 300 million people get in—when 95% of the rest of the world is on the other side of the drawbridge?"

CHAPTER 5

I talked with her long into the night on that second visit, with her aides coming and going. She went into far more detail about the motives behind the March, the groups she had met with before deciding to organize it, and most of all, how she saw the history of the tangled relationship between Mexico and the U.S. over the past two hundred years.

One of the things that she said had been drummed into me years ago by a friend who had studied U.S.-Mexico relations in college. In those days, he called himself a Chicano. Maria used a phrase that my friend Jorge had first introduced me to thirty years before: "We didn't cross the border, the border crossed us."

What this meant, my friend explained as we sat in the dorm at Occidental decades ago, was that the idea of the border between the U.S. and Mexico, which has really only existed in its present form since 1912, was far less important to Mexicans than the deeper history of Mexico. That deeper history, which Jorge called *el Mexico profundo*, was the story of the Indian peoples, the *indígenas*, who inhabited it long before Cortés. The fundamentals of those stories were the long centuries of movement of vast numbers of people north and south across the present-day border, driven by drought, conquest, and the horrors of colonial occupation after Cortés. From the long view of those centuries of history, the recent barriers to north-south movement were shallow attempts to repeal events deep in the culture of the peoples of the Americas.

Maria talked about everything but herself that night, but I ended up learning a lot about her by what she said—and what she didn't.

By then I had done some research on her background. Her press guy—she had a press guy named Roberto Rodriguez who became a great source and a good friend—told me that she had attended three years at UCLA and went back home to Michoacán after she decided she couldn't take the attitude any more. When I asked him what attitude, he said she didn't like the way Mexicans were treated in California. He also said that she had a 4-point grade average. Later, I checked—it was only 3.89. But she was a double major, in anthropology and American History.

She would have gotten a 4-point, but she got one F. As Roberto told the story, she had taken a speech course, and for the final, each student had to write and deliver a speech. She gave hers in Spanish, and when the professor demanded that she translate it, she said, "I already did, sir. If you didn't understand it, that is your problem." She flat-out refused to give it in English, since there was no specific language specified in the course assignment. So the professor flunked her. According to Roberto, the real punch line was that the speech was a strong critique of bilingual education for elementary students in the U.S.

After she went back to Mexico, she finished her classes and graduated from UNAM, but she had to take an extra year because her courses at UCLA didn't give her the same standing at UNAM, so she had to make up some courses. I assumed that would upset somebody a great deal in the registrar's office at UCLA.

She had grown up in East Los Angeles and Michoacán, in one of the thousands of families who moved back and forth between the U.S. and Mexico before the border tightened. She had a paternal grandfather who had been with Pancho Villa, the story went, and it was he who had recognized how bright she was and demanded that she enroll in U.S. high schools and then at UCLA. Roberto said her grandfather had never abandoned his dislike of the U.S., but he wanted the best for her and saw that her future would be going back and forth across the border, needing to understand the U.S. in order to do what he believed she could do for Mexico.

After she finished her course work at UNAM, she had joined a group working with the Catholic Church, in a project organizing Indians in Michoacán, Chiapas, and Oaxaca. She had learned Nahuatl, the base language of several of the Indian groups, and had organized public health campaigns that increased immunization and developed clean water supplies, often running into problems with the central government and conservative bishops of the Church.

She had won many allies among the native groups doing this work, and she was clearly drawing on those contacts in organizing the March. There was a loose network of these groups throughout Mexico, and she had become an informal leader within it. She was also involved with the National Indigenous Congress which had been formed in 1996, partly in response to the Chiapas uprising. She had been a leader of several delegations in negotiations with the Mexican government, which has had enormous problems dealing with the indigenous peoples in Mexico. The negotiations met with little success.

There are 56 distinct cultures and a hundred languages among the Indian population in Mexico, which make up between eight to ten million of the total Mexican population of more than 100 million. The Indian regions of Mexico had by far the worst rates of malnutrition, health care, and illiteracy. The word "Indian" made little sense in Mexico, but the alternatives—indigenous groups, native groups—were all equally unsatisfactory, so Indian became the least unacceptable default term in English. In Spanish, *indígenas* was used most often.

Maria's commitment to this work was mentioned repeatedly by all of her staff, who saw it as a big part of who she was and what the March was about. They said it came from her own roots in the Purépecha regions of Michoacán and from her religious orientation.

Roberto said to me on one of those first nights at the staging area, as we were sitting by a campfire near the headquarters tent, "You will never hear her talk about her religion. But watch what she does, my friend. Right now she is so deep into this thing, she is living so much in the here and now, that you can't see that part of her. But she is a much deeper spiritual person than any of the rest of us—she lives it, she breathes it."

He pointed out to the crowds and the tents, now stretching for acres and acres across the little valley. "Watch how she treats the children in the group, and their mothers." He shook his head, looking quickly over at the door she had walked out of. "A priest who is with us told me the other day that she is not really a Christian, she is a Mexica Marianist—if such a thing is possible. She believes in the Virgin, motherhood, and the Aztec way." He smiled, seeing the look of incredulity on my face. "It is a fairly complicated mix."

"A Mexica Marianist? What on earth is that?"

He threw up his hands. "It's a contradiction—and it's who she is. The Mexica and Nahuatl parts of her go back to *el Mexico profundo*, the deepest parts of our pre-Columbian history. The Marianist part of her is wholly Roman Catholic, but with a feminist core, a belief that Mary represents the heart, the best of Christianity, a mother who sacrificed for her son so that others could gain what she lost."

"Like you said—complicated."

"For us. Not for her. She puts the pieces together in a way that no one else could. She knows that the whole Catholic thing in Mexico comes in on top of ancient religions that revered the earth mother as the source of all fertility. Some anthropologists think that is who the Aztec sacrifices were really made to—not the fierce man gods, but the woman gods who held the fertility power. And so that gets all tangled up with Mary as the Virgin of Guadalupe, who adds this new softness along with the sacrifice. Only now it is her sacrifice and her son's that matter, not a sacrifice to a distant woman god."

It was an extraordinary blend, but I had come to realize that's who Maria was.

CHAPTER 6

In the morning, I went out to see what the March looked like up close and try to get sound bites from some of the marchers. At that point, Maria was true to her word—I had complete freedom to go anywhere in the camp and talk to anyone I wanted.

I saw a family breaking down their tent—which consisted of folding it up and putting each of the three sections in backpacks. A father was shaking off the tent while his wife was getting ready to feed three children who all looked under ten. She was cooking what looked like beans at a campfire shared by several families.

"Good morning, señor, I am an American journalist," I said. "May I talk with you?"

He smiled, but with some reserve. "Of course. We are honored to talk with you."

I started with the obvious questions. "Where are you from and why are you on this journey?"

He answered with obvious pride. "We are from a village near Puebla. We are members of this body"—he used the Latin word *corpus* instead of the Spanish *cuerpo*, with the religious overtones of the Latin—"because we believe in what Maria Dolores has told us, and because we hope to receive some payment for the lands of our ancestors in California del Norte."

"Are you worried about what will happen at the border?"

His look at me was the inevitable, flat stare of someone answering that question when asked in a yanqui accent. "We always worry about the border. I have crossed it eight times and my family has been with me in two of those journeys. But this time will be different, I think. This time we will not be sneaking across in the middle of the night after crawling under a fence with some coyote who may abandon us when the searchlights come on. This time it will be bright daylight and we will hold our heads up high." He smiled and gestured over toward the center of the camp where the headquarters were. "This is what *she* has given us—Maria has given us the dignity so that this time we will cross with our heads up high."

Then he added, proud again, almost defiant, with the line that was already becoming a familiar refrain, "*En todo caso,* how do you stop a million people?"

Later that day I walked through the tents with Maria and her core group, watching her stop and talk with some of the families. Roberto was right—seeing her with children was a revelation. She did not just bend down and talk with them for a moment, as many adults would. She sat down with them at their level wherever they were and lowered her voice so only the children could hear. And as she talked with them, she continually touched them, patting them gently on the back, stroking their faces or arms, running her fingers through the long hair of the pre-teen girls. With them, she listened intently when they spoke, giving each of them in turn more attention than I can ever remember seeing an adult give to kids. Her face, always alive and alert, softened visibly into a smile of such warmth you could believe they were all her own children. And of course, in a way, they were.

The few times I got close enough to hear her, she was asking them how they were feeling about the "long walk" to come, whether they were getting enough to eat, where they were from. They loved her, obviously, they knew who she was, and they would have done anything for her.

> *In Mexico, the plans for the million-person march to California are continuing. More than 125,000 people have gathered in Puebla, people who have come from all over Mexico to walk to California to demand what they believe to be their ancestral lands. Their leader, Maria Chavez, is confident that more than one million Mexicans will have joined the marchers by the time the group reaches the California border. She expects this to happen around January 1st.*

> *I interviewed several of the marchers today and they told me that they are strongly behind Ms Chavez and prepared to walk for the next hundred days to achieve their goals. Many of them have made this journey before, but never in such large numbers. They have high hopes for this trip, and they believe deeply in their leader. But it remains to be seen what happens when they get to California.*

> *In Cholula, this is Sam Leonard for NPR.*

CHAPTER 7

Somewhere along the line about ten years ago, I had decided to stop drinking. It had partly to do with the woman I was seeing at the time, who didn't drink. But it also came out of a calculation I had made about the net results of the habit—its cost, the physical wear and tear of the morning after, and the genetic odds of my ending up like other people I knew who seemed to need the stuff.

But I retained a vice, and in Mexico it was an easy vice to satisfy: I loved cigars. I hated that they had become fashionable in certain hotshot business circles sometime in the mid-1990's, but I loved them so much that I could even ignore the fad. The vice eased itself into my daily life with the availability of good Havanas and my even deeper enjoyment of the kind of quality Te Amos grown in the San Andres Valley and available everywhere in Mexico.

So finding out that Roberto shared this vice was a strong, unexpected bond. We spent some good blocks of time driving in my Highlander, sitting on a hillside during my favorite time of the day, long-shadow time just before sundown, or sprawled by a campfire at the end of the day. Some of my best reporting on the March came without a pen moving or a tape running, just talking with Roberto over a slow-burning Te Amo or, less often, a serious Cohiba, about the March and what it meant to Mexico, to California, and to each of us. That time of year, at that latitude, sundown came around 8 pm. So our conversations came at the end of the day, with dinner finished and enough light left to let the day cool off and the evening settle in.

I used my Highlander as a base of operations. It was far less fancy than the mobile studios sent down by the California media, but it carried everything I needed, with room for up to ten kids in the back. When I had to leave to fly out for interviews in Sacramento or elsewhere, I'd just toss the keys to Roberto or one of the staff, knowing that they would use it to transport kids, food, or old folks, or for some other good purpose.

One night while we were still in Cholula, Roberto asked me, "So what is your California story, Sam? Everyone who grows up in California has stories about Mexicans—what are yours?"

So I told him. My father was a high school principal working his way up the ladder in a series of small schools in working-class towns. Those schools always had a lot of Mexican and black students. In those days of the early and mid-1950s, a lot meant 15-20%. Most of Southern California was still fairly segregated, but we lived in smaller, more out-of-the-way towns which were more integrated. I played football, which was another melting pot experience. When the guy hit you, it didn't matter what color he was or what language he spoke. I was neither big nor fast, so getting along with the guys you were blocking for or whoever was blocking for you seemed like a great approach to racial relations.

Dad called them "Mexican kids" when they behaved well and "those *pachucos*" when they didn't. He forbade me from wearing black corduroy pants because "that's how the *pachucos* dress." The summer I was 14, I picked apricots with a work crew on which I was one of only three Anglo kids. I have never worked harder, but I didn't come close to working as hard as the much smaller Mexican boys. And every one of whom picked more than I did.

The "lazy Mexican" stereotype never made much sense to me after that. I also learned an extraordinary amount of Spanish that summer, almost all scatological and sexual terms, some of which come quickly to me to this day. I could always swear in Spanish much better than I could speak it.

I had a torrid romance while in high school with a Mexican girl—a lot more torrid from my side than hers. We dated sporadically as she moved in and out of the latest of several tangled episodes with other guys. Her name was Rose Maria Luisa—part of her attraction for me was the music of saying all those first names together. She had spectacular long black hair and lovely, soft, full lips. To this day, I can summon in a flash the memory of warm summer nights with her, sitting in my family's '56 Ford station wagon, parked in the hills outside Elsinore watching the lights come on across the valley, kissing like crazy and aching for what never came next.

My exposure to race relations in Southern California was not always smooth, however. My car was "keyed" several times after football games, with choice phrases written on the hood that summed up what some of my classmates felt toward Anglos. And there was a memorable squaring off at a rural crossroads one night between the "townies" and the rural kids, who were mostly Mexican, which was broken up by the cops before anything got very serious. But I was lucky enough to be able to hang out with some of the best and worst kids in the various racial groups that made up my classmates. I ended up thinking you could sort out the bastards individually better than you could by race.

After college, I was drafted into the Army. I served my basic training at Fort Bliss in El Paso—one of the great democratizing experiences that middle class Anglo kids miss out on today. Service in Vietnam was another set of lessons about merit—language and race meant a hell of a lot less than if you could count on a guy when you needed him.

My joining the Franciscans—or coming close, as the Franciscans would put it—was partly a reaction to Vietnam and partly a reaction to my pablumized Protestant upbringing. When I got back from Vietnam, I thought I wanted anchors, and the Church seemed to have some solid ones.

As it turned out, my timing was tragicomic. I tried to join the church in the middle of the largest exodus of priests and nuns and novitiates in the history of the Catholic Church in the U.S. It was a little like a guy walking into a stadium at the end of the fourth quarter with the home team behind by thirty points, and trying to figure out where everybody was going. Even a deep contrarian streak wasn't enough to keep me from realizing that this was not for me. But some of the theology stuck, and I usually thought of myself as being of the Church in the way that thousands of former clergy still do.

I was in the seminary long enough to work out three proofs for the existence of God: Bach, babies, and breasts. Then it began to dawn on me that I was supposed to get by on the Bach alone. It didn't seem like it was going to be enough.

It also became clear that the Franciscans, for all the great work they do around the world, had a lot to answer for in California and with the People of the South. Father Serra was a Franciscan, and the missions were the centerpiece of much of early California history—some good, a lot of bad for the California Indians.

St. Francis himself was part of the draw, as he was for all Franciscans. The Brother Sun and Sister Moon media hype, the repackaging of Francis as an early hippie, never moved me much. It was an unqualified commitment to the poor that seemed the core of what the Franciscans were originally trying to do, and still did at their best. But as I got deeper into the Church, I had more and more trouble getting past all the *stuff* it owned and all the rules about who had power and who didn't.

I came to believe that it was impossible—for me at least—to get past those rules and the hierarchy to what Francis was really all about: the redemptive struggle to act for and be with the least of us. So I decided instead to tell the story of that struggle where I found it, using journalism as a poor substitute for ministry. It *was* ministry of a sort, but it seemed to me a far lesser brand.

Later, after I had left the Franciscans, I had worked in a statewide media effort with a guy who had grown up on the Yucatan peninsula, José Alarcon. José was the first Mexican American to graduate from Stanford Law School. He had moved back to Modesto and bought a radio station that broadcast all over the valley, including in its audience thousands of agricultural workers who would listen to the station at nights around the fires in their campsites up and down the Valley. José had shown me a side of the "pickers and growers" controversies that few Californians ever get to see, and it was part of how I saw these issues and wrote about them.

Again, what was so damned obvious was how hard the work was. Growing up, I had gotten two messages from my father, and he never tried to sort them out or make them consistent. He was a bigot, like most men of his class in that time and place. But above all, my father valued hard work. He had escaped from a class that worked with their hands by working with both his head and his hands, and he never forgot it. When it came down to it, the racist part of his message was no match for the part that was about a work ethic. "These people," as he would call them, simply worked harder than anybody else in California.

A final piece of the puzzle, I told Roberto, was going past Manzanar, the former prison camp for Japanese in World War II. We passed the camp site on the road many times, going up to camp and fish in the Sierras and then later, after my folks retired and moved up to the Owens Valley.

I knew kids who had lived at Manzanar—whose parents were shipped there in buses in 1942, and who had grown up playing baseball there. I had gone to school with them in the 50's, after they had gotten out and gone back to where they had lived before the camps. They didn't like to talk about it, but somehow, deep down, I figured out that it was wrong to make people who were that smart and that decent live in a place that desolate. It was just wrong. Earl Warren approved it and FDR approved it and 99% of Californians approved it—and it was just wrong. It was the first inkling I had that civics was going to be more complicated than my fifth grade textbook.

I finished my long answer to Roberto's question, and stopped.

"That explains the California part, Sam. Where did your thing with Mexico come from?"

"It was what journalism was about in California when I was growing up—the migrant strikes, Cesar Chavez, the demographic earthquakes, the Border, the Fence, Pete Wilson's worst campaigns, Proposition 187, all the rest."

I explained to Roberto that another part of it was watching some of my co-workers handle their lives and their work. I shared an office with another reporter when I was starting out in Fresno on the local paper. She had grown up in Fresno and Oaxaca, and she lived with her mother in what I gathered was a fairly traditional family. She was younger than I was, tall, nearly thin, with short, dark hair she always wore in a kind of pageboy cut. An unforgettable part of the end of most days was listening to her talking to her mother, talking softly, rapidly, moving so quickly from Spanish to English and back again that I couldn't follow either language. Listening, I felt I was hearing the future, hearing her total ease with two languages and two cultures and two ways of living.

What I gradually absorbed from overhearing Juanita's talks with her mother was a sense of how many thousands of young women there were like her, making this journey across the boundaries between their two homes and their two lives. Realizing how much these young women were our future, I came to see that my own contribution would be, at best, to leave some of what I knew as armaments for them to use, in doing the work they would do for the rest of their lives.

"The other part is," I said, wrapping up with Roberto, "I've always liked maps. I always got good grades in geography. And you can't look at a map of Southern California or the hemisphere or even the U.S., unless it is one of those stupid maps that blanks out Canada and Mexico, without seeing two obvious facts: how close the border is and how long it is—the longest in the world between nations so alike and so different. The longest contiguous border, somebody said the other day, between two nations that are fundamentally about economic disparity."

"So you think this journey is justified," he asked, watching for my reaction.

"It's not my job to think what this journey is. My deal with Maria, and with the people who pay me, is that I write and do broadcasts about what is happening on this march." I paused, thinking about what I wasn't saying. "But if you are asking me whether I think all of these people deserve a better life, sure they do. Whether crossing into California is the best way to get it is what I am not sure about, and, for now, what I am not judging."

"For now, that's good enough," Roberto answered with a smile.

CHAPTER 8

After I filed the second batch of stories, NPR wanted me to go to Sacramento to interview the Governor and see how the state was going to respond to the "invasion." So I flew from Mexico City through Phoenix and on to Sacramento. I had an interview set with the Governor for the next morning, so I checked into the Claremont, a truly second-rate but well-located hotel in downtown Sacramento.

I had gotten the interview through a good friend, Bill Page, whom I had known at Occidental. Bill had worked for the Governor as his chief of staff since he went to Congress the first time, and knew him as well as anyone. He had spent most of his working life in Republican politics. Tall, thin, he looked like an investment banker, but he owned an art gallery in Sacramento with his Japanese-American wife, where they sold East Asian art of all kinds. After the March was over, he sat down with me and gave me a lot of background on what had been happening inside the Governor's staff. It helped me understand some of what happened, some of it making sense for the first time.

Governor William Hearn had been a college president at the Cal State campus in Ventura County, and then a congressman for five terms from a district based on that area. Then the Republicans wised up and ran him for Governor as a solid moderate against a lackluster Democrat who started out ten points ahead. Hearn got the soccer moms, took some of the minority vote, especially the middle class Latinos who vote, and a bunch of Dems who got sick of rich guys running for office in California with nothing but their checkbook going for them. He raised tons of dough from the usual Republican groups and from prison guards and similar law and order groups. It helped that he was running against a Democrat who was so cautious that he checked three weather forecasts before he stepped outside.

In Congress Hearn voted about half the time with the right-wingers and half the time more independently. Of the thirty Repubs in the California delegation, he ranked in the bottom third for party loyalty. As a professor, he had written two books about California's Governors that had won most of the nonfiction prizes awarded in California. The first one was about the Governors of the first half of the twentieth century and the second one, which he finished while he was in Congress, covered the period from World War II to 2000.

I had never met him, but I had talked to several Sacramento reporters about Hearn. They said he spoke passable Spanish, was a Vietnam vet, and was still married to his first wife with three good-looking kids. He liked opera, hiking in the Sierras, and country-western music.

He was supposed to have a fierce temper and had actually slugged a Democrat in Congress who had called him a "right-wing Neanderthal from Lalaland." In later explaining this, I was told by a friend who had covered it for the McClatchy papers, Hearn said it wasn't being called a right-winger or a Neanderthal that had really gotten him fired up—it was the accusation that he was from LA. He was very proud of having grown up in small-town California, places like Fillmore and Ventura and Bakersfield, as his father moved around in his salesman job.

As the staff aide ushered me into his office, the Governor was finishing a phone call. His hair was all gray, he was about six feet even, and looked as fit as a sixty-year-old man could be. He stood up and shook hands, motioned me to a sofa beside an armchair on the other side of the room from his desk, and got right to it.

"Bill Page tells me that you have met with Maria Chavez twice. What do you make of her?"

I never like it when I am the one being interviewed, so I responded by saying, "Governor, I am not sure what I think of her. What do you think of her?"

He frowned. "We have a lot of so-called intelligence on her, gathered by our own people and by the feds. But most of it is psychobabble or conspiratorial, and I don't think this woman is up to conspiracy. What she has done has been wide open, letting you and the other press in, letting all the TV crews in." He paused. "I guess I worry that she seems to think she's a Mexican Gandhi. She understands the power of numbers and geography." Then he shook his head, seeming puzzled. "She sure seems to have a keen sense for PR, doesn't she?"

I responded, "She says that this may be just the first of the peaceful marches from South to North. She talks a lot about millions of have-nots coming peacefully into the lands of the haves. She says that tens of millions of people have been doing this for centuries—the movement from South to North is hardly a new thing. But she knows that doing it all at once is different. No one has ever done that as a show of force—or a show of numbers, or whatever she is doing."

Hearn shook his head and smiled. "I suppose we should wonder why it has taken so long. It is an old rule in politics that you can only defeat big money with big turnouts—she is really a politician, isn't she?"

"She seems to understand how it works in this country."

The impression I was getting was that he really hadn't made up his mind yet what to do about the March. This was a smart, deliberate guy, not a reflex-acting, old-style politician. I asked, "So what are you going to do?"

"I want to talk to her, but at the right time. When somebody is trying to pressure me into doing something, my instinct is always to want to talk to them. I want to see what kind of a person she is, if she is really in control, what she wants most and what she will deal away. Things like that. So I'll talk to her. I think this thing can be headed off—I think there are some things we can negotiate along the way, at the right time." Then he stopped, and gave me a hard look. "But she is not going to come across that border with a million people—not on my watch."

"Governor," I asked more formally, "are you going to request federal troops?" I knew that his relations with the current administration in Washington had not been good, and so this was a tricky area.

"I don't know yet."

"Are you being advised by your own law enforcement officials to request federal troops?"

He asked to go off the record, and when I agreed, he said "Of course. They always want to answer a threat to the border or to public safety with force. But I want to see if she can be persuaded not to cross the border—if there are some things we could do with the feds, the Mexican government, or on our own to keep her from coming into California."

"Such as?"

He asked me if he could stay off the record. When I agreed, he said, "I don't know—I assume the land grant thing is just a negotiating ploy. But maybe she wants some help with economic development, and that may make sense given the amount of trade we have going both ways across the border now."

I shook my head. "She says she wants more than a few more *maquiladoras*, Governor."

He waved his hand, dismissing the difficulty of making a deal. "Well, we'll just have to see how the conversations go."

"It could come down to whether you and she can carve out any common ground, Governor. Do you think you can?"

He frowned. "That's supposed to be what I do in this job. So I'll give it a hell of a shot. But there is no way we are going to let a million people walk across a national border and set up camp. The minute we do that, the second million start walking." Then he smiled. "I'll look for common ground, but I don't see us giving up any land."

He got up, signaling that I was out of time, then gave me a puzzled look. "Do you think she is really going to have a million people when they get to the border?"

I answered, "I don't know, Governor, but if she's a hundred thousand off either way, will it matter?"

"I suppose not." He shook his head, almost sadly. "There are just no rules for this—no one has ever moved this many people this far all at once without a war being on. And now part of our job is to make sure that there isn't one." He looked thoughtful. "You know what they are saying, don't you? They ask me 'How do you stop a million people when they all come at once?' And to tell you the truth, I haven't heard a good answer yet."

As I walked out of his office, I kept thinking that he really didn't know what to do yet and that he was going to be very, very careful figuring it out.

After my interview with the Governor, I called a journalist friend who had been in Sacramento covering state government for twenty years. Paul Reyes was a clear-headed liberal who saw how badly the Democrats sometimes screwed up and wrote about that side as easily as he wrote about the right-wing follies that broke out every now and then in state politics.

Over coffee, he told me a lot about Hearn, filling in some of the question marks.

"This guy is a moderate, Sam. He is a moderate because he is smart and doesn't buy into the BS sloganizing on either side. He is a moderate because he hates the nuts on both sides. And he is a moderate because he is careful, he takes chances but only after he has really scoped it out. In Congress, he was a major pain in the ass for the leadership. They just couldn't count on him, because he made up his own mind. But he had such good press for his committee work and, after the second election, such a solid seat, they put up with him most of the time."

"What is he like on immigration and race issues?"

"Not bad, but not that great either. He never played the border card the way Wilson and the others did. But he never stuck his neck out very far. He voted for more Border Patrol, and he voted for The Fence. I guess the only time I remember him getting clearly on the other side of the Party on immigration was when those school districts started taking legal action to send invoices to Mexico for educating "their" children—kids born here whose parents were undocumented. He has a thing about education—it must be the college professor in him. But he said the districts were turning their backs on two hundred years of American history—that what public schools are supposed to do is educate people who come here from the rest of the world and that California had done that for millions of people already and that was part of what California is. He took some flak, but it blew over when the courts threw out the suits."

"Not bad for a Republican, I guess."

"Yeah. When the issues came up as civil rights, he was also pretty good. He voted for retaining the revised version of affirmative action after the national commission report came out in 2001. He talked at the time about making affirmative action income-based, but there weren't many votes for that."

So now I had Hearn's own response, and Paul Reyes' view of him. He would be a formidable opponent for Maria—if that is what she wanted. I filed my broadcast and headed back to Mexico City.

In Sacramento, Governor Hearn said today that he hoped that the marchers from Mexico could be persuaded not to cross the border into California. He plans to talk directly with Maria Chavez, the leader of the marchers, to determine if some compromise may be possible. But he stated strongly that no land in California would be given to the Mexican marchers. Governor Hearn would not reveal whether he has asked for federal troops to block the border. But I learned that plans are under way for a sizable military force at the border if the marchers try to cross.

In Sacramento, this is Sam Leonard for NPR.

CHAPTER 9

By now, it began to look like I was going to be on a shuttle circuit from Sacramento to Mexico City. NPR was delighted with the access I'd gotten, and I had begun to write some longer feature pieces that my agent was selling to different outlets. After a quick stop at my apartment for clean laundry and more audio tapes, I climbed in the SUV and headed south to the staging area.

I hated not being able to stay longer in my apartment. I had fixed it up as both workspace and living space, furnished with things I had picked up in Mexico and Central America. Some Huichol weavings and Mexican prints covered two walls, with a facing wall of books that went back forty years. The prints were my favorites, a Toledo, two warm Orozcos, a Tamayo, and two by David Siqueiros. I had my music, a decent amplifier and a tape-CD deck with some first-rate speakers.

The apartment was not large, a living room, bedroom, and small kitchen, but the living room opened onto an inner courtyard through double doors that I usually kept open. The inner courtyard walls were a stunning deep blue color, reminding me of the "Blue House" Diego Rivera and Frida Kahlo had lived in, now a museum here in Mexico City. My courtyard was full of multi-colored bougainvillea and had a small fountain that was usually running. The apartment was the best space I had ever lived in, and coming back to it after being on the road felt more like home than any of the houses I had owned in California.

But this time, it was just a pit stop. I had gotten a late start, and the drive down to the encampment had taken me until dusk. I pulled into the screening area and met with Roberto. By now, the number of marchers had grown to 200,000, and I could see the signs of the larger number in the campfires spreading across the hillsides. Roberto invited me to a planning meeting in the "command tent," as they had come to call a meeting room they had set up in a large tent at the center of the staging area.

The tone was serious, not festive, and clearly some of the staff were worried about the whole idea turning into a dream of Maria's that they couldn't bring to reality. The journey was going to be very, very hard. It was 1,800 miles of walking from the staging area in Cholula to the border crossing in Tijuana—and some of the marchers had come from further inland, so they were going to have to cover more than 2,000 miles. For all my years in Mexico, I was still used to thinking of that as a trip to Chicago from LA that took about 3 ½ hours.

Walking, it would take over a hundred days. A hundred days of worrying about road traffic, weather, and above all, food. Several of the staff were worried about the children, and they were trying to arrange as many trucks as they could get to carry the kids as much of the way as possible.

Maria was usually not at these meetings. Instead, she used her time to meet with the many groups that were part of the March, keeping them focused on the March itself and smoothing over the rivalries among the groups. She also spent a lot of time moving around the camp, letting the throngs see her and talking with the children. So her time for focusing on the details of the March was very limited. She had organized a loose Governing Council that included her top staff people and representatives of the major church, native, and labor groups in the March. The Council met every night for an hour or so.

Her staff seemed to know when to take a decision to her and when they could make the call themselves. When the issue of the trucks for the kids came up, they quickly agreed that she would want to decide the tradeoff between trucks and food supplies. They knew how concerned she was about the children, and wanted her to decide.

They also debated a long time about how far the marchers could go in a day. This obviously affected the time it would take, which affected the amount of food and supplies they would need. They finally agreed that 20 miles a day was feasible, with Sundays as a day of rest and no walking. That meant it would take about 105 days to go from the staging area to the border. They were planning to leave on September 16—the day of Mexico's celebration of independence known as "El Grito." So they should arrive at the border around New Year's Day.

The logistics of the food alone were staggering. They were planning to provide an average of 1.5 million meals every day along the route, more than 2 and a half million at the end of the journey. It would take between 40 and 50 million dollars just to feed them over the whole march—and that was just the one-way cost. But she had organized the food supplies so that the March organization itself only had to provide 5 million in cash. Some of it was very skillful financial management, and some it was truly loaves and fishes—she counted on it being there, and it was.

After sitting through a few of these meetings, I realized that there was one subject that never came up: the return trip. I asked Roberto once what their plans were for the return—or if any of the marchers were planning to return. It was one of the few times he completely clammed up. "Ask Maria," he said, but in a way that made clear I wasn't going to get anything from her either. So I decided to wait until we got closer.

The story of who paid for all of the supplies never came out, and it led to a lot of conspiracy theories. I gradually pieced most of it together from the staff, and after the whole thing was over, I did an article on the financing of Maria's March that was buried. By that time no one cared much how it had happened.

But it was a fascinating story. Roberto told me some of it one night. "She realized while she was at UCLA that there is this whole generation of American heirs and heiresses who are tired of being embarrassed by their millions and have decided to use it for something they care about. She had read somewhere that more than forty trillion dollars will be transferred from the richest 1% of Americans to their heirs from 1995 to 2045. And she realized that they were not all right-wing conservatives. While she was at UCLA she had met a few of them, oil and software and biogenetics heiresses who were in her classes. She was good at cultivating them, they saw that she was something special, and she filed their names away. When she contacted them two years before the March began, they were far more helpful with their own funds than she had ever imagined. Even more valuable, they had plugged her into the network of dozens of their counterparts throughout the U.S.. A total of twenty million was raised before the March even began, and the second twenty came in after we got started and donors realized the March was really going to happen."

Roberto continued, "The Rockefellers and families like that have always been interested in anthropology—trying to find out where they came from, maybe. One of the fourth generation heirs funded a lot of Maria's work with the native groups in Mexico. When she asked him for help with contacts and the early fundraising for the March, he was there with his checkbook and his PDA full of names. That and her UCLA contacts got her started."

"She also met rich kids from all over the world who were students at UCLA, kids who were sent their by their parents to get a world class education at bargain rates, even paying foreign tuition. There were students from Hong Kong, Iran, Saudi Arabia, Germany, Taiwan, Korea, South Africa, Israel, and Malaysia. Rich kids are the same the world over—they have a sense of privilege and a sense of guilt, and they hate their parents but can't break the tie, most of them. There are always a few of them who care about the right things, and a few of them can add up to a lot of money in no time."

Roberto finished the story. "So she filed those names away hoping that some of them would be making big investment and charitable decisions one day—and a lot of them are."

But there was another side of the financing that Roberto didn't bring out, which I discovered looking at some campaign finance reporting documents in Sacramento. In California, by the early 21st century, there were twenty gambling casinos owned by California Indian tribes. Some of them had not completely lost their progressive roots and—with huge irony—had funneled some of their profits from middle class Californians' gambling addictions into support for the March.

In some areas, the issues of California Indian rights had passed beyond justice to comedy. People would do anything to get their hands on gambling profits, the cleanest industry of all, requiring only gambling addicts and people who just couldn't count. In 2000, a tribe consisting of one adult and seven children tried to build a gambling casino on their property. Another tribe that had sold a part of their land for fifteen million dollars in the early twentieth century was reclaiming it, now that it had appreciated several times because it held hundreds of homes of Anglo "settlers" who wanted to live on the Colorado River.

A few rumors surfaced at the time of the March, but I could only verify them several years later. The statewide audit of casinos a few years after the March also helped. That audit, undertaken as a result of scandals and some of the tribes over-playing their hand in campaign contributions in the recall election of 2003, forced some of the casinos to be shut down completely. Online gambling also hit the casinos hard, and their peak came around 2002, when they began a decline from which they never recovered. But they were there for Maria, and funneled several million dollars to the March.

What this "early money" meant, as it does in U.S. politics, was that she could recruit and hire staff and equip them with technology and connections that helped enormously later on.

Once I began moving around the staging area, I realized just how much they relied on technology and telecommunications. This "misguided group of peasants," as one Mexican politician had referred to them, was equipped with laptops, satellite hookups, and cell phones everywhere, it seemed. Roberto had explained that one of their funding sources was the heiress to a chain of electronic superstores, and she had offered Maria either cash or hardware. Maria took the hardware, and you could see the results everywhere on the March. It was how they planned to stay in touch with the huge body of marchers once they were strung out along the route, and it was how they were coordinating the food, trucks, and other logistics. Later I saw how well they used it for their public relations.

It would have been incongruous if it hadn't become so common in the first decade of the 21st century. All that wasteland, no electric wires in sight anywhere, and the communications van would roll in, set up with all its satellite dishes on top, the communications team would file in and sit down at the ten workstations, and the downloads and uploads would begin, invisibly plugging them into what was going on around the world as well as any computer nerd back home in Silicon Valley.

One day I asked her about it. "Where did you get into all the technology? Is that from UCLA?"

She smiled. "No, it started a long time before that, back in Michoacán, when I was just a little girl." She reached into her desk and brought out a framed picture, and handed it to me. It showed a little girl, held up by what must have been her father in a crowd of people, looking at a television set mounted in the center of what looked like a typical village plaza.

"This is you?"

"Yes, with my father. I was two years old, so I don't have a clear memory of it, but this picture was one of our family treasures while I was growing up. It shows us in the plaza in Los Reyes, a town in Michoacán, in June of 1969. We had come down from the mountains from our own village with thousands of Purepécha, because the government had broadcast an announcement that a historic event was going to be broadcast on TV. In those days—pre-cable, pre-satellite—there was TV only in the towns, none in the villages. So when something big happened, we came down from the mountains and watched the TVs that were set up in the plaza."

She took the picture back and gazed at it with a soft smile of memory, then looked up at me. "This is a picture of me watching the first men landing on the moon. My father showed this to me over and over as I grew up, and I was so proud, as though I had somehow been part of it. A little Indian girl in a Mexican village, and I had seen them landing on the moon. My dad didn't make a big deal about them being *norteamericanos*—he said 'Look, Maria, people like us, human beings, and they went to the moon.' And something of the miracle of what humans could do, what we were capable of, has stayed with me ever since. So today," she gestured over at the bank of computer and terminals on one whole wall of the RV, "we do all that we can to use all the tools we can get, to show what humans can do and how they should treat each other."

From a single TV set in a village in 1969 to globe-spanning Internet connections decades later—another part of the journey of Maria Chavez.

CHAPTER 10

I kept interviewing people I met as I walked around the campgrounds. One older man saw me with my tape recorder and motioned me with his hands to come over, showing that he wanted to talk with me.

I began, "Isn't walking to California a hard journey, a long way?"

"Walk to California?" He laughed. "That is what we *do*! Some of us have done it every year for ten or fifteen years. We walk to California, pick your crops, sleep in caves or in the fields or in our old cars, send our money home, and then we come home for the three months of the year when you have nothing you need harvested. In some of our villages there are hardly any men for nine or ten months of the year!"

He smiled again. "This time, we walk to California for something better than five dollars an hour. It sounds very good to many of us."

I also spent a lot of time with her staff. Her inner circle consisted of about fifteen people who had been part of her organization for the past three years. None of them served as a clear deputy, and she seemed to consult with all of them in daily sessions held after the morning Masses and Protestant church services.

Roberto, who functioned as the press officer, was one of the Harvards, but only by virtue of a Nieman Fellowship he had won for his coverage of immigration issues for the San Antonio Press. He was actually a Cal Berkeley graduate from Guadalajara who had apprenticed in several small weekly papers in the Central Valley of California before he went to Texas. He was tall and good-looking, told great jokes, and was reputed to be a serious ladies' man—but he had clearly set that aside for the time being.

I ended up spending more time with Roberto than any of them except Maria, partly because he was the press guy and partly because we got to be good friends and he was so easy to talk to during our cigar time in the evenings. We had some clashes when I wanted more information than they were giving—her "open-doors" policy had some holes in it, it turned out. But he was always straight with me. He had spent so much time in the U.S. that he could anticipate what I wanted. He didn't always agree with my take on the problems of the March, but he was honest with me when he could be.

Maria's personal aide, José Robles, was also her cousin. José served as a combination bodyguard, valet, and confidant. He said very little, but was never more than a few steps away from her. When you saw the two of them together, the family resemblance was clear. He was short and stocky, with hair long worn in the Nahuatl style, which many of the marchers had adopted.

I once watched him handle an obviously drunk young man who had started walking toward Maria's tent saying he wanted to talk with her about something. With great care but also a surprising amount of strength, Robles took the young man by the arm, talking quietly to him all the way, and walked him over to the nearest of the trucks. Within seconds, he was deposited in the truck and the truck was moving away toward the highway south. I never saw the young man again.

The leader of the Ivy League group, as the press corps inevitably labeled it, was a woman from Mexico City who had graduated from the Yale School of Organization and Management. Isabel Salinas, thin and strikingly blond, was unrelated to the former President, which was the first question she had to answer from nearly every U.S.-based journalist. The second one, she told me one afternoon as we walked, was some variation on "why are you here instead of working for Pemex or Teleméxico or some other multinational firm?" Her answer was obviously well-practiced: "Because I can always do that and because Maria Chavez asked me to help."

Her counterpart among the Mexican university graduates was a young Mixtec Indian from Oaxaca named Hugo Morelia. He had a doctorate from UNAM in anthropology and a master's degree from Santa Clara University in California. He was very quiet and handled contacts with many of the groups from all over Mexico. He knew seven of the tribal languages and had prepared big notebooks filled with information about the leaders of each of the groups who were on the March. He had a very quiet voice and said little in most of the meetings I attended, but Maria and her aides depended on him a great deal, and anything he said about the reactions of the various groups that were part of the March was always taken seriously.

There were no Anglos, with the exception of three of the dozen or so priests who conducted services for the core group and seemed to serve as her emissaries to the rest of the religious officials who were part of the March. All three of them had been in Mexico for the entire term of their service as priests, and all three had worked in non-Spanish speaking parts of the countryside.

I had gotten to know a few of the UNAM group of Maria's staff and spent some time with them. One day just before the March began to move north, we met after the staff meeting. They talked about why they had come on the March and what it meant to them to be involved in such an historical undertaking.

One woman from Veracruz named Alicia Muñoz said she had signed up the minute she read about the March on the Internet, which is how Maria had done the initial recruiting. She knew her life would never be the same after the March, whatever happened at the end. She said that she expected she would spend her life working in the movement which she was sure would come out of the March itself.

Alicia was trying hard to make me see what the March was about. "You just don't understand," she said. "This is a country of more than 100 million people. One hundred million! And even more amazing—almost *two-thirds* of them are under 30! There is no way we have jobs or college educations for that many kids—no way. So this March has to be about more than land in California. It has to be about jobs here, also."

The Mexican university graduates were very different from the U.S. ones. In the staging area, there was a separate section set aside for sweat lodges for the tribal groups that used them for meditation, purification for the journey ahead, and as a part of their regular cleaning ritual. Once they set up the sweat lodges, the Mexican team used them regularly, while few of the U.S.-educated ones did. The Americans had set up their own tents and were almost always in them, working the phones, working their portable Toshibas and IBMs, working on the logistics and the finances of the March.

There was one group of the U.S.-based students who were called "the plumbers." When I asked why, Roberto laughed and said they were responsible for the water and sanitation on the March. One of the heiresses she had gotten to know at UCLA was the daughter of the portable potty king of California, who had invented the state-of-the-art, environmentally acceptable version of truck-towed portable toilets. A few hundred thousand people create lots of waste when they are mostly living outdoors, and the plumbers' group was responsible for this challenging aspect of the journey. Roberto told me that one of the student teams had invented a recycling device that they were using to fertilize the gardens they were planting along the way, in each of the camps where they stopped for the night. The student team had applied for a U.S. patent for the device, according to Roberto.

In contrast with the Americans, the Mexican graduates had no central headquarters. They came to the staff meeting that every morning, and then they dispersed throughout the marchers, meeting with the organized groups and talking to people all day long, as though they were running focus groups. In a way, that was exactly what they were doing, taking the temperature of the different groups, talking with their leaders, trying to see what was on their minds, and bringing it all back to Maria and the senior group.

And then there were a few, a very few, who transcended all these categories. They were born in Mexico, attended U.S. universities, studied in Europe, and had jobs in Mexico and the U.S. and Europe. They were Mexicans who were at the same time world citizens. Hanging out with a few of them during the trip, I found that they talked as easily about museums in Barcelona and restaurants in Harvard Square as they did the villages where they were working on research projects to set up internet access as a public utility.

Taken together, all of these young people collapsed the traditional categories, and in doing so, flashed a momentary preview of what Mexico could be at its best, a bright, exciting group of new leaders, not the cold, economic technocrats of Salinas' era, but a far more socially conscious group who knew the technology, knew the global economy, but also still knew their country.

Isabel was the informal leader of several of these category-crossers, and they took in every word she said and then argued late into the nights with her and each other. I had sat with them once or twice in these sessions, and ended up learning more about what the future leadership of Mexico might be like than I had ever been able to gather from mere reporting.

Late one afternoon, as we were walking back from some interviews with the marchers, Isabel Salinas told me what she had learned watching Maria working among the groups that were coming in from around the country. "I saw her in those meetings with the National Indigenous Congress that began back in '96— she was amazing. There were people in those meetings from all over Mexico, and some of them couldn't agree on how many noses they had, much less on ideology. And Maria would sit there in the meetings and almost never say anything until the meeting was more halfway over and all the initial posturing had begin to repeat itself. Then she would speak up in her little voice—the one you have to listen to—and she would lay out the compromise that no one else could see and then speak about how much we needed unity above all. Over and over, she was able to call them to a higher vision of what they could do than they could see by themselves."

She paused, and looked out at the hillsides, which were beginning to show the pinpoints of hundreds of cooking fires in the early dusk. "And that is why so many of those groups are here—they just got to trust her in all of those meetings. When she said she was going to do something, she did it. She could always use the UCLA network to get some resources when she really needed it, and she became the only person the other groups could all count on. She was a bridge and a broker, she knew how to get resources and she knew how to keep all these groups from fighting with each other."

These were her team, an extraordinary group of people. They welcomed me, but with a definite reserve. They knew Maria had made a commitment to give me access, and they wanted to honor that, but they also knew that she had taken a risk and that I hadn't been tested yet. They didn't want loyalty—they understood I was a journalist—but they wanted a better sense of who I was and how I was going to describe what they were doing. For most of them, it was the most important thing they would ever do with their lives, and they wanted someone to get it right. So they watched me, and I watched them, and we waited.

CHAPTER 11

As the time for departure drew nearer, Maria's actions took on even more symbolic intent.

On September 1, Maria loaded up the trucks and some RVs they had gotten their hands on and took about a hundred of her core group, the people who had been with her the longest. They drove up to Mexico City, and made a series of visits to three national shrines in and around the city. First they went to La Plaza de las Tres Culturas in the northern section of the City, then to the Basilica de Nuestra Señora de Guadalupe—the most sacred place in all of Mexico to Roman Catholics, and finally to Teotihuacán, the ancient city which is the site of the Pyramids of the Sun and the Moon.

At each of the sites, she held a simple ceremony, dedicating the trip to the memory of the builders of the ancient sites and to the Virgin. She had allowed TV and film crews to accompany her, and the footage they got was very powerful. It was shown all over Mexico, on Spanish-language stations in the U.S., and on nearly all California TV stations.

By then, the California TV stations had developed a fascination for this woman from Mexico who said she was coming North with a million people. They had sent several feature reporters down to cover the preparations for the March, and their coverage was getting great ratings.

Part of it, one of the LA TV reporters told me, was a strange fear that this really would be an invasion of "those people," and part of it was wondering if she could ever get it together or if it was just some stunt that would end up with the marchers staying on "their side" of the Border.

After I had joined the core group with Maria at the first stop, the Plaza of the Three Cultures, I returned home and watched the rest of the coverage on TV in my apartment in Mexico City. Again, I marveled at her knowledge of camera angles. The drama of a single woman walking through these immense monuments with thousands of years of history was a great visual display of how deeply she was immersed in her history. At the top of the pyramids and in the Basilica, she was filmed kneeling in prayer for a long time.

When I talked with her later on the trip about her tours of the monuments, I asked her why she had done it.

"We needed to show people—the people going with us and those watching us around the world—what the trip was going to be about. We needed to remind them what Mexico is about, the natives, the Spanish conquerors, the invasions by the U.S. and France. In those places our history is visible, above the ground, and we needed to wrap ourselves in some of that history as we got ready for the journey North." She paused. Quietly she added, "I also needed it, for myself, to get ready."

"How did it affect you?" I asked her.

"It was very…" she stopped, looking for the word…"sobering. It felt almost like a physical warning to me about how hard the trip was going to be and how difficult the struggle would be once we crossed the border. What happened at those places, at the Basilica and Teotihuacán, set the roots of our history for centuries afterward. I was humbled, because this March may also affect our history." She paused, and looked at me, with an uncertainty in her tone I rarely heard. "It *has* to."

"Which site affected you most?" I asked her.

"I have been to them all, dozens of times. But this time I think it was the inscription on the plaque on the edge of the Plaza—the one that commemorates the final battle between Cortés and Cuauhtémoc. It says that the battle," and she recited from memory," 'was neither a triumph nor a defeat, but the painful birth of the mixed race that is the Mexico of today.' It tells us all we need to know about who we are."

Despite the look of deep sorrow that had come to her face as she recalled the words, I did not realize then how personal her remarks were. But I could see how much the words had affected her.

After they came back to Cholula, they visited a bright yellow church, the Santuario de los Remedios, which is notable for being built on top of an Aztec pyramid, Tipanipa. Then they went into Puebla, to the battlefield where 2,000 Mexican troops had defeated a French army of 6,000 on May 5, 1872. This, of course, is the battle celebrated by the Cinco de Mayo Fiesta.

The theme of her visits to the monuments was Mexico's history, which has hundreds of themes. But in these trips, she was spotlighting the battles against the Spanish, the French, and the U.S. One way of reading the message was that they were getting ready for another battle, this time against the idea of the Border and whatever California put on the other side to block them.

Roberto tried to explain some of it to me after the monuments. He was talking about what the colonial era meant and how heavily it lay over all that Mexico does and is today.

"We are Spanish in a part of us, we always will be. But the other part is filled with a memory of those terrible numbers we can never forget: when the Spaniards came, there were 25 million of us in what is Mexico today. By 1800, there were only three million of us left. Their diseases killed most of us, war and the cruelty of the colonial system killed the rest."

Isabel and some of the rest of the staff had joined our postdinner cigar ritual. They were all wound up from the tour of the monuments and wanted to talk about it. I asked them, "What do you think the Mexican government will do once you get this thing under way?"

Roberto answered first. "They will stand back and see what they can get out of it. They will pretend that they are neutral, even though they hate the U.S. as much as the rest of us sometimes do. But they will resist to the death doing anything real about the lives of the people on this march who have the most to gain—*los indios*."

"You don't think much of your government."

He shook his head with a look of disgust. "They are venal in ways your government never dreamed of. Maybe it is still partly your fault—maybe living in the shadow of a great power makes a nation's leaders think small. But these people think so small it is pathetic—it is all about keeping their tiny group of oligarchs in power. That is all they care about, it is all they ever think about. They have no sense at all of what this nation could be. Finally, we have more than one national party. But it has made no difference to the goals of the government."

Isabel spoke up. "In some ways, this march is as much about influencing the Mexican government as the U.S. It pressures them to acknowledge the demands for land and good jobs. It underscores the cynical use of the U.S. as a pressure valve for change in the Mexican economy and political structure." She looked over at Maria's tent. "If we are successful—if we get any piece of what we want—next we will march on Mexico City if we need to. It is a much shorter walk. And the whole world will still be watching."

Then I asked them how they thought the March was connected to the Marxist strains in peasant movements throughout Mexican history. Roberto laughed, and it was not his usual friendly laugh.

"None of us are Marxists," he said. "That Cold War crap is something you and the Russians kept alive for forty years for your own reasons. Maria and the rest of us have no problem with a foreign investor coming to Mexico and making a profit. But we want them to come with respect—respect for the people they want to work for them and respect for the land they are building on."

Isabel picked up the theme. "Look, Sam, we know how the world works. We know that markets in Hong Kong and London and New York can strip our country of value if they think this is not a safe place to do business. We all want Mexico to be a safe place for investment—just as much as we want the jobs that

will come from it. But the biggest barrier to that safety is not a peasant uprising—
it is the stinking corruption at the top of our government for the last fifty years
that has been blocking serious, sustained investment."

She went on, angry now. "You know, I was assigned to read Adam Smith once
by a professor at Yale. I thought I was going to hate it, having to read this anti-
quated old fart who is quoted by everybody who defends free market capitalism.
But you know what? They quote him wrong! They leave out the fact that he
wrote *Wealth of Nations* to explain what to do about *poverty*—not about how to
make a few investors rich."

She glared at me. "Sam, it's got nothing at all to do with Marx. The rest of this
century people without resources will either be refining Gandhi's tactics or Bin
Laden's. Your country had better hope it's Gandhi's."

She went on. "Gandhi saw that it was going to be about North and South for
centuries. He knew that the so-called haves and have-nots would be unable to
avoid each other. And he knew that the numbers in India were so huge that they
carried a weight of their own once they squared off against the British."

She stopped talking, and walked away from the fire, then whirled back to face
me. "You've seen that map Maria keeps on her wall. Look at it, Sam—look how
close we are! One hundred million people—that close. How long can Hearn and
his people not see that?"

Hugo, who rarely spoke in these discussions, came up to the fire at that point.
"Sam, what we are trying to do makes Marxism irrelevant. It is about people and
connections and microchips. You have seen the technology we are using. The
democratization of technology cannot be blocked. The great joke on those who
think they control it is that they *cannot* control a great part of what they have created. The illiterate people on this march can know in minutes what every stock
market on the planet is doing. They can know the effect of this march on the
price of Teleméxico at the end of every single day that we walk."

It was a long speech for Hugo. He was more charged up than I had ever seen
him, walking around the fire, with all the others' heads nodding at every phrase.
"No one has ever tried to put the power of people together with that kind of *connection*—Maria is the first one to see what it means."

"We have many weapons that we are taking on this march. Some are high
tech, and they will help us tell our story and find out how it is being told by others—including you. But we must never forget—"he turned to the others as if to
remind them, "that the most important weapon of all, the one that got us here, is
our feet. Without all those people out there willing to walk all those miles, none
of the technology means anything. It is people power that will get us to Califor-

nia, not microchips. We owe everything to those people, and the weapons *we* use are to redeem and honor what they have already given of themselves."

All that could be said after this soliloquy was what we heard next—Maria's soft "*Verdad*, Hugo." She had come up to the campfire and was listening to him quietly with the rest of us.

PART II

▼

THE MARCH

CHAPTER 12

Maria had planned very carefully for the beginning of the March itself. Again, she used symbols masterfully, choosing September 15 as the night for a final dedication Mass. The March actually began on the morning of the 16th. She was deliberately invoking one of the most revered holidays of Mexico, El Grito de Dolores—the day in 1810 when Father Miguel Hidalgo y Castilla, in the small village of Dolores, called the lowest class of Mexican society to revolution against Spanish rule. The words he used—the Cry of Dolores—are still uttered by Mexicans at midnight on September 16: "*Mexicanos, viva Mexico!*"

So the day had overtones of our 4th of July, because what Father Hidalgo had done was to challenge the Spanish colonial regime at its core. On their march to Mexico City, Hidalgo's forces took a statue of the Virgin of Guadalupe and carried it with them.

Maria knew exactly what she was doing. Using the most sacred symbols of Catholic Mexico, the Virgin of Guadalupe, and the memory of the battle for independence from Spain, she was insulating the March from any hostile action by the Mexican government. They would find it far more difficult to intervene once the symbols of the Virgin and El Grito had been invoked, and Maria knew it.

Mexico had an election in 2000 which had not settled much. It was won by a candidate who opposed the PRI, the party that had governed Mexico for seventy years. At the time it was treated as a major breakthrough. But little permanent change had happened in the years since the election. The hopeless rivalries between the opposition parties of the left and right had resulted in a stalemate, and the new president was unable to deliver on the sky-high promises he had made. As a result, he had turned his administration into the most cautious, do-nothing-risky government in Mexico in a long time. So they were very unlikely to get involved in any political or economic moves that were not a sure thing.

As the sun rose in the East, all the marchers stood waiting, facing southwest on the 190 highway. Ironically, the first several kilometers were going to take us south, because we were swinging around Mexico City to the west, rather than going back up through the City.

The tents were all folded and stored in the trucks before dawn, and a quick meal was served. The statue of the Virgin which had been outside Maria's tent was set up on the lead truck, raised on a sturdy platform ten feet above the truck bed so it could be seen for a long way.

Maria came out of her RV and walked slowly to the head of the March, stopping on a rise in the highway. She was in a deep blue dress, holding a few flowers someone had given her. Her face was austere, but when she lifted her head and saw the marchers strung out along the highway, waiting, silent, she closed her eyes for a moment. She murmured some words, and then crossed herself. She turned to José and nodded. He pulled out an ancient trumpet and blew a few bars of *Carabinera*, a revolutionary song that had been recycled by the Zapatistas and student demonstrators in Mexico City.

As she took her first step, she half-turned for a moment, and over her shoulder, said in a clear voice, not shouting but loudly and confidently *"Mexicanos, vamos a California!"*

As she stepped off and began walking, the group nearest to her repeated it, and then we began to hear it rippling through the crowd for several minutes, as each section of the March heard the group ahead and then spoke the words. It was an oral, Mexican version of a stadium wave, but far more solemn, awesome in the power that lay just beneath the soft rumble of the crowd, as the words receded, repeated on down the seven miles of highway now covered by the marchers.

And so began the March.

CHAPTER 13

The first day was mostly sunny, with clouds off to the west that looked full and heavy. But they didn't reach us and the day was an easy one, inviting the throngs to a walk that was more downhill than up. We were walking through the lower hills, on our way to Cuernavaca.

But the second day began to remind us how far this was going to be. The rainy season continued through September and October from where we were all the way to the Pacific. The rain began softly in the morning of the second day, at about 10, and then increased throughout the day. The festive nature of the first day was still hanging on for some marchers, but trudging on through the rain soaked it out of most of them. By mid-afternoon those at the front of the March had made about 25 miles from the stepoff of the first day, but the crowd was now strung out along ten miles of highway.

We were in the foothills southeast of Cuernavaca, which we would swing around using the bypass highway. We were still at lower altitudes, with some higher passes to go through in a week or so. But here, the fields beyond the side of the road were filled with fruit trees, mangoes more than anything else, and vines with late-ripening watermelons and cantaloupes.

The trees and plants on the trip were a botanists' dream—if botanists ever set off and walked for 1800 miles instead of staying in one place at a time. We would be walking through seven different vegetation zones—and that was only along the Pacific coast, from the marshes just west of Tepic up more than a thousand miles to the end of the Sea of Cortés. We would see coastal mangroves along the Gulf of California, pine forests along the higher edges of the Sierra Madre like those we had started out through this morning, and plenty of first cousins of California's trees—oaks, junipers, alders, ashes, cottonwoods, and willows. And palms, and palms, and more palms, over a hundred varieties on this trip, and hundreds more throughout the rest of Mexico. Short, squat fan palms and impossibly skinny, tall ones, and dozens in between.

If the people weren't so fascinating and the mission wasn't so extraordinary, the plant life along the way would have been a great story in itself.

I moved over to Roberto and asked him how it was going.

"We're doing all right," he said with an easy air. "We knew the rains would come for the first few weeks, and this is probably a good way to remind everyone that it will be wet for the first part of the March. We've got some reports from the back of the March that we're losing a few people, but it's probably just the sightseers who weren't serious about going all the way. *No problema*, Sam," he smiled. "For most of them, the rains are what happens this time of year, and walking in it is what they do every day."

They had equipped some of their trucks—they had over fifty by now—with wide flat beds that could be folded up. Tarps were hung over the back of the truck bed for the children and older marchers to ride under during part of the day, and it was working well. It meant that only a few thousand marchers could get shelter at any one time, but people would hop on and off, grateful for the dry time.

We moved through a small village that was spread out along one side of the highway, and I could see some of the buildings as we drove slowly by. In some cities and villages, the doors alone were an art museum. Red, orange, blue, yellow, green—colors and combinations that could get you banned from a neighborhood association in Southern California for all eternity. Only in Ireland, on a trip there in my Franciscan days, had I ever seen as many different-colored doors—and there, unsurprisingly, they tended to be the doors of pubs. Here, doors were a celebration of the colors of life itself, and there were no rules that I could detect other than *go for it*.

Mexico is a feast of color, of walls and roofs, courtyards, doors, and fences painted colors that Anglo eyes first see as a bizarre joke, and then learn to savor. You can tell you have been in Mexico a long time when you go back to the U.S., and you begin to feel sad to see the miles and miles of beige housing tracts, because they lack so many different kinds of color.

I had stopped taking pictures on the trip after a while, because I kept running out of digital chips for my camera and because I had plenty of pictures of Mexico by then. But this village was early on the trip, and so I took some shots that captured a small slice of the rampant colors: Green treeline rising above a blue roofline, red and orange doors, and a faded yellow wall, so faded it looked like yellow came here to die, leaving only a faint memory of what yellow once was, clinging to the few places where the paint or the wall itself had not fallen away.

That night, Roberto and I wound down with some Te Amos, talking about the March. Then he turned it personal again.

"Sam, why aren't you married?"

"Roberto, why aren't you?" It was the predictable parry, a response that kept the truth about my own history at bay, pressing for his.

But then he told me. He said he had come close several times, but he had always had problems finding a woman who would put up with his traveling. He moved back and forth across the border in his work, to California for his education, to Mexico City for graduate work, to Harvard to do some teaching after being awarded the Nieman, to Spain for several jobs while he was writing a book on the Conquest as it affected the native peoples, and then to three state capitals while he was working his way up the ladder in Mexican journalism and a year-long, unsuccessful effort at TV news.

"I never could find a woman that wanted to live in that many places, Sam."

So I told him I had been married. My ex-wife was a lot more than the proverbial good woman with a wandering man—but that covered some of it. My own wandering, like Roberto's, was work-related and ambition-fueled, not the other kind, but in the end it didn't matter. She finally left because I traveled so much with the reporting and didn't want to get off the bus. She called me a "workaholic," which I never answered to, because at that point I was working hard at staying on the near edge of being an alcoholic. The work stuff was just there. She had always wanted more kids and had three with her second husband. We stayed pretty good friends because we liked each other, and because our daughter usually made it easy for us. Elisabeth forgave her mother and me for most of the divorce, and used the rest for leverage.

I tried to sum it up for Roberto. "I like women. I married one, I've fathered one, I've lived with several, and I've loved a few. They help me figure out who I am and who I could be. Some of them forced me," I paused, to try to get it right, "helped me to choose who I want to be and then to live with the choice. I resist their power over me, but I relish their ability to change me." Remembering, I added to myself that the best women in my life have all challenged me to travel an upward curve, to become more than I thought I could be. Sometimes they were right.

CHAPTER 14

Along the route, every morning there were church services. Masses were given in the open, with priests officiating from the back of a flat bed truck that was outfitted with an altar. By the time they got to the border, it took ten services to cover the whole crowd.

The first Sunday morning after we began the March, I went up into the hills off the 190 highway below Cuernavaca to watch the services. The sight of a half million people divided up into groups of 50,000 singing and kneeling in unison was something I will never forget.

It was also a sight that CNN showed over and over. There was one shot of an enormous crowd surrounding a stage built up on the back of a flatbed truck, with an altar and a cross in the center of the stage. As the sun came up, the priest who was presiding at the Mass raised the cup for communion and hundreds of thousands of people crossed themselves and then kneeled. The statue of the Virgin was on the raised platform near the altar. It made great television—and it also made it obvious that these were not violence-prone, crazed Mexicans coming to loot Southern California.

It was not just Catholic services, either. Maria knew that Protestants are the fastest growing churches in Latin America, and she had invited them to be part of the March early on. Hugo and the UNAM group spent a lot of time with them, making sure that the Catholic symbols were not all that was visible on the March. There were separate Protestant services, with their own ministers and lay leaders, and they were given full representation in the Council.

Many of the Protestants were evangelicals, and Roberto explained to me that Maria had delegated three of the California-born staff to work as liaison to these groups—and to make sure that their counterparts in California churches knew they were coming.

The country we were passing through in this first week was very beautiful, and very sad. The sloping, tree-covered mountains, and the blue, often cloudless sky were reminders of how unspoiled much of Mexico still was. But the poverty of many of those who lived along the highway was also unmistakable. Inevitably, with this many people to draw from, begging was visible, and the dilemma was obvious—if those who had little on the March gave a little, then the word would go out to those ahead that a lot of people might give a little to them, too. We all struggled with it.

With the winter rains, the hillsides shifted shades from brown to brightest green. The California hills do the same thing, as February rains brighten into March, and green velvet hillsides become a temporary feature, giving way to summer's yellow-brown residue as the weather shifts.

Yet for all the scenic beauty of the mountains and foothills, as we came back into the coastal plain in the weeks ahead, we would pass into long strips of highway, with the leftovers of an automobile culture spread out alongside the road: junk yards, parts "stores" that were more like parts flea markets, repair shops, and gas stations. Mexico was not yet at the level of the near-total uglification achieved on some of California's worst highways—the 99 in the Central Valley and the 60 in Southern California come to mind. But it was getting there.

We passed through towns with colonial churches with ancient brown, aged walls, standing next to gas stations with ads for every imaginable remedy for constipation, irregularity, and erectile dysfunction. The taste police had never gained a foothold here, and we could truly see what the global marketplace has to offer the poor and near-poor of the rest of the world: better laxatives.

Maria was always a presence along the way. Some days she walked, and some days she moved among the marchers in what they quickly came to call the "Mariamobile." It was a remarkable, well-equipped headquarters office, which had been rigged up in a 44-foot RV that an anthropologist friend of hers from UCLA had given her. He had retired in Mexico and used it to move around among the pre-Columbian sites he loved to study. When he heard about the March, he donated it to Maria for a year.

It was a perfect set-up, big enough to have a private area where she could meet and take an occasional 10-minute nap. It had phones, TV, satellite hookups, and a bank of laptops that was formidable. I once watched her access the Library of Congress on some land grant research that she was doing with one of the UNAM graduates; it took them only about three seconds to connect.

The route that had been chosen was not an easy one, but it was the most direct route for walking or driving. Roberto explained it to me one morning using their topographic maps.

"We leave Cholula and head down the 190 toward Cuernavaca and Toluca. Then, we move over through Morelia, Zamora, Guadalajara, Ixtlan, and on to Tepic. The longest part is the walk north from Tepic, when we first hit the Pacific coast, through Los Mochis all the way up to Guaymas, when we turn back inland to Hermosillo and then back along the northern edge of the Sea of Cortés to Cobarca and on to Mexicali and Tijuana. From Hermosillo to Mexicali is nine hours by bus, through El Gran Desierto, so we are going to use trucks for as much of the desert segment as we can."

"When we cut over toward Baja California del Norte, we hit one of the worst parts of the whole trip. The road there runs along the edge of the Sierra del Pinacate, along the northern edge of the Sea of Cortés. It is so desolate your astronauts used it to simulate the surface of the moon when they were training for the lunar landing. It will be December, but it will still be very rough."

"In each area," he went on, "we will pause to honor the local groups. This is Maria's way of showing that we respect our traditions and that we are made up of many groups from all over Mexico."

And throughout the March in the months ahead that is what they did. As the March entered each of the regions identified with a given group, Maria would stop and invite the local leaders to meet with her. These meetings became ceremonies themselves, in which she exchanged gifts, acknowledged the history of the group, talked about the purposes of the March, and invited the leaders to designate some representatives to travel with her. She was never refused, and the head men—they were always men—clearly appreciated her honoring them with the formality of the visit. She did this with the Huichol in Nayarit, the Pima, Yuma, and Seri in Sonora, the Tarasco in Michoacán. There was a memorable celebration with the Yaqui tribal leaders at the head of the Valley of the Rio Yaqui, between Guaymas and Ciudad Obregon in Sonora. The Yaqui are a tribe of native people who "make the Apaches look like wimps" as Roberto put it.

As each of the groups Maria met with came to meet with her and the marchers, they brought delegations of their own members who joined the March. We had left Cholula with a little over 250,000, and in groups of 10,000 to 20,000 at a time, the March was growing. By the time we reached the coast, we were up to 450,000.

By prearrangement with Maria's Mexican university teams, each group joined the March bringing something to sustain itself and something for the rest of the marchers—bread, blankets, pharmaceutical supplies, wood, or charcoal. Some groups from the mountains along the coast even brought goats and small cows that they milked along the way.

She had scheduled daily food deliveries with each of the local groups she had worked with during the past decade. Tuesday was the delivery from Veracruz, Wednesday the delivery from Chiapas, Thursday from Guerrero, and so on. As the March moved up the route towards California, the schedule shifted, and the more northern states took over a larger part of the load that the southern states had been carrying in the earlier days of the March. The logistics were staggering, but her crews of MBAs had worked it all out many months before the March began, using her extraordinary network of contacts with local groups throughout Mexico.

I watched her food crew working one day, and it was amazing. They had laid out a daily schedule on a huge spread sheet that filled up the largest monitor they had, tracking each shipment and when it was scheduled to arrive at the March. GPS maps of each of the delivery routes coming from the nearby states to the March, and they had sent out trackers that were attached to each of the trucks, so you could watch the trucks getting closer and closer to the March area as the display kept changing.

In some of the villages and cities we passed through, local sellers relocated the weekly market from the center of town out to the highway, hoping that several hundred thousand people would buy more than the usual weekly shoppers. When this happened, we would come up to the market and watch thousands of our marchers throng around the stalls and blankets covered with produce and other food.

CHAPTER 15

I went in to interview Maria again after we had been on the March for a week. The same three things, and nothing else, were still on the wall of her tent: the Virgin of Guadalupe, the Pyramid, and the map of the land grants in California. I looked at them and then asked her, "Can I ask you a question?"

She tensed a bit and I could tell she knew it was going to be a hardball. "Is there anything you do that isn't about symbols? The visit to the shrines, the statue of the Virgin, all that—what are you trying to do with these symbols?"

She looked at me with the harder look, the *am I sure I did the right thing by letting this guy inside* look, and said "Sam, symbols are how people live. Walk down Main Street in Disneyland sometime and tell me that symbols aren't important. Look at your own politicians' TV ads—they're all about symbols." She looked at the side of the tent where the picture of the Virgin was hung. "Our symbols tell us who we are—and who we were. Both are very important to this journey." She paused and then asked me, with a smile this time, "Why do you ask such hard questions?"

"I have to ask you the hard questions. If I don't, then I just turn into a propagandist."

Thinking about it, and wanting to give her a better answer, I went on. "I lost some friends in California politics by asking them hard questions. But it's what I do. A politician I really respected once said I asked harder questions than anybody else covering the campaign." I laughed at the memory. "I felt high for a week."

She smiled slowly. "I could see how it could cost you some friends. And I can also see that you really like to do it, even when it hurts the people you are asking." She paused, and then seemed to decide to go on. "It is a way you make peace with yourself, isn't it, for only writing about all this? Because you are not *doing* it, you want to make sure that those who are...those who are making trouble or running for office are genuine."

She had nailed it so completely, I had to turn away so I wouldn't have to look at her. "Something like that."

We talked some more about the route of the March and I got up to leave. When she saw me glancing at her desk, she casually moved between me and the desk. I had noticed some papers with lines and arrows on them. I realized she was trying to keep me from seeing them, so I risked the question, "What's that?" motioning to her desk.

"Oh just some media stuff."

"What is it?" I asked again.

She paused for a long time, looking at me, then frowning. Then she decided. "You will be able to figure it out anyway after a while. It looks contrived. But remember, we must make the story clear—we must!"

She moved aside, and what she revealed was a set of maps of the March sites for the past five days and for the next five days. At first I couldn't make any sense of it, with arrows going all over the place and elevation marks. Then I saw the lettering along the side—"TV, CNN, stills." Basically, it was a plan for camera angles and visual shots, and as I looked at it further, I realized how totally planned each day's images were, down to the last shot.

It was not surprising, given the importance she had given to media. But seeing it laid out in black and white confirmed how deliberate she was about images. "The peasant movement with all the right camera angles?"

She looked at me with an almost pitying look. "Come on, Sam, it is what Reagan did at Normandy in 1994, it's what Bush tried to do on the aircraft carrier during the Iraq war in '03—it's what every president of your country and mine does with his inauguration. Sam, this is what we were just talking about! It is how we tell stories in the 21st century, instead of sitting around fires with the elders. The cameras are our history; they are our guarantee that some of what we do will be told truly, not just by the winners. Even if we pick an angle that makes it look good, we cannot make it look good if those people out there on the hillside do not make it look good. All we are trying to do is to make sure that their story gets told well."

"So this is all just a media stunt?" I was getting steamed.

"No, no, Sam, that's not it at all. You are telling the story we need for history, and I know you are trying to get the balance right—to tell it fairly for us and also for those who run California—those we must confront. That is just as important as the visuals. But we must have the visuals also. Don't you see? We need both weapons—the images and the truth."

I was irritated, but I knew she was right. I had to admire her single-mindedness in doing all she could to tell her story. Yet I still worried how far I was straying from the balance she was talking about.

I could not yet tell when she was lying or shading the truth, and it bothered me. In reporting, I had learned to watch all the signals given off by a liar: eyes at an off angle, tilted head, smiles that didn't quite fit. But she was so steady and so unwavering that she gave no signals to read except what she said. It was unnerving, and sometimes it made me even more suspicious.

Of course, it might have meant that she always told the truth.

So I kept trying to get further inside the March and go beyond the stories I was getting from the top.

After three weeks of walking, the March came to Lake Patzcuaro, passing along the north side of the lake heading toward Zamora de Hidalgo. In early fall the lake was not full, but was still a welcome blue break in the green and brown landscape. Several of the groups stopped and joined the native fishermen from the area in catching fish for the evening's meal.

As they walked past the lake, I flashed back on a strange, yet wonderful pastime of my mother's. She had a cabin in the Sierras, which she had bought with some money left to her by her mother. Far from fancy, it was a family get-away where I and all four of my siblings could crowd in with our parents and rough it for a few weeks each summer.

A few yards from the cabin was a small gem of a Sierra lake, Lake Mamie, where rowboats could be rented by the hour or day. My mother had gotten into the habit of taking a boat out into the lake by herself and "luring," which meant dragging a very large magnet at the end of a long cord and pulling up metal fishing lures which fishermen had lost on the bottom of the lake. She would do this by the hour, quietly rowing back and forth so that she didn't disturb the fishermen on the shore or in other boats. On the cabin's largest wall, she had fastened a corkboard, which contained hundreds of lures. Back in my apartment in Mexico City, I had several of them pinned on a wall, as mementoes of her and her hobby.

Late in my parents' marriage, as tensions rose, I later realized, the lake had become a refuge for her, where she was totally in control of directions taken, where there was peace, no alcohol, no shouting, just the lake, the pine trees, the bluest of skies, and the jagged peaks of the highest Sierras in the background. Years later, I took my daughter there and tried to help her understand what a special place it was, for me and for my mother. I have several treasured pictures of my mother, in boats in the lake and along its shores, calling up the best memories of the quietest of times. They were pictures of peace, peace in the water and the mountains and the sky and the quiet.

As I continued on past the lake, I hoped that peace was also what lay ahead at the border.

One of the strangest moments on the March was when we passed Ajiic, about 150 miles out of Mexico City, south of Guadalajara, where there is a sizable colony of Americans. In fact, some of them live in a fenced-off area of RVs and mobile homes with a big sign calling it "The American Colony."

I had been spending the day with a youth group from Chiapas, interviewing them and just watching them interact with the rest of the marchers. When we passed the Colony, the kids from Chiapas listened carefully as I tried to explain who these people were.

"Am I understanding you, Señor Leonard?" asked one teenager from a youth group sponsored by the National Indigenous Congress. "They came here from California to *live*? They're from where we are headed?"

I tried as hard as I could to explain that not all Americans had a lot of money and some of them wanted to retire in Mexico because of the climate, but as we passed the Colony sign, what I heard was the kids murmuring quietly to each other, "*Los norteamericanos locos.*"

After the first two radio broadcasts I had done, I had started to get calls from the print media in the U.S., wanting exclusives on my written coverage of the March. The word about my special access to Maria and her staff had gotten out, and producers and editors wanted to lock me up for their outlets. I started to get calls from several of them, wanting to talk about exclusives.

Every reporter likes to be wooed, but I also felt uncomfortable trading on what Maria had given me. Yet I knew that more coverage was exactly what she wanted. I was beginning to see that the access she had given was double-edged, that I was going to hear things no other reporter had gotten—and then have to decide whether to use all of them.

The producers were the most persistent, but I knew how badly TV would screw up the story, and I never considered them. But two of the editors offered me sizable advances on a book made up of dispatches I could file along the way. One of them was working for WeekReport, which has the biggest circulation of any newsmagazine in the world. I had done some stories for them from California and they hadn't butchered them too badly, which was the standard you had to set working with outlets that had as many editors as reporters. The editor was a woman, Gerry Swan, who had been a former news anchor who had crossed over the line from TV to print. She had a reputation as a hard person to deal with, but as someone who knew her stuff.

I thought about it for a few days, remembering that my daughter's tuition was coming due again. Finally I went ahead and agreed. I made a deal with myself that half of the advance would go to a fund Maria had set up for medical expenses for the March. Then I tried to quiet the little demons that were whispering how this new role was going to cause me trouble down the line.

CHAPTER 16

The first baby was born two weeks after we started out. The captain of that group had alerted Maria and she came to the tent where the *curandera* had just finished cleaning the baby and the new mother. Maria had asked me to come along and I hung back at the opening of the tent, but Maria motioned me in. The father and his brothers were waiting outside the tent.

There were three women inside, the *curandera*, the mother, and her mother. The baby was a boy, and the new mother was holding him proudly. When she saw it was Maria, she began softly crying, and then held the baby out to Maria.

"Please, Maria, bless him."

"I am not the one who should bless him, sister. We will get a priest to do that. But I would be honored to say a prayer for him. May I?"

"Oh yes," said the mother, whose name was Juana.

And Maria held the baby, who was awake, and looked up and then closed her eyes, lifting the baby, and said "Lord God, who has brought this man child to this family, thank you for this gift. May this child come with us on our journey to California and return home to a better place. May the love his parents feel for him tonight be with him all of his days, and may he grow to be a good and caring man. And may he honor his mother as our Lord honored His. Amen."

She handed the baby back to his mother and touched her face gently, saying "Thank you. You have given us all a great gift, and we will always remember the first little one who joined us on this walk. What is his name?"

Juana said "We will call him Pedro because his father is a fisherman. We are from nearby, from Lake Pátzcuaro, in Michoacán."

Maria said good night to her. Her prayer was the first time I had ever heard Maria talk about the marchers going back home, and I wondered what she meant by it. But in the stir of returning the baby to its mother and then Maria's quietness as we walked back to her tent, I knew it was not the right time to ask her.

Later that day, as we walked along, the marchers ahead of us began pointing at what looked like a large cloud, but was moving toward us much too fast and too low to be a cloud. We could hear the murmurs of the crowds ahead gradually becoming an audible word, "*mariposa*," with an echo of "*papalotl*"—the Indian word for butterfly.

It was the annual migration of millions of Monarch butterflies from the eucalyptus trees on the slopes of the Pacific near Monterey to the Oyamel forest ecosystem in Michoacán where they winter, in one of the most remarkable migrations in nature. If you go up into the mountains and find the right hillside, the butterflies coat the trees and in the afternoon drop to the ground where they form a solid yellow carpet for several square miles. In March they head north, with some groups navigating across 2000 miles to Monterey, on the California central coast, and others heading northeast into Texas, Georgia and other southeastern states.

CHAPTER 17

Knowing I was a reporter, marchers would come up to me and shyly give me things they "wanted to get in the newspaper" or "on the radio." I really didn't know what to do with them. Some of them were wonderfully descriptive of the March, and I tried to use them in my broadcasts or written pieces I was sending out. I did it with attribution where I could find the person again. I kept all of them, because they gradually formed a mosaic of the experience of the March from way inside it in a way my reporting could never do. It became a part of the story I didn't want to tell, except in their words.

Then Maria upped the ante. One Sunday morning about two weeks into the March, she ended the Mass that was held nearest the head of the March by coming up and making what she called "a small announcement." The announcement was to ask the marchers to "give Señor Leonard your stories so he can tell the *norteamericanos* who we are and why we are on this journey."

Imagine several hundred thousand people being asked to give you a piece of paper, and knowing that thousands of them would do it—because Maria had asked. I was going to need my own trailer to haul it. But she knew she had unleashed a movement—a flood of raw lyricism that proved, as I sifted through it along the March and for months after, to tell the story with a depth I could never have reached.

Some of it was written by teenagers, some by others who took down the words of the *viejos,* the elders who came along with the rest of their families. But as always, Maria played all the angles. She had also brought along her own historians, not completely trusting us outside journalists to get it right, and each of them wrote a part of the story. Later I read some of what they had written, along with the scraps of paper given to me by the marchers, these young and old writers who cared so much about getting the history of it right and telling the story so that it honored those who walked.

> A priest from Oaxaca: *To see the movement across the land, the people crossing the land with an inevitability to their walk, their march northward. One foot in front of another, not trudging, disconsolate, but with a sense of a job to be done, a job sometimes with a laugh in it, or a grimace at a rock in the shoe, or a tug at the hand of the little ones who were trying so hard to keep up. Watching for a soft, shaded place to stop, knowing that there were long stretches where there was no shade at all. But knowing that God would somehow be our shade, somewhere along the walk, some time when we needed it.*

A poet from Veracruz: *And the land let us pass over her, and the land kept us moving, promising us an easier walk as we went up the grades, then comforting us as we eased down the slopes. And the land was harsh and soft, then bright, and then shadowed. The land was ours, but we must pass through it on the way to the other that had been ours and might be again. Who could know? We would do our best, we would walk and do our jobs, and then we would see what happened. But as we passed, the land reminded us of all we had come from, and we remembered the good parts, and so the land comforted us.*

An old man from Michoacán: *I have walked this road more than twenty times, going to El Norte to pick crops and send money home to my family and my cousins. But I have never walked with my head high before. Always going up I was worried about being caught at the border. Always coming back I was worried that something may have happened to my family, left alone for nine months. Always the worry. But this time, we all go together. This time we will cross in daylight, and we will go to share a part of what we and los indios de California had taken from us so many years ago. This is the best walk North I have ever done!*

A teen-aged girl from Puebla: *This is hard, and we have so far to go still. But I have met many friends here from other parts of Mexico and I like talking with them as we walk. And sometimes we see Maria and that always makes me feel we are part of a bigger thing that all these people are doing together, like a big family. The other day she stopped and talked with us and I felt so proud when she said we were the ones that were doing the hardest work and that we should carry our pride with us in every step we take. I feel that pride today and I know will feel it for the rest of my life. Maria has given us so much, we all love her for what she has given us.*

A college student from Chiapas: *What I believe is most important about this March is how mixed a group we are, and how much we represent all of Mexico, not just the middle classes. Maria works so hard to keep us unified, and to over-come the old walls between the light-skinned and the darker ones. It is such a pow-erful reminder of what we studied last year in school—the irony that the Spaniards themselves were the product of 700 years of mixture of Moors and Iberians. Those poor fools acted as though they thought they were all blond Aryans—and they were really partly African when you come right down to it! And now with the DNA studies and modern archeology, we know that we all go back to Lucy, the first ancestor, and she came from Kenya. So the March is a reminder that the walls of color are the real enemy and those who build them are the ones we must confront.*

An artist from Quintana Roo: *We began in the green parts with the rains and moved through the mountains, walking down to where the brown overcame the green. Along the edge of the dark black highway we moved, looking into the hills. It was brown for so long, then the sand was a terrible yellowish white. Then at last we saw the blue of the Sea of Cortés and we knew we were getting closer. More brown, more sand, more hard, grey rocks. Then finally we came back into the cities of our North and their South, where signs painted with all the colors of the rainbow called us to the stores and the goods we could not buy.*

A historian from UNAM: *This walk has taken us through our history, from Cholula, the sacred heart of the Aztec empire, to the defeat of the French in Puebla on Cinco de Mayo, past the monuments of the capital city, Tonichtitlan, Teotihuacán, La Plaza de lasTres Culturas, and the Baslica, on to the September 16 celebrations of El Grito de Dolores and Father Hidalgo's courage. We moved on through the passes where Cuauhtémoc fought the Spaniards and up into the mountains where lived the Purépecha who were never conquered. Then on to Sinaloa where the modern pirates live, recalling the buccaneers who sailed off both our coasts centuries ago. We crossed the deserts where Pancho Villa hid from the Americans and where Geronimo retreated to build his warriors' strength again. Each step we have taken has been on the sacred land of our ancestors, as we go to claim what they once held in the other lands that were once ours and should always be. Each step shows us the power of our bodies in motion, surging to the North again, as the power of our numbers erases boundaries and overcomes borders.*

A graduate of Stanford who returned to his grandparents' home in Guadalajara to live: *On this journey we are seeing that California and Mexico are inextricably bound together, Siamese twins raised by different families, rivers that diverge at the source, then run side by side their whole length, flooding at times and running into each other, then receding and becoming separate again. We cannot deny that we are brothers and sisters—the closest of cousins—any more than the Israelis and Palestinians can pretend that they do not spring from the same roots, however far they travel from where those roots first grew. Pablo Neruda says about lovers in his poem The Potter: "…juntos, somos completos como un solo río, como una sola arena—together we are complete like a single river, like a single grain of sand." Mexico and California are like those lovers, but at the same time we have such a sad history of so much hate and fear. Lovers and haters, but this journey may add to the story of the rivers that connect us, that make us one.*

CHAPTER 18

The movement of the March had a shape each day that was similar, from tight to long to tight again. The camp would begin to break at sunup, and by full light at 6:30 or so, the March would begin. The camp was usually set up in an oval around the highway that was the main route, but as the day moved on, the March elongated, as some moved further ahead and others fell further back. Then toward the end of the day, the front of the column would begin to slow first, tightening and bulging the column until the tight oval re-appeared again as camp was set up.

If this shape had been seen each day from 10,000 feet above the March, it would have resembled a mammoth inchworm, squeezing in and bulging each night, and then stretching out into its full length throughout each day's march. Later, I actually had a chance to see the March from above, and it proved to be as alive from the sky above as it was on the ground.

The children were remarkable—remarkable to a *norteamericano*, at any rate. They walked, they rode on their mother's (and, less often, their father's) backs in dozens of different kinds of colorful wrapped garments and slings, they rode in the trucks from time to time when their parents could watch them close at hand. And always they talked, chattering like birds of the air and fields, chattering away all day. They talked about the sky and they talked about the earth and the birds and the trip itself and what California would be like. They talked with shy pride about their villages. They played with toys made of string, pieces of wood, and even dirt mixed with water they had picked up along the road. Thinking about the mammoth superstores in California that sold nothing but children's toys, each more elaborate and expensive than the last, I wondered what one of these children would make of those vast expanses of molded plastic and C battery-driven action.

Maria had appointed captains and lieutenants from the UNAM graduates and tribal leaders to organize the units of the March. Each lieutenant was responsible for a unit of ten thousand marchers. Each unit bore the name of a Mexican hero, general, or pre-Columbian god or goddess. The food, the line of march, the medical care were all organized on this "tens system," as they called it. So each lieutenant was in charge of a small village on the move, reporting to a "March captain" who was in charge of ten villages. People were given armbands when they joined the March and told which group they belonged to.

One day when Roberto was explaining how this worked to me, I remembered some Old Testament and asked "Doesn't this have something to do with Moses?"

He laughed and said "She told us to memorize this, but," and he pulled out a little notebook he carried in his shoulder pack, "but I can never remember it. Scripture was not my thing in school." He flipped through the pages, then stopped and jabbed at a page. "Here it is: Exodus: 18:25: 'And Moses chose able men out of all Israel, and made them heads over the people, rulers of thousands, rulers of hundreds, rulers of fifties, and rulers of tens.'"

And so did Maria. Hers was not an exodus—but a return to a part of what she defined as homeland. And her organization of the groups was extraordinary, as it had to be to keep order.

To keep the groups cohesive, in the evenings as the groups grew larger, there were singing contests and even some cooking contests among the groups. One night I attended a combined sing-off/cook-off between the Benito Juarez unit and the Cuauhtémoc unit. It was uproarious good fun, with twenty thousand voices raised in singing ancient Huichol songs and the smells of cooking all mingled together on a small hillside outside Morelia. It was a cool evening, and nearly everyone had a coat, serape, or blanket wrapped around themselves.

The contest was remarkable. What they had managed to do with the daily allotment of beans, rice, tortillas, and a few baskets of fish was unbelievable, and would do credit to any Mexico City restaurant. Someone with a warped sense of humor decided the "*gringo journalisto*" should be the judge, so I started tasting. I quickly realized that both on the merits and in the interests of good will I'd better declare a tie. When I did, immense cheers rose from both sides.

Later that evening, I had a question for Roberto which I had been holding back. Now seemed like the right time. "Roberto—why did the team pick me to do this coverage from inside?"

Roberto smiled. "I wondered when you were going to get around to this. *She* picked you, Sam. We had three students start a year ago, going through clips on the Internet from every Spanish-speaking Anglo journalist in California. There are 310 of you, if you want to know. We filtered it down to 16 and that's when the Franciscan thing came up. She went for you from the first meeting. Some of our team wanted several other choices, but she stayed with you from the first."

"You're flattering me, man, and it isn't good flattery—you're saying all that made me stand out was that I dropped out of seminary a hundred years ago?"

"No, Sam. It was what you had written that got you into the cut. It was also your age that made some of us feel you wouldn't jump on every mistake we made trying to get a big scoop, whether it made us look bad or not."

I laughed, not happily. "Great—so now it's my failure in the seminary *and* my being an old fart that recommended me. I'd hate the see the guys you turned down."

"They were mostly women, Sam, and two of them were gorgeous, you ugly bastard."

He refused to take me seriously, so I gave up trying to be offended. Whatever her reasons, I was here and it was the story of a lifetime. I guess I owed the Franciscans more than I thought—although if I had stayed in, obviously I never would have done the story.

CHAPTER 19

The last hurricane of the season was named Laura, and she did not start out like a song. She was a bitch, forming out in the lower Eastern Pacific, a bastard child of that year's La Niña water temperatures. Maria's meteorological staff had been watching her from the first, using their satellite links to monitor the three-day plots to see whether she would come ashore anywhere near the March.

We had progressed up past Guadalajara to just outside Tepic. Roberto had alerted me to the possibility of a bad landfall and I found my way to the "weather RV," as the satellite vehicle with the weather links had inevitably been named. As I ducked inside out of the rain, I could see Maria and most of her core staff crowded around the biggest monitor with four satellite shots arrayed in quadrants. The lights from the monitors cast a shifting glow over the room, as the satellite continually refreshed the radar map on the screen. Everyone was so quiet I could hear the friction of the computer operator's fingers on the pad as he moved the mouse.

Manuel Carranza was the head guy in the RV. Roberto told me he had a Ph.D from the University of Hawaii in meteorology and knew more about Pacific hurricanes than anyone in Mexico. He finally spoke to Maria, quietly.

"The U.S. National Weather Service has three plots, depending on the winds from the west. I have two more plots, and the last one is the one that really *nos chingas* the worst." He hit two keys on his keyboard and two dotted lines were imposed on the map. One led from the eye of Laura up into the Gulf of Cortés, and the other swung further south, right into Nayarit.

It was where we expected to be in two days.

"Either way, we're going to take a hit," said Manuel. "But the southern plot is the one that scares me, because it comes ashore with 130-knot winds. We don't want any kids or old people out in that if it happens. We don't want *anybody* out in that if we can help it."

Maria closed her eyes for several seconds, and then spoke. "When will you know for sure?"

"We're getting downloads every hour," said Manuel. "We're replotting every time we get new wind data and a new satellite shot. I can give you an update at midnight, but we won't really know until twelve hours or so before landfall where it is coming in. We just won't know." He shook his head, angry that he couldn't give her a better fix on it.

But Maria pressed him. "What's your best guess? You know more about this than the guys at the Weather Service—what's your best guess, Manuel?" She was almost begging him, hoping for the best.

He didn't want to look at her. "Maria, it's going to come very near us. We need to use the next two days to get ready. The March has to stop and we need to get ready."

Maria made a choking sound, and swayed, and the group moved toward her. She stood up and waved them off. "No, I'm OK. Let's move into the main tent and talk about what to do," she said, already moving toward the door.

They talked for two hours, looking at all the options. They talked about digging shelters, they talked about trying to take cover in the nearest town, San Pedro, they talked about everything they could think of. But the bottom line was that they had almost a half million people out in the open and finding shelter in forty-eight hours for that many people was an impossible task.

The trickiest part of it was getting to higher ground, while at the same time staying away from hills that would turn into mudslides and streams that would turn into rivers that could sweep people out into the Pacific in a matter of minutes. They had loaded the latest topographical maps of the area onto the big desktop server that Maria used as her base computer, and they kept zooming in and out, trying to find the safest place. Finally they picked a sheltered valley that was about a day's walk from where we were, back up into the hills.

Maria was worried about the loss of life, but she was also upset at losing four or five days as a result of leaving the main route and digging in. They had planned the trip carefully, and this was going to throw their food and travel calculations off.

We turned inland, and after a hard struggle through coastal hills rising into the high ranges beyond, we got to the site they had picked, going uphill through heavier and heavier rains and slippery dirt roads. I had to use the Highlander six times to pull small trucks out of the mud. It was about four in the afternoon, and almost as dark as it would be well after sundown on a normal day.

Manuel had been right. Laura was going to make landfall about three miles up the coast from where we would have been if we had kept on the planned route.

Maria was furious that afternoon, because the governor of Jalisco had called offering to airlift her out with his personal helicopter. "Do they think they can lure me off of this march with a *helicopter*?!" she spat at me as I came into her tent after she had gotten the call. "How dumb do they think I am?!"

As I started to answer her, José came running into the tent. "Maria, come here, you've got to see what they found."

We slipped and slid our way up the hill toward a huge rock at the base of a cliff that was covered with vegetation. Maria went around the corner of the rock, and stood facing the cliff wall. A deep cave had been cut into it, clearly manmade, with enough trees and brush in front of it that it was a low-grade miracle that anyone had found it. The crew that had found it had cut away some of the brush to make an entrance.

"How bad is it—what about bats?" she asked.

"We haven't been in it yet. We're going in now with lights and smoke."

"Hurry, the rains are getting worse. Manuel says we only have four or five hours or so left, and we need to know how many people will fit in there."

As the advance party headed back into the cave with torches, the entrance was lit up and then slowly darkened as the lead group passed further inside. From the mouth of the cave we could see the glow from the torches fading as they moved deeper into the cave. A few shadows were cast on the small part of the wall of the cave we could see from below, then it was dark.

A few synapses flashed, and for a moment, I was back in my History of Civilization class at Occidental, sitting in the auditorium and hearing the lecture on Plato's great essay about the cave and the nature of reality.

But this was not some abstract philosophical debate; it was life and death for hundreds of thousands of people. What would Plato have thought about the March; what would the Greeks have made of the theory of passive resistance? Glorifying war and sacrifice of the individual for the community, what would they have thought of moving one million people across boundaries for peaceful purposes?

Maria's team worked for another hour checking out the cave, chasing out a few bats. As they were exploring it, they found altars and tools that were definitely pre-Columbian. I went back down to the floor of the valley and helped tie down the supplies. Maria was hard at work when I caught up with her as the first large group was moving inside. The rains were coming harder, and she was helping a group of children get inside the mouth of the cave.

She turned and saw me and said, clearly delighted, "Sheltered by our ancestors, Sam. I had begun to worry that God and the gods had both forgotten us. But now I know we will be OK."

I could only laugh at the way she had put it. "Maria, you need to explain your theology to me some day when it isn't raining so hard. Are you just not monotheistic, or what?"

"Oh Sam, you are reverting to your Protestant roots. God created the gods to give us something easier to understand. It's so simple, really. Come on, get inside."

After an hour of packing them in, more than 50,000 people found room inside—almost all of the younger children and the oldest of the marchers. The rest of us were dug into the hill outside the cave where the rocks were largest. The truck crew had driven the trucks and RVs into a small group of trees at the mouth of the valley and had tied them down with the strongest ropes they could find. As the darkest hours of night finally came, we felt the winds picking up. We could hear trees breaking in the valley below us where the mouth of the valley was open to the west. The winds blew harder and harder for two hours, then began to fade so quickly it seemed like an illusion.

"It is the eye," Manuel said quietly, "the eye is passing over us."

It was still pitch dark, but the quieting of the storm made it seem as though it was growing brighter. After a half an hour or so, the winds started to pick up again and then a faint glow became visible at the far end of the valley, which faced east. It was the sunrise, and it brought more wind, but nowhere near as bad as we had felt before we found the cave.

"It's heading south," said Manuel. "God help the people down in Michoacán. That's where some of the slides were worst when Greg came ashore in 1999."

Maria led the group in prayers, both of thanksgiving and for the people still in the path of Laura. As the sun came up, we headed back down to see what had happened to the trucks.

CHAPTER 20

We got back on the route after a day of cleaning up after the hurricane and thanksgiving services. The only damages were windshields on a few of the trucks and a few broken arms and scrapes among the marchers who had been under the trees near the opening to the valley. We were only a few days behind schedule and the mood of the marchers seemed good, grateful for their escape from the worst of the hurricane.

Maria invited me over to her RV, once she began using it regularly now, every other night or so, to talk about the day and how the March had gone. It wasn't an interview as much as a wind-down, for her, obviously, because she had been carrying the load of the whole thing. For me, it was also a good time, because I was out and around the March trying to capture who these people were and what the March was about. We talked about what had happened during the day, problems that would come up tomorrow or the next day, and how she was going to work with her team to resolve them. It was all on background, we had agreed on that from the start, and she very rarely said that I couldn't use something she had mentioned.

We had gotten past my irritation at her manipulation of the media. I knew it was part of her whole story, and I was trying to work out how I fit into the big picture of media manipulation. So getting to know her at close range seemed part of the job.

And the fact was that I also enjoyed her company. When we met at the end of the day, she was tired, but she had great reserves of energy. I came to realize that our talks and her time with the children were both part of her recharging at the end of each day.

When I met with her in the evenings, it was usually in her RV. She had decorated the inside with native peoples' art from all over Mexico, so it had a warmth and personality that made it her home, not just a base of operations. Her own communications equipment was all rigged in the back, where the bed went—she told me she was small enough to sleep in the tipped-back drivers' seat, so she didn't need the oversize bedroom.

When we talked, she sat in one of the two captain's chairs in the mid-section of the RV and I took the other. We usually had coffee—she had an inexhaustible supply, she said, and admitted the addiction to strong coffee which we shared.

José and some of the young men he had recruited as guards were usually sitting outside the door. They talked in a soft murmur, and whenever I could hear what they were saying, it was always the same topic: they were replaying the day, what had gone well, what had been problems, how to anticipate problems the next time. If they had been in the army, it would have been called an after-action report. But for them, it was just winding down the day to see how the next one could be better.

The smells of the end of the day came in through the open door: the camp-fires, the coffee, a few lingering smells of dinner cooked over open fires. And, less pleasantly, the diesel smell from the other RVs that were hooked up to the rest of the world through their communications set-up.

One evening she started out by asking me when I was going to write my novel. "All journalists are trying to write a novel. So when is yours coming out?"

"I have read too many good ones and too many bad ones to try. I'm afraid mine would end up one of the bad ones. I am better at the short stuff."

"What is your favorite?"

"I have too many favorites. Do you know William Brammer's book *The Gay Place?*"

"Never heard of it," she said.

"It's three novellas really, set in Texas politics in the late 1950's. Brammer worked for Lyndon Johnson and it gets LBJ down perfectly—he's the Governor in the novellas."

She laughed. "Texas in the 50's—now there was a scene that was great for Latinos. Why don't you write about the differences between Texas politics in the 1990s and California politics—there's a novel."

"Too close to home for me," I said.

"What's your favorite line from a novel?"

I started to answer, and then stopped. "If I tell you, I have to apologize first."

"Why, is it sexist?"

"No—it's Eurocentric."

She laughed. "What else could you be, *norteamericano?* Tell me."

I closed my eyes and recited *"And her long fair hair was girlish, and girlish, and touched, with the wonder of mortal beauty, her face."*

She smiled and said softly, shaking her head, "You're pathetic. A romantic and a blondist, both. Who wrote that?"

"James Joyce, from *A Portrait of The Artist as a Young Man*. So what's your favorite?"

"Novel or line?"

"Both."

"Novel, probably Carlos Fuentes' *Terra Nostra*. No one line, really. Maybe the section in *Labyrinth of Solitude*, by Octavio Paz, on the meaning of *chingar*. That is so funny and so tragic and so dead right about Mexico. I love that."

"I'm glad you didn't say *The Old Gringo* was your favorite."

She laughed. "You aren't old, Sam—you're just safely into middle age. That's not a bad book, not a bad movie, either, but not one of his best."

Then she shifted, quieter. "Tell me about your parents, Sam. I always think I can know people better if I understand who their parents were."

"You and Freud and a few other people."

"Maybe. But tell me."

"My Dad was a teacher. He worked hard, he valued hard work, he believed in education above all. It changed his life and he believed it could change other kids' lives. I went to a reunion once attended by a lot of his former students. All night long, they kept coming up to me and telling me how much he meant to them— that he pushed them to do better than they thought they could." I paused, thinking. "On the things this March is about, he was fundamentally prejudiced, but he was fair. If that makes any sense."

She smiled. "I had an English teacher like that. You could tell he didn't expect much of us—he started out thinking we were inferior. But when he saw the spark, he would help you. He gave me a book by Isabel Allende one time—I guess that was as far into Hispanic literature as he got. And he stopped the Anglos from making fun of us whenever he caught them at it. They still did it, but not around him."

"That's it—that's part of who my father was. He was very demanding. He had high standards." I paused, remembering. "My mother did, too, but she was easier to be with."

"What did she give you?"

"The music, all the music. She was our church organist and played the piano at home, for herself sometimes, and always at holidays. She was reserved, like all upper middle class women of her time—but she had her passions. The music was there all her life, but her later love was the Dodgers. It was a total commitment with her, and Vin Scully was a near-religious figure in her home in the retirement village where she lived." Then I did my poor imitation of the best voice in radio: 'Hello, everybody. It's time to pull up a chair and listen to Dodger baseball.'" I went on, remembering. "The wonderful thing is she lived long enough to see them win the World Series in '88. She died in December of '88."

I asked her, "And yours?"

She said, quietly, "It is such a trite story, and so powerful. They worked incredibly hard so that their kids would have a better life. And we did. End of story."

"Come on—there's more to it than that."

"Yes, I guess so. Mama was stronger than most mothers from Michoacán. She had gotten it from my grandfather who had all these wonderful stories about Pancho Villa and the revolution. No one knew if they were true, but Mama revered him and when he would come it was like fiesta all the time he was there. He seemed huge—most of the men in my family are very short and he was almost six feet tall. Papa Pedro—what a man! He was the one who made us come up to LA for my high school. My father didn't want to come but Papa Pedro insisted and then Mama took over. My father gave in, and once we got up north, he really did fairly well. He had a little gardening company he ran out of East LA that did hundreds of the lawns and yards in Pasadena and Altadena."

"There was a day…" she said, and then paused, and reached up, with that breathtaking move that women do, lifting her arms over her head and unclasping something behind her neck, and took it off. She cupped it in her hand and gave it to me. I held it up and then recognized it.

"It's a Phi Beta Kappa key. From UCLA?"

"Right." She was watching me, smiling her about-to-laugh smile. "Got one?"

"As a matter of fact I do—or I used to, before I lost it in a move. Why do you wear it?"

She answered quickly, the smile fading. "So one or two of those hot shots we are going to meet with in California will know I'm not just some scruffy little Indian girl from Michoacán. And to remind myself how proud my father was the day I won it."

"Maybe you could just have somebody carve you a chip of wood and pin it to your shoulder."

She laughed out loud, delighted at my irreverence. "Sam, you're accusing me of being aggressive! I would never want to be aggressive—it wouldn't be lady-like." She said the last word as though it were a synonym for disgusting.

She paused. "When I left UCLA—" a brief cloud of sadness seemed to pass over her face—"my father was very upset for a while because he had been in the U.S. long enough to know what it meant for a little Latina kid to graduate from a place like that. He was so proud when I got in—he could never understand why I didn't stay."

"Why didn't you?"

"It was how we were treated, even then, and I had some very messy family things—"she suddenly stood up frowning and brushed her hands together dismissively—"and we are not going to talk about them now, Sam. I have to go to work."

It had been such an easy, almost intimate conversation, and she was ending it so abruptly. Obviously, we had gotten too close to some very painful stuff for her. I wondered if it would come up again, or if it was just another of Maria's secrets.

CHAPTER 21

After recovering from the hurricane, we had continued up the 15 headed toward Mazatlán. As we went over the next two weeks' route in detail for the first time, a glaring problem almost jumped off the map. I asked the obvious question.

"What is she going to do about Sinaloa?"

Sinaloa, a long coastal state shaped like an alligator with a fat tail, had become the drug capital of Mexico, where growing, processing, and distribution headquarters of the major Mexican drug cartel had been located since the late '90s. It was a very lucrative business, involving marijuana grown in the hills, major heroin processing, and even some cocaine distribution centers which received product from Colombia and other growing centers around Latin America. Some U.S. authorities thought that the Sinaloa cartel had reached the critical mass of the Medillin cartel in Colombia in the early 90's. The marchers' route up the coast went right through the strongholds of the cartel.

Roberto and the rest of them looked at each other. No one spoke for a few seconds. Then Roberto said "We will deal with local groups as we come to each of their communities and we will consult with them on our routes."

For the first time I was disgusted with his obfuscating. "That sounds like a press release, Roberto. Come on—I asked what she's going to do. Does she know yet?"

What I didn't realize then, but saw clearly later, was that they had been debating the Sinaloa problem fiercely among themselves and had not yet come to a decision about how to play it. Although I kept asking, no one would answer. We were a week away at that point, so I decided to wait and see what happened when we got there.

The next day, Roberto came by my Highlander as I was packing up. "She wants you to listen in on a phone call she is going to get at 8 a.m. from Governor Hearn. Come quickly." We were at that point still two hours later than California time, so I assumed Hearn had decided to call her as his work day began.

When I got to her command tent, she had assembled the ten people who made up the core of her inner circle. I recognized all of them except a new face, who was introduced as Judith Izquierdo. She had joined the group the week before and was helping with the Mexican press, I was told. She was a striking-looking woman with short, black hair and a remarkable resemblance to the famous Frida Kahlo self-portrait. She almost always looked angry about something.

The call was just being set up when I got there. Maria was leaning forward toward a speakerphone that was on the table in front of her.

Maria began as soon as Hearn came on the line. "Good morning Governor, thank you for calling. I should tell you that I have some of my staff here and Sam Leonard, a reporter whom I believe you have met."

"I know Sam. Good morning to all of you. Thank you, Miss Chavez, for taking my call. I want to see if we can find some way to avoid any confrontation at the border that might be dangerous for your associates and for those at the Border as well." He paused. "Do you think we can work our way through this?"

He had begun by going to the heart of the matter, as his reputation suggested he would. And he was trying to put the pressure on her for a solution. But if he had intended to put her on the defensive, he was a long way from figuring out how to deal with Maria Chavez.

She answered, "Thank you for your concern about the safety of our marchers, Governor. We are coming to California, as so many of us have in prior years, to seek economic justice. What are your plans to respond to our requests?"

There was a longer pause before Hearn responded.

"We recognize the needs of those who are with you, Miss Chavez. But the land claims you have referred to have been settled long ago. And I know you are aware that there are already more than a million of your countrymen who are in this state illegally as we speak, many of whom use our services. We do not see how we can respond to these new demands when we are already overburdened with those who are already here."

"Governor, we should set aside the legality of the land claims, for the moment. I will send you some of our materials on that question today. I am not sure you have been advised in enough depth on the full history of those claims." She went on. "As to the efforts you are already making, we would be more convinced if you and your predecessors hadn't proposed legislation and initiatives to cut off many of those services to Mexican nationals in California."

"Miss Chavez," and this time his tone suggested that he was clearly getting fed up with her lecture, "we don't seem to be communicating. I am concerned about the safety of those people who are traveling with you. Bringing them illegally across that border will be seen as a provocative act, and I will be under great—" he caught himself, realizing that he was in public, "I will act to reflect the consensus of California citizens that such an incursion should not be allowed."

"Governor, if safety is your concern, I am sure it will not be necessary to proceed with your mobilization of the entire State National Guard south of Bakersfield."

As always, her intelligence was extraordinary. I wondered if it was computer hacking, infiltration of local groups, or just careful reading of the California newspapers that had led to this latest nugget.

When he spoke next his tone was steely. "My job is the safety of the people on this side as well as anyone who comes into this state. We are going to be prepared for whatever happens. I want to be very clear with you, Miss Chavez—any confrontation will be your responsibility for crossing into our state without permission."

"We understand. But we are coming in peace to seek justice. I hope your state will meet us in that spirit, and not with armed force, Governor."

"You can't just walk and suspend property rights, Ms. Chavez. That isn't how it works here."

"Well, that isn't how it worked in the 19th century, Governor, and in most of the 20th. But in the 21st century there are just too many of us and too few of you and it isn't going to work that way any more."

She sighed, as if giving up on his understanding what she was trying to say. "Don't you see—we are the best friends you are ever going to get in this world. None of those people coming with us are going to fly airplanes into your buildings—they just want the chance to clean the planes and the buildings, so their kids can ride and work in them and their grandchildren can build new ones. These people embody the American Dream; they want to work and they want a better life for their kids."

They signed off coolly, with no agreement to talk again. It had not been a positive encounter, as I saw it. But the hard-liners among her young lieutenants were delighted, predictably, that she had "really told the gringo off." She was quiet, looking at some notes she had made while they were talking, frowning as if she had not said all that she intended.

So with the first contact between the two of them, the serious negotiations had begun. Maria knew what she wanted, to cross into California and get something for the marchers. The Governor knew what he wanted, which was to keep her on the other side and show California voters that he had stood up to the "invasion." And I knew what I wanted, which was a good story that stayed peaceful.

We had become, with the movement of the marchers and the passage of time, a fierce triangle of wanting—and there was no way we could all get what we all wanted.

CHAPTER 22

I called the Governor's office after the phone call, hoping to get on the list to see him. I was surprised when the press office called back and said I could see him the next morning. I caught a ride on one of the food transport trucks to Guadalajara and got on a night plane to San Francisco. I was in the Governor's office by 10 am.

He was clearly irritated at having to deal with the press so early, but he got down to it. "You heard her. We aren't on the same wave length—we are barely on the same planet." Then he cooled down, and said something that came from way out of left field.

"Look, I've got a proposition. I've been reading and listening to the pieces you've been filing from along the route. She's obviously made a decision to let you come way inside and report what she is doing and why."

He went on. "I've also read some of your stuff from when you covered California politics. You're hard on elected pols, but you're fair. Bill Page tells me he knows you and knows where you're coming from." He paused and looked at me as if he were trying to make up his mind about something. "You want this to turn out right, don't you?"

It was a strange thing for him to say, because it sounded like he was accusing me of bias.

"How I want this to turn out doesn't matter. I'm just reporting what is happening."

"Sure, sure. Look, I'm not saying you're one-sided. But when you've written about the Valley, you've made sure to describe what it is like for the migrants, and you go out of your way to talk to them. You have the Spanish and you make the effort. But you also talk to the growers. Right?"

"I try to, Governor. That's part of the story."

"OK. What if I let you shadow me for a day, all on deep background, as we try to deal with this. I want you to understand how we are trying to handle this thing, so that we don't cross across like some kind of ogres or *norteamericano* tyrants. You can't write what you hear, but I want you to see that we are preparing the most humane response to this"—he struggled with the words—"this *population blackmail* she has aimed at us."

"Governor, I appreciate the offer and of course I would accept it. But if you read my stuff you know I have been hard on some of your predecessors. Why aren't you making this offer to a more," now I had to pause for a safe word, "*compatible* reporter?"

He waved his hand as if shooing a fly away. "Simple. You have the credibility—they wouldn't. I am willing to take the same risk I think she has already taken—that you will tell it fair. Is that a good risk?"

"That's for you to decide. But I sure am trying to tell it as fair as I can."

"That's all I can ask for. Someday, somebody is going to write a history of the early 21st century California governors, and all this will be part of it. I want to be sure my part isn't told by some third-echelon state bureaucrat who went to a few meetings and had no idea of what was really going on."

He was referring to his own histories, of course. The next question was obvious. "Why not write it yourself?"

"I will, of course, but it'll be filtered through my own take on it. When I was doing the books on the Governors, their own memoirs and their notes were the least helpful material I had, because they had no perspective. I want someone with the perspective to see what is happening. Will you do it?"

It was a hell of an offer, and I knew it. I agreed, and we worked out the logistics. I would show up in two days and he would let me shadow him, telling the people in meetings that it was all off the record.

Getting ready for the day, I spent some time with Jim Rose, the Governor's press guy. He filled me in on some of what had already happened. Like the Governor, Rose was anxious to get out the full story on what the Governor had tried to do to avert a crisis. Rose was the archetype of a press secretary, a medium-height, balding, somewhat overweight guy with a quick smile and a storehouse of political lore that went back to the 50's in California politics.

Rose told me that they had already had a series of exploratory meetings to try to develop a response. The meetings usually included Rose, Colonel Abel Cox, the Governor's military liaison officer to the National Guard, General Bullard Lewis, Commandant of the California National Guard, Susan Connor, the Attorney General, who was a hard-right member of the Governor's party, the head of the Highway Patrol, and various staff aides to Hearn, including Bill Page.

The mood at the first meeting after the phone call, according to Rose, was angry, given the tone of the call. "Who the hell does she think she is" shouted Susan Connor, "telling you that she's coming anyway after you told her not to?!"

The Governor answered calmly, "She's the leader of a movement that has defined success as getting here, Susan, and we're just going to have to assume from now on that she'll try everything she can to pull it off. Now who has any ideas about what we do when she gets to the border?"

The discussion went back and forth, from closing the border completely to demanding paperwork from the marchers—as if they were coming as tourists— and on to rubber bullets and tear gas. Although the hardliners clearly wanted a policy decision that anyone who crossed illegally would be detained and transported back to the other side, a few minutes with a calculator made clear that locking up one hundred thousand people or more would take every available bus, cop, and jail cell in southern California. As the meeting went on, the logic of the question "how do you stop a million people?" became clearer, and the Governor's face grew stormier and stormier.

"Let's assume we can turn most of them back, somehow," he said. "What are we going to do about these land claims she says she can justify?"

Susan Connor shot back quickly "That's nonsense and she knows it! These claims have all been settled over a century and a half ago."

"Do we agree with that?" the Governor asked his legal counsel, a Stanford Law School graduate named April Parks.

"Actually, Governor, she may have some claims that have merit." Parks glanced at Connor, who was getting ready to explode again. "It depends on what arguments she is using. Our research seems to indicate that if she has claims based on the original families who sold—or were forced to sell their property to Anglo buyers, she may have a point. The earlier Mexican legal status of the land claims has never been completely clarified. The change from Mexican—really Spanish—law to U.S. law clearly put the *Californio* landowners at a big legal disadvantage. Plus if she can show that any of the original sales were under duress, she may have a further point."

"You have *got* to be kidding!" Connor shrieked. "Where do you get off saying she has a case?!"

Parks answered calmly, "It all depends on how you interpret the Treaty of Guadalupe Hidalgo, Governor. After the Mexican-American War of 1846, the Treaty was negotiated in 1847. The official map of the Treaty, called the Disturnell Map, which is housed in the National Archives in Washington, D.C., shows a homeland area in the American Southwest which is labeled 'Ancient Homeland of the Aztecs.' This map, according to Latino groups in California and their associates in Mexico, proves that Mexicans are not 'foreigners,' but indigenous to Arizona, New Mexico, Colorado and Utah. There are oral traditions of Hopi, Pueblo and Lakota Indian elders that appear to confirm that Nahuatl-speaking peoples are their relatives. And a great deal of anthropological work in the past twenty years has come up with new evidence that the tribes who settled the area around Mexico City all came from much further north—which some ethnicists argue may entitle them to status as separate nations much like our own Indian tribes."

Connor was about to have a stroke. "What does some old map have to do with this invasion? Using that logic, people living in Siberia today own California!"

Parks went on. "If the Disturnall map is interpreted as giving standing to Mexican claims to parts of the Southwest, those claims can be extended to lands originally owned by Mexican nationals in what they called Alta California before the 1847 Treaty." She looked down at her notes for a moment. "The rest of their case rests on what Anglo law did to Mexican land owners in the 1850's and 1860's when the owners of the Spanish land grants sold their lands or lost legal battles to American settlers. Once California became a state in 1850, the legal standing of the Mexican owners was altered in favor of the new Anglo settlers. Basically, the rules were changed to make it harder for the *Californios* to keep their land."

Rose told me that the debate continued, but nothing was resolved. Finally the Governor called it quits and they agreed to meet again the next morning.

CHAPTER 23

Two days later, after taking some brief R and R fishing at Lake Tahoe and visiting some friends over on the eastern side of the Sierra, I walked in the L Street door to the Capitol at 8 a.m. and went to the Governor's office. He was just beginning a breakfast meeting and motioned me to a side chair. It was his own staff, and they went over four or five legislative things that they had to decide in the next week. Then he opened the March part of the meeting. He explained the ground rules covering my being there, and aside from some raised eyebrows, no one said anything.

From the very first, the Governor's aides had split into two camps. One group thought that the Governor could get a lot of mileage out of turning the marchers around and chasing them out of California. The second camp felt that there were huge risks in using the level of force it would take to make a million people do something they didn't want to do. Bill Page, as chief of staff, tried to keep the two groups from attacking each other all the time, and was able to enforce peace on most issues. But this one was different.

The Governor had hired some staff assistants who had been referred from business groups, big contributors, and the national Republican Party, and they were mostly the hard-liners. Bill Page told me that Hearn was less comfortable with them than the pragmatists, who had been with him longer. The pragmatic group included two Latinos who were the real thing—honest conservatives who thought that moderate Republicans were better for Latinos than Democrats who took money from the alcohol and tobacco lobbies and then talked about their commitment to children but kept taxes on alcohol far below most other states.

The pressures outside were also building. In California, as in other parts of the U.S., radio had become an outlet for some of the worst extremists. Maria's heading for the border had unleashed a firestorm of reaction on what was loosely called "hate radio" and the "e-hate" on-line networks throughout California. The worst of the hatemongers began calling for "God-fearing true Americans" to go out and stop the "invading aliens," as though the marchers were coming from outer space. There was talk about the militia forming vigilante groups to block the border. And some of the hard right groups were back to proposing that Mexican-American kids be thrown out of California schools, as though it was their fault the marchers were coming.

The Governor got right to the point. "Where are we on the March preps?" he asked Page.

In my work watching pols, I had come to see that they had two basic styles of running meetings with staff. The take-charge guys ran the meeting themselves, and threw out their own ideas for people to react to, pressing the group to buy their ideas and suppressing dissent most of the time. The listeners encouraged their staff to fly the ideas themselves, urged them to debate, probed for evidence, and then made the final call later. The listeners were often the guys who were most secure in their own ideas, because they had to allow debate among their staffs. FDR was a listener, LBJ was the opposite. After the first five minutes, it was clear that Hearn was clearly a listener.

Page ran through the options that had come out of the earlier meetings. "Basically, Governor, we have three choices. We can try military force at the border on our own or working with the feds, we can try to get the feds to persuade the Mexican government to stop them on their side, or we can negotiate with her before they get here and give her enough to turn them around before they cross."

Rose said "We can probably scratch the second option, based on what we heard yesterday."

He was referring to the reports from the Governor's representative in Washington, a former congressman who ran the state's Washington office. He had flown in and briefed the Governor with a full report on the federal options.

Apparently within the past few days, when it became clear that Maria's marchers had a very good chance of making it to the border, the feds had panicked and went to the Mexican government to try to get them to stop her on their side. The Mexican Cabinet met for several days and decided there was no way they were going to get into it. Running errands for the U.S. government was never a very good route to electoral success in Mexican elections, and there were four state elections coming up in the next six months.

There was a big back and forth, and the feds threatened to cut off border cooperation projects, and the Mexican President said he did not like the pressure he was getting, and it all dissolved in a lot of "We'll get back to you" and "Let's watch developments and confer later…" But the bottom line was the Mexican government was taking a pass on the whole thing.

"All right," Hearn said, "what are the military options?"

This part of the picture was still emerging. They couldn't tell for sure what military resources would be available. As Maria had noted in their phone call, there was a now well-publicized plan pending to mobilize over 60% of the state National Guard. This would mean about 15,000 troops. If the California Highway Patrol, local police forces, and sheriff's departments were added to it, a total of 30,000 armed officers would be available.

But, not surprisingly, it turned out that very few city and county elected leaders were anxious to strip their local law enforcement forces of all or most of their sworn personnel.

The Governor was still reluctant to call in any federal troops. Some of his staff were beginning to argue that the federal option was the only one they had left. His National Guard head, General Lewis, was almost apoplectic when he heard the Governor argue against any federal troops.

"Governor, you are asking me and my forces to hold off a million people. We are going to be outnumbered fifty to one. We just can't do that and you shouldn't ask us to do that. We would have to use very heavy armed force against that many people. It is the only option we have left if you refuse federal troops."

Page looked impatient, shaking his head. "Wait a minute, Bull. To the best of our knowledge, these people are not armed. Are you saying you can't patrol a border crossing a few hundred yards wide and keep them from coming through without shooting them? Why not just shut the border so they can't get through?"

At that point, the Governor's deputy counsel, Elena Villarreal, spoke up. "Governor, disruption is just what terrorists want, and she is basically just another terrorist. A terrorist tries to disrupt normal life so badly that the population rises up against authority. Once you shut down the border physically so she can't get through, you shut down $100 million dollars worth of business every day. That is exactly what the little b—"she caught herself—"that's what she wants. She *wants* the economic disruption that would cause."

I had been told by friends who covered the Governor's office that Villarreal was the most interesting of the Governor's staff. She was a 35-year-old Latina who was part of the in-house conservative crowd. She had apparently spent a lot of time on immigration issues, especially illegal immigrants who had been arrested for breaking California laws and were in detention. She was definitely from the "book 'em and bus 'em back" school.

She had graduated from Boalt Law School and had been on the law review there. Some people thought she was future Attorney General material. Other people felt that she was far too outspoken and had crossed the line between acceptable Republican behavior for Latinas and outright betrayal. She had hooked up with Hearn after working for one of his primary opponents—a Republican conservative who had been too far right even for California Republicans. Rose, who retained an eye for great-looking women, described her once as "Salma Hayek plus," meaning that she had a superb body and a lovely face to go with it. From the looks of her, he got that right.

They all said that Elena was a true conservative—a "we worked hard as hell and none of these illegals is going to get what we got" Southern California conservative. I made a note that I should spend some time with her and wondered what her history was.

Page glared at her. Apparently they had tangled before. "All right, we can't block the border and we don't want to shoot the first thousand people who come through. What's left?"

They talked about the third option—persuading Maria not to cross the border. The Governor asked Bill Page to fly down to meet with her to explore that option, and it was the only time in the meeting that things got hopeful. I kept quiet, but I didn't have high hopes for those discussions.

Then they returned to the question of what the national administration in Washington would do. The fact that there was a national election coming up complicated the federal reaction to the March. Four years before, the winner had gotten 31% of the Hispanic vote—which was itself a flawed concept, a little like referring to the *left-handed vote*. There *was* no Hispanic vote nationally, there was only a Hispanic vote in many states—nearly all of the big ones, with many different kinds of Spanish-speaking groups in the U.S., from right wing Cubans to *independista* Puerto Ricans to Mexicans and Central Americans. Their politics ranged from relentlessly middle-class to radical left. Perhaps the only thing they agreed on was that criticisms of Hispanics or Latinos or whatever they wanted to be called would make them all mad.

So staying away from a confrontation at the Mexican border looked like smart politics, because for every group that would welcome it, there was another that would bitterly oppose whatever the feds did—or didn't do. So the White House was hoping that Hearn's head-strong temperament would emerge, and end up with him taking the lead in a way that they could point to as an explanation of why they stayed out.

The other risk to the feds was the downside of anything that affected the flows of commerce across the border. Interrupting that flow, as Elena had made so bluntly clear, would cost millions a day. The feds would let the Border Patrol and the INS do what they were going to do at the Border to keep things under control, but the economics of the Border had changed greatly in the past ten years.

Bill Page told me later that Hearn's people in Washington had learned that the White House had done six different simulations of what would happen at the border, bringing in the Border Patrol and Homeland Security staffs and setting up mockups of the border crossings. Each time they ran the simulation, hundreds of people were killed, which then led, in the simulation, to two things: the California economy tanked and the President's popularity ratings plummeted. So staying out looked like the best bet, unless Hearn forced their hand.

Finally, Hearn and his team returned to the possible responses if the March did come across the border. They went around and around, talking about tear gas, stun guns, dogs, rubber bullets, and other options. But no consensus emerged. Once they started repeating themselves the second time, the Governor clapped his hands once and said "Thank you, people. Let's take a look at this again at the end of the week." The meeting quickly broke up.

As people were filing out, Hearn asked me to stay for a minute. When the room had cleared, he sat down with a sigh and said "So what did you think?"

"Great Danish, Governor. Where do you get it?"

He frowned at my non-response, and then laughed softly. "They make it in the basement every morning. If you get here at 5, it's fresh and hot. They always have a plate for me because I drop in once or twice a week. It's my best perk in this job." Then he leaned back in the chair, all business. "OK—what did you think?"

"Your guys seem a long way from knowing how to deal with this."

He nodded, still frowning. "No one knows how to deal with this. Always before, when this many people moved at once, they were refugees from war or famine, and somebody had the basic job of setting up tents and feeding them. But these people are here to get something from us. They aren't refugees—they have their own food system already set up." He paused. "If this many people were an invading army, you bomb hell out of them or put up serious barriers. But any barriers we set up would be a bigger inconvenience to our own citizens than to them. Elena's right—the two economies are much too tangled up with each other to be able to just shut the border until they go away."

"Once Ms. Chavez got ten people headed in this direction, I began to lose my options." He rose and began pacing. "So much of the business of this job is reacting, reacting well, with all the skill we have, knowing what your reaction may create, but reacting, not acting. This is probably the biggest reaction we'll have on my watch."

"So what are your goals, Governor?"

Then he turned angry again. "I want her *out* of here—I want her to go home again. The only question is what it will take to make that happen, and maybe what will force our hand. If more people get hurt—or if she gets hurt—we're way short of options. Then it becomes whether she can control her people. I know I can't control our forty million."

He looked at me with a sharp look. "You don't think Bill is going to get any-where with her, do you?"

"You read body language pretty well, Governor," I said. "I just can't see her getting a million people this far and then getting talked out of it for a few new factories."

He sat down, and leaned back in the chair, shaking his head. "There are a lot of people around here who will be upset if I don't shoot all of the marchers or use nukes. That would get me in the history books, I suppose." He went on, warm-ing up. "She is doing a great job so far of keeping this peaceful, and some of the liberals in the press are going to town on us. The rich people in the U.S. vs. the poor people in Mexico—it sells papers and keeps them glued to the TV. But it's bull, Sam!" He was beginning to pace, frustrated that he had only me for an audi-ence.

"You bet we have been selfish and done some God-awful things in our history. But there is no nation anywhere in human history with as much power as we have who have used it for anywhere near as much good. Nobody, nowhere!!" He was angry now, a historian in full possession of his facts. "The British Empire—give me a break. The Romans? Where was the Romans' Marshall Plan to help their defeated enemies recover? The Greeks? The Chinese at their peak? And not the Aztecs either. Virgin sacrifices and altars to gods who kill children? These are our moral superiors?!"

He was angry, as much at his powerlessness as at the media victories Maria was winning. We talked some more, inconclusively, and he kept the invitation open and told me that he had asked his staff to talk with me as I wished.

Later that week, as Page related it to me in an interview after it was all over, Hearn had met again with his military staff. They got nowhere, and at the end of the meeting, tired and frustrated, Hearn said "I just wish somebody would wave a magic wand and make this whole thing go away. I am sick of it, and it is going to come to no good. She won't listen to anything that we have said and she is going to take this thing into a collision that none of us is ready for. She just won't listen to reason—we have got to think of some other way of stopping her."

The remark seemed innocent enough at the time, a careless remark by a usu-ally careful politician. But like a small stone rolling down a rocky slope, it started many other, more dangerous shifts in the substrata of California's most militant haters.

What had happened next, Page told me off the record after the March was over, was that the Governor's staff liaison to the National Guard decided that the

Governor's statement was his authorization to begin working with the militia groups in San Diego County. There were four of these groups, loosely affiliated gun nuts, ex-military types, and survivalists, and they used the hills in eastern San Diego County as their staging area for what they called "war games." This being California, they each had a small arsenal stashed in their various underground headquarters.

These groups had met after getting the indirect contact from the Governor's aide. The aide had called a big contributor who had worked in the past with an international arms dealer. This guy had agreed to serve as the cutout so that the Governor's office role would be masked. He and his staff had then approached the other militia groups, and all agreed they would work together to stop the March if it ever got across the border. Over the next few weeks they had actually developed three different plans, one of which was to mortar the marchers as they came out of the Pendleton area into San Clemente, the first town north of the military reservation.

The other two plans, as I learned from a surprising source later on, both involved assassinating Maria.

CHAPTER 24

After the meeting with Hearn, I headed back to the Claremont and called Elena Villarreal to ask her for an interview. She agreed and we met across the street from the Capitol in the Hyatt coffee shop. It was the first of three meetings I had with her, and the guys who warned me that she was "interesting" didn't come close to it. She had worked for Governor Hearn for three years as assistant legal counsel, but Rose had told me she had some problems fitting in. After I talked to her, I could see why.

As I had already seen, Elena Villarreal was a striking woman, with long, dark hair that she wore that day in a braid. She had what would have been called, using unquestionably sexist language from an earlier era, a lush figure. She had a brutal way of talking that took some getting used to. She would get so worked up about certain issues that she would revert to a caricature by saying "boolsheet" in the most atrocious Mexican accent imaginable. You wanted to laugh, but you could never tell if she really thought it was funny or not. Clearly it was not how she talked the rest of the time—she could hold her own in high legalspeak with the best of the law review types I had ever met.

But she could be profane in English and Spanish like no woman I had ever known. She was an equal opportunity cusser, with the swearing punctuated by a lot of talking with her hands, increasing her volume as she became more passionate about the topic. In some of our meetings over lunch or dinner, I saw waiters and waitresses cringe at some of the things she said in a volume loud enough to be heard across the room.

The first time we talked, I was trying to figure out who was on the other side of the table and it looked like she was doing the same. Her first question was "Why the hell did Hearn let you into our meetings? Do you have something on him?"

"Not a thing," I said. "I think the guy is secure enough to let a reporter see what you all are trying to do to solve this thing. He knows that Maria Chavez has let me cover the March from inside, and he knows that part of this whole thing is how well both of them explain what they are doing."

"Have you fallen for her boolsheet?" she asked with disdain.

I recognized the hard guy tactics I had experienced in a thousand interviews. It was time to talk about her, not me. "Why does she upset you so much?"

She glared at me, then seemed to get herself under control. "Look, my dad was a cop and his dad was a cop. I went to law school so I could hang around with cops and not feel left out. We are a law and order family—we believe that assholes who break the law should be locked up for a long time, wherever they come from. It's that simple. These people are breaking the law—or threatening to—and we should get some cells ready for them if they cross. We don't need concrete cells to make jails or prisons. Put the jails on trucks and buses so we can take them back home—or set up jails in tents out in the desert the way that sheriff in Phoenix does."

She leaned back and smiled, clearly enjoying watching me try to figure her out.

"Have you shared these *solutions* with the Governor?" I asked as politely as I could, beginning to think of her as partly deranged.

"He knows where I am coming from, but it is too soon to get this blunt in the public debate about all this. Some of the wimps around him start wetting their pants when I talk this way. And they just don't understand the facts of the case."

She went on. "Maria knows how this economy works better than most of you guys—she's studied the connections between California and Mexico for a long time. When China hit the global economy around 1995 with 50 cent an hour manufacturing plants that could make anything they make in Mexico *maquiladoras*, dozens of companies moved thousands of jobs to China. So in response, starting in 2000 U.S. and foreign investors in Mexican border states shifted their production to short-term delivery components, making just-in-time stuff that California companies need quickly. There are auto assembly plants all over the West Coast that just stop whenever the border closes, because critical components are made in Baja and Sonora. There's an entire industrial complex that was deliberately built just south of the Otay Mesa border crossing in Baja to move parts into the Southern California economy. Face it, they can still produce those parts at one-tenth the cost in California."

She stopped and shook her head. "You close that border and you close down a big piece of the sixth largest economy in the world—California's. And Hearn is not going to let that happen for very long, whatever the cost of letting her cross. She has us—she really has us."

She leaned forward. "Sam, let's do the numbers. Every single week, 750 million dollars worth of trade crosses that border, and another 200 million comes across and then goes to the rest of the U.S.. That's 40 to 50 billion a year. You close that border and to the California economy, it's the same thing as Hollywood shutting down—or the entire aerospace industry. The California economy *is* the Mexican economy, and vice-versa. So if that border closes for 2 or 3 weeks while we just sit there, our governor has to explain to his business backers why he put a 2 billion dollar hole in the California economy."

It was a brilliant analysis, with numbers she had mastered completely—all the more impressive because it argued against the outcome she wanted.

She paused and gave me another hard look. "What do you really think about all this? Your stuff from the March has been pretty sympathetic. Are you just another soft old liberal, or what?" Then she gave me this huge smile that was just as disconcerting as her words.

I was becoming irritated at her act. "My politics don't matter. I report what is happening, here and on the March. But I have to tell you I admire the hell out of people who are walking 1,800 miles for what they believe in. A lot of people in this state start whining when they have to walk more than 100 feet from their car to the front door of the mall."

I had lost it, and it was just what she wanted. Then she threw me a wild curve. "You know, Sam, you're really cute when you're mad."

I broke the conversation off at that point, telling her I had to file a report to NPR on deadline and was then heading back down to rejoin the March. She looked disgusted, as though she had just gotten an invitation to a fundraiser for the ACLU. I told her I wanted to talk with her again when I came back to Sacramento, and she agreed right away.

CHAPTER 25

The next day, I met with the Governor's top guys, Bill Page and Jim Rose, to try to make sense of it all. They were still a little nervous about my access to them and to Hearn, and I had to assure them that I understood that it was all on deep background and I could not use any of it in direct quotes. Then I asked Page what he thought the Governor was going to do if they crossed the border.

"No one knows, least of all him. We are going to play this out day by day and try to resist the worst pressures we are getting from both sides." He clearly did not want to talk any more about their immediate options. "You know, Sam, this whole thing didn't start a few weeks ago. This goes back through a century and a half of this state's history."

He paused, and continued. "This state has always been schizophrenic about these things. We've been on both sides of history from the very first days of California. Sure, we passed the Oriental Exclusion Act, but we kicked hell out of Proposition 14—the first anti-civil rights initiative in 1964. Republicans led the fight against it in those days. It was wrong, and we defeated it."

Rose chimed in. "And then we passed those red meat initiatives 187 and 209 that beat up on immigration and affirmative action."

"But for God's sake," said Page, "no other state in the nation has a minority college enrollment of 45%. Unless you count Hawaii."

Page had worked with Hearn in the Cal State system, and he warmed to his topic. "At our worst, we are rednecks from the valley and Beemer-driving stockbrokers from southern Orange County. But, Sam, you know, you've covered this state—in those same cities and towns there are Latino and Vietnamese and Taiwanese valedictorians. And older kids who are getting PhDs—mostly at public expense—whose grandparents came here from Oklahoma in the '30s. Grapes of wrath time."

Rose added "And it isn't just a white vs. minorities thing, either. It's a lot more complicated than that." He leaned back in his chair, shaking his head. "I was in LA last month and we had some hearings on immigration. The worst stories we heard were about the garment industry in LA where Asian owners rip off undocumented workers. You watch, Sam—if she crosses over, some of the worst opposition to her will come from Latino middle class voters who have paid their dues and want her to stay the hell out of their country."

Page also filled me in on the continuing discussions with the federal administration.

"We have gone around and around with the feds. They have never liked Hearn politically, so it doesn't look like they'e going to do anything that would make him look good. Some of those guys are still afraid he will run for President against one of their creepy right-wing buddies. And to make it worse, Hearn is on the record now saying he thinks California can handle this, and they may just call his bluff and let him. And they agree with us—if we close the border everybody loses money and she just waits us out until we open it again."

He went on. "All those guys can count votes, and it won't do their chances with the Hispanic vote much good to see us shooting or gassing a million or so Mexicans on the 6 o'clock news all over the country. Not to mention how it will play in the rest of this hemisphere."

From media friends in Washington, I got pretty much the same story. No one in the administration wanted to help Hearn, and they thought he would have to take the heat either way—if he let them in or blocked them from crossing the border in force. So it looked like they were going to stay out of it. It wasn't a military invasion, after all—it looked like a domestic problem, and so the state would be allowed to handle it.

The feds had a fallback position as well. If the marchers got across the border, they could use the troops at Pendleton, which sits right on top of Interstate 5. There were 50,000 Marines at Pendleton, spread across 200,000 acres. They were the final federal presence, there if needed to restore order, but uninvolved in the first phases, when it would be only Hearn who was in the spotlight.

We talked some more, but by then I had gotten tired of all this speculation about what might happen. These were two tough veterans of the political wars, but like everyone else, they were just trying to guess what the voters wanted. I wasn't going to get any more from them, and they couldn't tell me a damn thing about what Hearn was going to do.

Then I realized that I was in Sacramento, and I had a foolproof way to read the voter barometer on the March. It was time to go see Cousin Pill.

CHAPTER 26

Cousin Pill, with whom my two brothers and I had grown up years ago in small Southern California towns, got his nickname because he was a whiner—no matter what game we played, after ten minutes Cousin Pill would run off to his mother crying that someone had cheated. Later, I realized that this was great training for elective politics.

And Cousin Pill, whose real name was Paul Andrews, took to elected politics like the proverbial duck to water. He ran for office six times from the time he was 29 and never lost. Now in his early fifties, he was the perfect politician, moving out in front of the electorate about two millimeters while looking over his shoulder to see where his followers were going. He was the best bellwether I knew for what the average guy in California was thinking. Except for dumping his first wife for a San Diego Chargers cheerleader in a sort of mid-life crisis, he was as close to the norms of this state as an elected guy could get. They loved him in suburban San Diego County, and he became minority leader of the Assembly only four terms into his legislative career. Once term limits hit, he kept bouncing around between the state Senate and the Assembly and even talked about running for Congress eventually.

Whenever I was in Sacramento, I visited Paul to see what the voters were thinking. With his knack for representing the common suburban man, he invariably embodied what 51% of California voters were thinking. So talking to him was a fine way to see what people around the state were thinking about Maria and the March.

"So, Paul," I said as I walked into his office, "How do you solve a problem like Maria?"

He was looking glum. "You got me—you've been out there with her and that ragtag army—what do you think of her?"

I laughed and said "She doesn't have an army, Paul, so far she just has a half million people who want some of what we have here. What do your polls say?"

Paul took polls on everything. He wouldn't dream of taking a stand on an issue until he had first taken a poll on it. One of my brothers who lived in his district once told me that he had heard Paul had taken a poll when he was thinking about leaving his wife to see how his constituents would react. So I knew he had already done polls on the March.

"A majority opposes her—a strong majority. But the softness in the numbers comes when you ask what we should do to them. 55% want to *negotiate*," speaking the word like it was some strange and perverse sexual practice, "and only 24%

want to load them up and ship them back at gunpoint or whatever it takes. And the crazy thing is, when we break the numbers down, the more churchy they are, the more they like her—even rock-hard conservatives who want to close the borders forever."

He frowned and asked "Is all this religious stuff real? My problem is that the fundies in my district and all over the state can't bring themselves to hate her because of all that religious mumbo-jumbo. They think she's misguided, but they just want us to pat her on the head and send her back home."

Technically, Paul was a born-again, but it didn't seem to have taken.

"I think it's real," I said. "She is very sincere, but she also understands how it plays here. I think she means it and I think she wants it to have exactly the effect that it is having." He shook his head in disbelief. I asked, "So what do you think the Governor should do?"

"I don't know. He is such a wimp sometimes, waiting to hear everybody out before he makes up his mind. But once they cross the border he starts to lose his options fast—people are not going to feel the same about her, once they see how much space a million people take up. It won't matter how much she prays when the cameras are turned on. They're gonna want her gone."

Later, as I was driving back down to San Diego to catch a flight to join up with the March again, I thought about what he had said, and I supposed he was right. The marchers had a temporary base of support, however threatening they seemed to some Californians. But then Cousin Pill was always right about the voters, eventually.

So I decided to stop off at the village green—the mall—to hear what some voters thought.

CHAPTER 27

Spending a day at the mall interviewing people was another way to try to sense how Maria and the March were coming across. The malls in Southern California, even more than in the rest of the country, had become the new village green, where citizens gathered and the events of the day were digested.

But the village green had never been full of so many leering adolescents with head sets and voice mikes. The purple hair and nose rings and baggy pants of the '90s had given way to the "tech look" favored by hand-held computer-bound kids with voice-activated games and chat rooms. They walked or skated around talking into their head set mikes and looking off into space or at their hand-helds, which meant that they were a real hazard to anyone just walking along.

But the older denizens of the mall—those over 30—were good sources for what Californians were thinking, so I used my winning smile and my fancy-looking tape recorder to get some interviews

This is Sam Leonard. Today I have been interviewing Southern Californians about their reactions to Maria Chavez and the March she is leading to California. Here are some of their comments.

> *I am talking with Mrs. Robin Jorgenson, who lives in Laguna Hills. Mrs., Jorgenson, would you mind telling me what your attitude is toward the march?*
>
> *I'd be glad to. I hope they all get tear gassed or zapped or whatever they have to do to keep the border closed, and then I hope they all turn around and go back where they came from. They have no business coming up here and trying to take our land.*
>
> *So you are completely opposed to what they are trying to do.*
>
> *That's right. We worked hard to buy a house here and we don't want a bunch of farmers from Mexico coming here to move in next door.*
>
> *Do you really think they want to move in next door, Mrs. Jorgenson?*
>
> *You know what I mean. They want some land, they said, and they keep talking about land that was stolen from them. That's crazy. I bought my house on land I leased from the Coniff Company, and the Company bought that land years ago fair and square. If these people want some land why don't they stay home and buy land in their own country where they belong? We don't want them here.*
>
> *Do you think they are going to get this far?*
>
> *No way. If they get through the border, my husband told me the Marines at Pendleton will stop them cold. They know how to deal with terrorists from other countries.*
>
> *Thank you. Mrs. Jorgenson. This is Sam Leonard, reporting for NPR from Orange County, California.*

I am with Mr. José Velasquez from Anaheim. Mr. Velasquez, what do you think about the marchers?

They aren't coming here. There's no way they're going to let them cross the border. They'll arrest a few, fire a few shots, and the rest will all run back home.

Excuse me, Mr. Velasquez, but it would appear to me that your own family came here from Mexico, didn't they?

Sure, fifty years ago just after the war when they needed pickers. Then we applied for amnesty and we all became citizens. But we have worked for fifty years and paid taxes and my kids have stayed out of trouble and gone to college. No way those peasants deserve what we have worked for here—just by showing up and asking for it. No way.

I am with Miss Ella Rovere from Mission Viejo. Miss Rovere, what do you think about the marchers coming up from Mexico?

Well, I am part of a study circle in my church, and we have been talking about these people for the past two weeks. We are trying to decide what the Lord wants us to do about them trying to come here. Some of the people in my group say it's already too crowded here and they hope they don't come. But some of us keep reading Luke and Amos and Micah and other parts of the Bible where it talks about caring for your neighbor, and we're trying to figure out if these people really are our neighbors.

What do you think, Miss Rovere?

Well I'm not sure. The Lord sure didn't say we were only supposed to help people that look like me. The way I read the Good Samaritan story, it says we are supposed to help out anybody who needs help whether they are our kind or not.

How do you feel about the marchers themselves?

*Well, you can't help but notice that they all seem to be good Christians with all that praying and those church services out in the fields that we see on TV. I don't know where we'll put them, but I guess they'll figure something out. You know, I flew up to see my sister in Stockton last year, and looking out the window of the plane, it seemed to me like there's still a lot of empty land in this state. I can't help but remember how neighborly people were when my family first moved here from Iowa thirty years ago. When you get right down to it, almost nobody is really **from** California—we all moved here from somewhere else, didn't we?*

Driving back to the airport, I tuned into a fundie radio station to see what this segment of Southern California had to say about the March. A radio preacher was talking about the history of California from a biblical perspective.

The history of Southern California is about taking. They took the water from the Owens Valley and made it a desert, they took the land from everyone who owned it, they took the clean air from all of us. And they made a paradise south of the Tehachapi, where there was cactus and sage brush. These are the sins of the founders, and what they created was uglier than the land before them. The ugliness is the price of the sin. So it is land as cursed as the South was by the sin of slavery.

These new people from Mexico are the old people, they have come to Old California and they have reminded us that all that is new here was once someone else's—someone else's water, someone else's land. It is a land born of theft, and cursed by the thievery. Now the marchers call us to account for the theft, and we have no answer. Our answer must be God's answer—and we must listen carefully. Is He saying they are the Canaanites who should be expelled from the Promised Land—or are we the Canaanites?

Only in California, I thought: an environmental fundie.

CHAPTER 28

After flying back into Mazatlán, I caught up with the March twenty miles north of Tepic. We were a day's walk away from the southern border of Sinaloa. I had kept asking what was going to happen, but Roberto still refused to answer.

At the morning staff meeting, there was brief discussion about the logistics of the day, and then Maria left her headquarters vehicle in a truck with Roberto. It was very clear that I was not welcome, and I assumed she was headed off for a meeting with the drug lords.

After about three hours they came back and Maria went straight to her RV when she got out of the truck. She looked tense and shook her head when Roberto gestured to me—I was standing as close as I could get to the truck to try to talk to her, but it looked like I wasn't going to get an interview yet.

Roberto came over, and I said "Looks like the negotiations went badly."

He looked at me with a strange expression and said, "No, they went well. We will cross into Sinaloa in the morning."

I was angry that they seemed to be expecting that I wouldn't ask any questions. "And how is that going to happen? Are we all supposed to pretend that billions of dollars of drugs don't go through here?" I was irritated that they had cut me out of this discussion, after she had promised to let me observe whatever I wanted.

Roberto shook his head, "No, we are not going to pretend. She met this morning with the Garcia brothers who control this province." He stopped, and the look on his face was almost pleading at this point. "Sam, can I go off the record?"

It was the first time he had ever asked me, and it just added to my anger. It was starting to look like she had given me this big buildup about getting total access back in Cholula and now they were going back on it. "Look, Roberto, you can tell me the story anyway you want. But I'm going to find out what happened here and so are a lot of the rest of the Mexican and American press who know what goes on here. No one is going to assume she just strolled through here and said 'Hi, guys' to the Garcias and they let her walk through their fiefdom with a half million people or so. So you can tell me off the record now and I will write whatever I can confirm. All right?"

He knew I could do it that way and that he really had no choice. So he said "OK—here is what is happening. She told them that we would go on through starting tomorrow and that we would make no mention of the drug traffic while we were on the route. At first the Garcias said they wanted some kind of tribute paid, but she got tough and said that we were ready for confrontation at the California border and if they wanted to have one here, too, we were ready. Apparently the older Garcia was not ready for a battle, although some of the younger hotheads in the family wanted to just start shooting." He shook his head. "Some of our drug dealers are not that big on human life when it starts to crowd their profits."

I almost lost it. "So we're just walking through and acting as if this is just another part of the countryside that we are passing through. You are going to ignore the thousands of lives these guys ruin—the cops they bribe, the judges and journalists and *cardinals* they kill!"

Trying to divert me with humor, he asked "Which bothers you more, Sam, the journalists or the clergy?"

But I wasn't having any of it. "Cut the crap, Roberto. Her moral standing goes out the window if you walk through here and act as if this is normal."

He shook his head. "You're wrong, Sam. We are going to get on with the March. That is always what has been the heart of what we are doing. We will not be sidetracked if we can help it." Then he got angry, too. "We are going to do exactly what the government of this country has done for decades—we are going to ignore this part of business life in Mexico. And we are going to do what your country does to ignore it, too—if you know anything about what's happened in Afghanistan since 2001."

Then, finally feeling cornered, he really got in my face. "And save your righteousness on this one, Sam. You know as well as I do that the drug business here is as much about the demand from your side as it is the supply from ours. Maria called it when we were riding back from meeting with those creeps. She said if they weren't the biggest economic development investors and job creators in Western Mexico, it would be easier to condemn them."

"Sam, you are trying to do a fair job, and most of us think you are succeeding. But when it comes down to it, you are just another *norteamericano*—who knows a little more about who we are and what we are trying to do. But you still see it with California eyes, not Mexican eyes. There is no way an Anglo can understand what is going on out there and how hard these people—how hard all of us—have worked to make this happen. When we started out, no one gave us a chance to get fifty people together to walk more than twenty kilometers."

Isabel joined in. "Sam, you are a naive, straight, Anglo male. You speak great Spanish and you know a lot of facts about Mexico. You've got a good heart, hombre. But sometimes you don't have a clue about what is going on here. You can't be anything but whitebread, Sam, however many tortillas you eat with us."

I was totally pissed. "So I'm just another whitebread guy who doesn't get it?"

Roberto wasn't backing down. "We didn't say that. But you are who you are, Sam. You see the drug thing through Anglo eyes, and you can't see California the way we do, like a huge suction pump that pulls in drugs, people, and anything it can buy cheap."

I kept at him for a few minutes longer but I got nowhere. Maria and her staff had clearly decided to let this one pass. They were going to play it their way. It was one more piece of evidence about how single-minded they had become about the goals of the March.

As I drove on up the highway toward Culiacan, I was again glad that I had decided to bring the Highlander on the trip. My daughter had once done a painful character analysis of me based on my car and its contents. It was painful because she was so observant, missing few clues about me and my lifestyle.

Somewhere in a marketing course she had picked up the idea that cars define their owners—or that owners use their cars to try to define themselves. My car, as I have said, was a compromise between power and greenish politics, a hybrid like myself, I guess.

But Elisabeth said it was what was in the car that was the point. That included, in considerable contrast to the rest of my well-ordered apartment and workspace, a jumble of books, papers, sound equipment and accessories, along with the extensive residue of a cigar smoker. I would load up the car with reading and writing material and then leave much of it in the car after I had finished a job.

She also claimed that the car made a statement about me and my music. The last time I went through San Diego with the car, I invested in a top-grade Bose system with twelve speakers. Usually, the CD changer was loaded with 8 classical selections and two country western albums for relief—usually country classicals from Willie Nelson, Johnny Cash, with a bit of Loretta Lynn and Emmylou Harris thrown in. I loved Linda Ronstadt's *Canciones* albums, and they also got some play.

On the March, of course, the market for Willie and string quartets was a bit smaller than the desire to hear Mexican ballads. So my rule was that anyone who rode along with me and brought their own music got to listen to it, but I controlled the volume.

I loved the car, and I loved driving it. Growing up in some of California's farther-out spaces, the idea of going a long way to get to somewhere was fine with me. Elisabeth said the insides of cars were an introvert's revenge on the rest of the world, and I didn't have to buy all of that psychobabble to see that she had a point. It was a control thing, and I was just fine with it.

CHAPTER 29

I decided there wasn't much reporting I could do passing through Sinaloa, so I went back up to Los Angeles again to try to get some more information about what the Governor's people were up to. Bill Page was scheduled to see Maria in four days, and I figured I could get back in time for that. I called Elena Villarreal to see if she could meet with me in LA, and we agreed to meet near the airport.

After the flight, I took a cab over to the hotel where we had agreed to meet. She was waiting for me in the lobby, and we went into the coffee shop.

I began. "Thanks for seeing me. Do you have any idea what is going to happen on this side?"

She was wearing a white silk blouse with a black skirt, her hair up this time. She looked sexy and sophisticated. I could see people occasionally staring at her from around the restaurant.

"We are still debating it, and there are still wets—don't you love Margaret Thatcher's old phrase—"she said in an aside, "and drys who are arguing whether we should use force or not."

"But you were the one who argued that the border couldn't be closed—that it would choke off too much business for either side to put up with a closure."

"That's right. She has done what she needed to—she has threatened us and now we are going to have to decide."

"What do you think they should do? Are you still on the bag 'em and take 'em to the desert side of the argument?"

For the first time, she looked uncertain. "It is going to be very tricky. We just haven't got the forces to stand up to that many people, and the Governor has decided there is no way he is going to ask for federal troops in addition to the Border Patrol. So we aren't sure."

She looked at me with a new expression, which I could no longer read.

"How old are you?" she bluntly asked.

"58. How old are you?"

"35. But I think older men are very sexy. They have such amazing experience—some of them, anyway."

She was so bizarre—you could never tell when she was being serious or joking. I had no idea whether she was really coming on to me or just trying to manipulate me, probably the same way I was trying to manipulate her as a source for my reporting. Who knew who was using whom? So I played it light.

"If you don't stop you're going to hurt my feelings."

"You have feelings?" she laughed.

"Somewhere in here," I mimed looking through my briefcase. "I have them in here somewhere. I never travel without them."

"I'll bet you do. I'll bet you're one of those old guys who is just incredibly sensitive beneath that world-weary exterior, Sam."

"You've got it."

She was quiet for a few seconds, looking at me with a softer smile. Then it widened and I could see something new coming.

She leaned toward me and lowered her voice. "I've never made it with an old liberal before. Young ones, but never an old one."

"Why, Elena," I whispered back, certain the waiter was watching and trying to match her cool but knowing I was failing, "are you propositioning me?"

"What's the matter, Sam, haven't you ever been propositioned before?"

Trying to recover, I shot back, "No that isn't it. I'm just trying to figure out where you even *found* a young liberal these days."

She laughed, kept the wide smile on and letting it get even wider, making me wonder what her lips were like up close. "Sam, I'm promising you. Not today, not now, but soon. I promise."

She leaned back in her chair and the spell was broken and I blinked with relief that whatever had just happened had stopped, since I had no idea in the world what to do next.

I tried to put it away. "OK. That's a deal. You tell me when."

"I will." Then, with a visible shake of her shoulders, she turned back to business, and we talked some more about the March and what she thought the Governor would finally do when he had to decide.

CHAPTER 30

After working on my notes for the book for a few days at a friend's house in Laguna Beach, trying to cool off from both Elena and the attack following the Sinaloa discussion, I flew back down to Los Mochis to meet up with the March. Bill Page was flying in to meet with Maria, and she had told me through Roberto that she wanted me to sit in on the meeting.

But first we had a major festival to celebrate on the road, one of the most fascinating of all the Mexican holidays—the Day of the Dead, celebrated on November 1 and 2. The Day is the blended holiday resulting from the Spanish attempt to convert the Aztec celebration of death and the continuity of life into an All Saint's Day, neo-Halloween festival. It was hugely popular in Mexico—but probably not for the reasons the Spanish Church hoped it would be.

Along the route, as camp was set up on November 1, families prepared for the festival. If they had been back in their homes, families would normally visit the graves of their ancestors and carry on their celebration in the cemeteries. Here, along the road, small altars were erected by each family, with pictures of their departed relatives. The Indian communities from Southern Mexico, where the Day is observed more widely than in urban and northern areas, were most active, and the parties went on throughout most of the night. The skulls and skeletons that seem macabre to North American eyes were everywhere, as our marchers recreated a familiar event in their lives in the middle of their journey.

Bill Page had been picked up at the airport by José Robles, who delivered him to Maria's RV around noon.

Bill knew he had a weak hand, but tried to play it. "Thanks for meeting with me, Miss Chavez. The Governor has asked me to explore with you what help we might be able to give you in persuading your followers not to cross illegally into California."

Maria looked at him with the hard look, the same one I got when I questioned her methods. "Mr. Page, how many jobs can you commit to?"

"We will do all we can to persuade the Mexican—"

She interrupted him. "Don't waste your time, Mr. Page. Those people in Los Piños will promise and promise and nothing at all will happen. That is all they are good for—promises. We will not believe those promises unless they are backed with American cash. How much cash are you authorized to commit?"

Page held himself in control, despite her attack. "That is something we could discuss if you will make a commitment not to cross the border."

But she shook her head, not in anger, but seeming frustrated that she couldn't explain herself clearly. "You don't understand—we really believe that some fair share of this land belongs to these people. If we stay on what you call 'our side,' it means we are renouncing those claims. And we will not renounce claims to land that belonged to the ancestors of these people. I just won't do it. If the Governor needs to tell the media in California that he has tried for a peaceful solution, fine. But we are still going to be peaceful—*we* haven't mobilized any troops."

"And I will tell you one thing more—we are going to be peaceful in the face of whatever provocations you or those disgusting rightwing radio creeps throw at us." She got the hard look, glaring at Page. "The governor is a historian—let's do some history. From the sit-ins in 1960 to Martin Luther King's assassination in 1968, fewer than 25 people in the civil rights movement were killed. Take it all the way back to the Brown decision in 1954 if you want to. During that time, with the help of a lot of courageous kids and their leaders, the civil rights movement changed the country." Her eyes got hard. "If we have to, we have a lot more than twenty-five people who will give their lives for this cause."

It was the most cold-blooded thing I ever heard her say. Later, she proved not to be anywhere near as ruthless as the remark threatened. But I knew she was trying to make clear that they were ready to take losses if they had to.

They talked some more, but it was futile. Bill didn't have enough to convince her to back off, and she wasn't ready to make any deals. She knew her biggest leverage came if she could get a million people inside California, and that was all she was focused on.

After Page left, the March stayed in Los Mochis for a Sunday rest day, and then began walking the long straight stretch of the 15 north to Guaymas and Hermosillo and the town with the strange name of Benjamin Hill.

Roberto briefed me on the week I had missed while I was in Sacramento and Southern California. They had had a rough time, with trucks breaking down and the food supply lines getting stretched further than they liked. They had to spend some scarce cash getting food from the locals, and even with the donations they received as they went through each town, it was getting tight. And they still had over 600 miles and the worst desert of the entire trip to cross.

We were now in the dusty area, where the semi-tropical vegetation of the coast had begun to give way to the beginnings of the desert. The marchers were walking more slowly now, through the eternal dust of Mexico, atomized earth mixed with the spilt blood and broken bones of centuries of martyrs, victims, and ambushed conquerors. It was no more or less violent that the genocide-stained prairies and woodlands of the North, but with less water, and so far dustier.

The groups were holding together fairly well, but there had been the inevitable incidents that were bound to occur in a group that large. Keeping the peace in a group of several hundred thousand was not easy. More than once I saw a group of troublemakers being evicted from the March for excessive drinking or fighting. There were three trucks that circulated through the crowd all the time with a kind of internal police force that wore red and yellow armbands. The crew that rode in these trucks were stocky and all wore their hair long, but chopped off on the sides. One afternoon I watched them come down on a fistfight so fast they scooped both the guys up who were fighting while the truck was still moving and tossed them both into the back of the truck. The crowd disappeared in seconds.

I asked Maria about it later that day and she got irritated at my question about her own "internal enforcers."

"You bet we have enforcers. Listen, Sam, once we cross the border, we are going to walk in broad daylight through some of the most hostile territory any of these people have ever encountered. It will be bad enough for us to be there. I don't want any provocation if we can help it, and I will send thousands of people back home if there is the slightest chance they are going to cause trouble. This is going to be a peaceful march—"

I couldn't resist interrupting her, "…if you have to beat the hell out of every troublemaker on the trip."

She tossed her head in anger, but then stopped and laughed, softly. "Oh Sam, you see too much sometimes. You really do." And she sighed. "But write what you like." And then the sly smile came, "…and if you *must* tell them about how we are sending all our troublemakers back home, well, we will just have to let that speak for itself with the people up North."

Maria had heard, through her excellent sources no doubt, of my deal to cover the Governor. "I hear you have an inside with Hearn. Is that going to compromise you covering us?"

"I don't think so. It means I know a bit more about what they are thinking and—" I knew what she was getting ready to ask me, "it means that I have to be as careful not revealing what I hear from them as I am with what I hear sitting in on your meetings."

"Poor Sam, always trying to be fair. You know, don't you, that you may not be able to split the difference, at the end. You may have to choose."

I knew, more than I wanted to tell her at that point.

I met with Maria again the second night after I rejoined the March. I had decided to drop the Sinaloa thing for the time being. She looked tired, but was much more intense than I had seen her. She had just received some faxes when I walked into her tent. She was smiling.

"Good news?" I asked.

"Welcome, Sam. Yes, I think it is." She tossed the faxes on her desk. "We had heard through one of our banking sources several months ago that the World Bank and a consortium of banks that have handled Mexico's international loans were scheduling a trip to meet with the President and his Cabinet sometime early next year. This confirms it. They will be arriving in Mexico City in mid-January. At the end of the trip they issue new ratings for our loans and bonds." She paused to see if I was following her.

"So you think it will help? How?"

"Those trips are basically inspections; they look at the books, they smell the air, they see what is happening that makes the country stable, or unstable. So obviously having a crowd this big wandering around makes some of them a little nervous. We think that gives us leverage. The Mexican stock market watches this kind of visit like hawks, and good news gives them a real rise."

"Did you time this, knowing that the ratings were coming out?"

"Sam, we have had to learn where *all* of the levers are—because usually they are used against us. This time *we* intend to use them." She went on. "If we can use the timing of international financial decisions in favor of this march, we will do it. And if we can use the tides or astrological charts or Mayan mythology—we will do it. We will use any tools we can get our hands on."

It was a bold and single-minded declaration, and after Sinaloa, I couldn't let it go by.

"And the ends justify the means, right?"

She was suddenly furious. "Don't you dare get philosophical on me! You've seen these children walking along day after day. You know what sacrifices their parents are making. I will do *anything* to get them what they deserve. And if that says that the ends justify the means—so be it!"

She was so angry that she turned away and motioned to Roberto, who had been waiting at the door. I was clearly not welcome—at least for the moment, so I walked on out. As I went back to my tent, I felt badly that I had provoked her, and at the same time, I felt fine—I had acted like a journalist for once, asking the hard questions.

But there were repercussions, sooner than I expected.

Some of Maria's team were growing concerned about my role, and things had been coming to a head. Whether it was my access to Maria, their jealousy, or the predictable unease about having an outsider this far inside their organization, who knew. But when it came, it was ugly and things were never quite the same after with some of them.

Judith was the instigator. She had always been distant with me, and clearly hated North Americans. So when she came stalking up while I was talking with Roberto after a long day of walking outside of Hermosillo, I had a strong feeling that all hell was going to break loose.

Roberto was talking about the next day's planned march when Judith interrupted. "Why are you telling this *gringo* spy our plans, Roberto? So he can call Hearn and tell him what we are going to do?"

Roberto tried to handle her by answering lightly, "Judith, if this guy was going to rat us out he would have done it a long time ago."

But she wasn't buying it. "How the hell do you know he hasn't already done it? You sit around BS'ing with him, and he knows everything we are doing." Then she turned to me. "Why don't you get out of here and go home, *gringo pendejo*? We don't need you hanging around trying to pick up garbage stories so you can do your stupid little radio shows." She was furious, and later we tried to figure out what had set her off, but no one seemed to know.

I tried to answer her. "Judith, look, I don't…"

She interrupted, getting up close to me and wagging her finger at me. "Shut up, *gringo*. Just shut up. I'm sick of seeing you around here, sucking up to Her—" she referred to Maria as if it were a curse "—and talking to everybody who doesn't have the sense to distrust you."

Isabel had come up and smoothly got herself between us. "Judith, come on, I want to talk to you about the crossing. Leave Sam alone. If he is going to betray us, he will just make his own problems. No one is going to stop us now that we are this close."

I was pissed that Isabel had seemed to side with Judith, but I could see that she was also trying to defuse the thing. I was getting disgusted with all of them, and said "To hell with it. I'm flying out as soon as we get to Hermosillo. I'll see you later." And I walked away, leaving them to their own argument about what a bad guy I was or wasn't.

A while later Roberto came over to the Highlander where I was setting up my bed roll. "Look Sam, Judith is weird, and she doesn't speak for all of us. She is just dealing with her own rotten history on the other side, and she was trying to take it out on you. She is a true believer, Sam. She has terrible family history with *norteamericanos* and hates everything about the U.S. Her grandfather was hung in Texas and a cousin is in jail in Arizona for smuggling."

I tried to keep it light. "I know you guys—you brought her along to make you look like moderates. I've covered California politics too long to fall for that stuff."

Isabel had come up. I asked her, "Isabel? What set that off?"

Isabel shook her head impatiently, and said "Oh Sam, who knows why Judith is the way she is? She detests everything north of the border." Then she seemed to be choosing her words more carefully. "A lot of people know you are trying to cover this thing right, but they have no reason to trust journalists from the U.S. Those of us who have gotten to know you know you try to be detached and ironic like a proper journalist. But come on—that just isn't who you are. Maria didn't choose you to cover this because of your sense of irony. She thought you cared about what we care about. And the rest of us just hope she was right." She was irritated, and she let it show.

It was high praise—and a professional insult at the same time. I was so tangled up with the two emotions that I finally I could only grunt and try to change the subject. But she wouldn't leave it alone.

"You're no longer a reporter, Sam. You've become our chronicler. The facts are at the center, but it is what you put around them that makes it matter. You are more like Ernie Pyle or Thomas Malory than some detached observer. They *cared* about what they wrote—and so do you." She saw I was getting angrier, and added, "I'm not putting you down, Sam. Who remembers Ernest Hemingway's journalism about the Spanish Civil War? It was what he wrote that went *beyond* the facts that made his legend."

Whether she knew how flattering that was or had just picked lucky words, I had no idea. But it worked. There aren't too many writers alive who can stay mad when they've been compared with Hemingway—whatever the point of the comparison. So I shut up for the night.

CHAPTER 31

After another week, we came to what would probably be the hardest part of the March. Even though it was December, crossing the desert was still going to be fierce. Both water and heat were going to be a problem, especially for the children. The trucks were able to carry some of the kids, but most of them were walking most of the time.

Edward Abbey, the famous desert terrorist of the American Southwest, called the Pinacate Desert "the final test of desert rathood....the bleakest, flattest, hottest, grittiest, grimmest, dreariest, ugliest, most useless, most senseless desert of them all." Granted that Abbey tried every way he knew to discourage people from coming out into lands he regarded as sacred, this was still saying something. The famous Arizona lawman Jefferson Davis Milton said of this area "Hell must have boiled over at Pinacate." The Spaniards called this part of the route from Mexico City to Alta California "El Camino del Diablo"—the Devil's Road.

The Pinacate, which covers a million and a half acres, was declared a national reserve in the 1990's. The desert is marked by ancient cinder cones from the volcanic period of the region's geological history. Lava flows from the top of the cones reach out into the desert, which rolls on for hundreds of miles until it comes to the well-named Gran Desierto, the largest dune field in North America. The sands are from the Colorado River's overflows, and are covered by thousands of animal tunnels, which create treacherous soft spots where you can sink in up to your beltline in a second.

Maria and her staff had decided in mapping their route to stay on the main highway north of Guaymas to Benjamin Hill, which was the long way around, rather than hugging the Sea of Cortés which looked shorter, but was a lot more dangerous. But at Benjamin Hill their route cut back northwest to Cobarca on to the northern end of the Sea of Cortés at Puerto Peñasco, then straight out across El Gran Desierto to Mexicali.

They had estimated that this part of the trip was going to take 18 days. It was about 300 miles from Benjamin Hill to Mexicali, and the marchers were exhausted by the 1,500 miles they had already come. Maria and the senior staff had decided to break for an extra day of rest in Benjamin Hill while an advance party went out checking for water supplies.

The name of the village was so unusual, I had to ask Roberto which wandering American it was named after. He laughed and said "Benjamin Hill is named after a *British* general who fought with the revolutionaries in the Mexican revolution.

It is very unlikely, Sam, that you will find any towns in this part of Mexico named after Americans—this is where Black Jack Pershing came in with the U.S. Army in 1916 chasing Pancho Villa. This part of Mexico has good reason to remember Americans, and not with much fondness."

I may not have known the history, but I had read up on the more recent economic journalism about the area. I shot back "Yes, and now the tourist industry in these states is the second or third biggest moneymaker. And most of their business is with the hated gringos, and the people who live here think of Southern Mexicans as lazy, backward southerners—just as we used to in the Northeast U.S."

Roberto smiled and said "You've got that part right. Our North-South problems are serious—the stereotypes on both sides are pretty bad. It is another thing that Maria has worked hard at bridging, but we still have to be careful about which groups to put beside each other when we make camp and lay out the routes of march."

And as we came into Sonora and then all along the route up to Mexicali, we had in fact been joined by tens of thousands of marchers from the northern states. You heard the distinctive *musica norteña* at night, full of saxophones, accordions, a 12-string guitar, and electric bass. They hooked the bass up to the truck generators and you could hear it in the northern camps until 10 or 11 o'clock at night.

Roberto explained it further. "The UNAMs spend a lot of their time working among the groups and keeping the norteños marching with each other and not all mixed up with the southerners. It is serious dislike, not just friendly rivalry. They see the future of the country differently, even among the working poor who are joining us. Because of the geography, the northerners see relations with the U.S. as live and let live, and they welcome the *maquiladoras* more than we do. They have gotten more out of NAFTA than the South has, and both sides know it. She deliberately recruited a lot of the UNAMs from the northern states so that we would have the credibility there when they joined us."

On the rest day, I noticed a lot of activity around a few of the trucks. I wandered over and saw a pile of four foot sticks and some thick paper. One crew was painting something on the paper, and a second group was stapling the finished papers to the sticks. When I got close enough to read what they were writing, it was clear they were making signs. The most frequent message brought back memories.

Roberto came up as I was looking at the project. He said, "You remember those signs they used to have at football games that were always on TV; John 3:16?"

I answered, "Yeah." The signs the work crew were making said "Luke 6.20." Ex-seminarian that I was, the lines came involuntarily. "'And he lifted up his eyes on his disciples, and said, 'Blessed be ye poor: for yours is the kingdom of God.' From the Sermon on the Mount."

"Yes. She believes it, and she believes that it will be a powerful reminder that the message she is carrying is an old one. We will have these up front when we cross the border."

CHAPTER 32

On December 12, the March had stopped for the day to celebrate Día de Nuestra Señora de Guadalupe—the day of the Virgin of Guadalupe. A "feast" was prepared, consisting at this point of a little meat and some vegetables brought in from southern Arizona and Sonora truck farms. Mexico's patron saint was well-honored, despite the exhaustion of many of the marchers, and the day of rest was even more welcome.

We set out again and by the 16th had come to Santa Ana, in Sonora. There was an air of anticipation throughout the March that afternoon, and Roberto had passed the word that there would be an entertainment that evening. The media people were all set up around the tents at the head of the March after the dinner meal.

I was pretty sure I knew what was coming next, and I was not disappointed. An old searchlight that had been picked up somewhere along the route was hooked up to a generator, and when it was turned on, every camera from every outlet around the world that had a crew on the March was trained on a small rise about fifty yards out from the main camp.

All was quiet, for so long that I began to wonder if something had gone wrong. Then, coming into view from behind the rise, was a boy who looked about 20, holding a rope attached to the most inevitable donkey in Mexico, on the back of which was, of course, a very pregnant and very beautiful Mexican girl.

A complete hush fell over the crowd. For the next three minutes, all that happened was that the boy and the donkey and the girl slowly moved about 100 yards from the small rise that had concealed them to another, off to the left. And the stars shone down and the desert night was silent. And several of the most hardened, cynical camera crew guys I had ever known were seen sniffling—but they all got the shot. And it was seen all over the world.

The night was December 16, the first night of Las Posadas, which celebrates Joseph and Mary's search for shelter in Bethlehem. Two homeless people in the desert looking for a place to shelter their child.

It was so corny—and it was so powerful, a truly sacred moment. I could not help thinking, with my internal editor hard at work, about the old Budweiser Christmas commercials, with the horses clomping through the snow and the frost on the window and everyone coming home, presumably to drink beer around the Christmas tree. That ad was so *manufactured*—and, at the same time, so unbelievably evocative for anyone who had ever lived in a New England Christmas, or wished they had.

But this one—this was real, and it was happening in a desert, far more like the First Christmas than New England ever would be. And in a few minutes some of the meaning of the March moved out silently and powerfully, out across the vast waves of telecommunication, in images familiar to hundreds of millions of people all over the world, from this desert in Mexico to living rooms all over the world.

As the crews began breaking down their equipment and the watchers went back to their camps, I saw Maria, who had wisely decided to stay out of the procession herself and was a distant observer over off the road. She waved and walked over to me. I wiped my own nose and eyes as unobtrusively as I could, and as she came up, she reached up and touched my forehead, smiling, and said "Did you know I can read minds, Sam? Shall I tell you what you are thinking?" Then, without waiting for an answer, she went on "You are wondering 'Did they plan this for a camera angle, too—did they plan to get to the desert for Christmas?'"

She was making fun of me and she was making fun of herself—a little. But the moment was so full and the kids on the donkey were so powerful that all I could do was throw up my hands, give her back a smile, and say "*Pax vobiscum*, Maria. *Y Feliz Navidad.*"

CHAPTER 33

As we started out the next morning, I got a call from the editor at WeekReport, Gerry Swan. She wanted to meet me in Nogales and sounded abrupt and irritated on the voice mail. She named a time and place that was not badly inconvenient, so I drove past the point where the March would turn west toward Cobarca and kept going north to Nogales. I got to the hotel she mentioned an hour ahead of her.

She had called twice before, saying she wanted to talk to me about the coverage I was sending. They were using some of it in the magazine and were saving the longer pieces for the book. Her messages were the usual peremptory New York "get back to me immediately" and I never got too excited about that kind of thing. The great thing about covering stories way out in the boondocks in the old days had been that no one could reach you. But cell phones and voice mail had pretty well screwed that up.

I was sitting in the bar having coffee when she came in, wearing New York clothes and looking hot and angry.

"Do you have any idea how many puddle-jumpers it takes to get here? I *hate* small planes!" She smoothed her wrinkled suit skirt, having taken off the jacket and thrown it over a chair, revealing a disproportionate pair of store-boughts that seemed to match her improbably blond hair. She ordered a drink and then spun around on the bar stool, glaring at me.

"Why are you holding out, Sam? I thought we had a deal."

"Holding out on what?" I thought I knew where she was going, but she was mad as hell and I wanted to see how she played it.

It made her even madder. "I'm not stupid, Sam. I can read, and I saw some of the coverage from Sinaloa. I know damn well something was going on down there with the drug lords. So where was your inside stuff, hot shot? We didn't pay you a big advance to get the same crap the rest of those guys are putting out. But you took a pass on the whole story. Not one word, and you were meeting with her and her team every day." She took a big swallow of her drink, and then asked me, "What's the deal, Sam—are you boinking her, or just soft on these people?"

I never made a big-money decision in my life quicker and easier. I put my coffee cup down on the counter, stood up, put some money on the bar, and said "See you around, toots. Read my cancellation clause. Not everybody works under the same rules you play by. And that is the last time you accuse me of anything."

As I was wrestling the Highlander on the road back to the March, I had time to think about it. She had obviously seen the few speculative stories that reporters had done when the March went through Sinaloa without incident. None of them got more than a day's play, and it had blown over quickly. My not writing about the drug kingpins' negotiations with Maria was only slightly visible from the vague inferences made by a few other stories, but they were few and none ran longer than a day. But Swan was no dummy, and she knew I had taken a pass on the real story, and she hated being played for a lightweight.

Then I started replaying the scene in the bar, and realized I had called her "toots." It was mildly satisfying—probably the most old-fashioned thing anyone had called her in a long time.

The book deal was dead, and it was just as well. I had let my checking account make up my mind when I took the original deal with WeekReport, and in my life that has always worked out badly. But the bigger question was what I was going to do the next time I got an inside story that would make Maria and the March look bad. Somewhere along the line I was going to have to decide whether I was really a journalist. I knew it would happen again, and I started wondering where. But I realized, thinking about it this time on the long drive back, that it was probably not going to lead to my being more critical of the March, whatever Maria's methods.

I had seen her motives at close range, and I knew they were good. The time with Roberto and the rest of her team had shown me who they were—good people who cared about their country, about the least of their countrymen. Their motives were closer to the reasons I had gone into the Franciscans than the reasons I had gone into journalism, and for the moment, I was all right with that.

The next morning, another bright, no-clouds day, I got a call on my cell phone. It was my sister Kathy, calling from Visalia, where she lived.

"Hey, Sam, how is it going down there? I keep watching for you on TV."

"Doing fine, Kid." She was almost fifty, but she was the youngest and was always the Kid or Little Sister in our family. "Why don't you just fly on down and tag along with us for a few days?"

"Why don't you just take a flying leap, smart guy?"

It was a family joke, unfair teasing really. She refused to fly anywhere, since she had encountered a small bit of "midair turbulence" on her first flight across the country twenty years ago.

"Look, Sam, everyone on the board"—she was a member of the school board in Visalia—"has been listening to your broadcasts on NPR and asking me what is really going on. They think I know the inside story because you're there. What's happening and how far is this going to go?"

"I think it's going all the way, kid. She is serious and these people are going to follow her and there is going to be trouble along the way and it will get settled somehow. What worries me is that nobody on either side has a good idea about how, so far."

"I am trying to understand this, Sam. But the board is in a hell of a fix financially because we have to pay to educate all these kids whose parents aren't legal. And this Maria wants to bring in a million more, and then millions after that?"

"Yeah, but come on, Kathy. You read that series I did on California education five years ago. It isn't Mexican migrants' kids who are costing you a fortune. It's the lawyers' kids who need medicine twice a day and specialized instruction and extra aides. Special ed costs you a hell of a lot more than Mexican immigrants, and you know it."

I was impatient with her, but I knew she was a hell of a lot more approachable than 90% of the other elected officials in California. There were more than 60,000 of them, and they were the key to part of Maria's future. If Kathy could see what Maria was trying to do, Maria had a chance.

"It's both, Sam—the languages and the special ed kids are both breaking our backs. And it's not just the Mexican kids, Sam. We've got fifty languages in the district now, kids from Iran and Iraq and Tonga and Afghanistan and all over the world. I know we can't run away from it—everyone wants to come here, and some of them fought on our side in some of our crummy little wars. But people up here are getting tired of doing it all without any help."

"It's how California works, kid. We are the port of entry—we get the computer scientists from India and Taiwan and the grape pickers from Guatemala, both."

"I know, I know. We can't run away from it. Our board is 3-2 Anglo now, but ten years ago it was all Anglo. And there is a Korean guy running this year who is more right-wing than any of us. He wants to set up separate-sex schools and go from 180 days a year to 220."

"Like the rest of the world." She and I had argued for years about California schools being exactly as far behind the rest of the world in test score percentages as they were in the number of days the kids went to school.

"You know, Sam, I read a book the other day about 'the new California.'" She laughed, with an uncanny copy of our mother's quick, staccato laugh. "It seems like every two or three years there is a new book about the new California."

"That's because there *is* a new California with two or three million new people every two or three years, kid. So what did this book say?"

"It was all the numbers stuff—50 million people by 2030, the crossover point that came in 2001, when there was no ethnic majority any more in California."

"The cross-over point in the schools came in 1990, Kathy."

"I know, I know. Let me read to you from this book, Sam. I kept thinking about it when I heard your NPR broadcasts about the March." She read "'Geography and demography create their own logic, their own power to compel change, eventually overcoming any forces resisting that change.' It sounds like what this Maria is saying, right?"

"It's almost word for word what she said to me the first time we met, Kid."

"We don't have to like it. But it's not going to go away, is it?"

"No chance. She says that there will be more of these things, that it's not just a one-shot deal."

"Good Lord. Then we'd just better deal with it, somehow. How are you going to stop a million people?" She laughed again. "Death, taxes, and Mexico. You can't get around any of them, can you, Sam?"

"Probably not, Kid."

I gave her my love and said goodbye. As I kept on walking, I wondered if her acceptance of the March, however partial and uncertain, would ever be shared by many of her 60,000 peers. She was bright, well-educated, and cared about the kids in her district. That was not true of many of the rest of the 60,000—not by a long shot.

CHAPTER 34

The next morning, several miles outside Cobarca, I was walking with Maria, talking with her and Roberto about the next week's schedule. A small boy, maybe 9 or 10, had been walking along with us, not saying much but just watching us. I said hello to him and asked him how he was doing.

"I am fine, Señor Leonard. I am very proud to be walking with you and Maria for a while." Then he frowned. "You and Maria and the leaders of the March are so brave. I wish my father could be so brave."

I stopped abruptly and pointed at him, the words pouring out of me. "You are wrong, young man, very wrong! Your father is much braver than we are, and he works much harder. He gets up every day and does everything he can to make a better life for you. No one thanks him, he just does it, it is his job and he does it because he loves you so very much, more than he will ever tell you. His work is how he tells you, not his words. You go back and tell him you love him—and do not ever say such a thing about him again."

As the boy backed away, eyes wide, trying to figure out what I meant and why I was so angry, Maria nodded at him and said, "That's right—go tell your father." The boy walked away slowly toward the nearest trucks. We kept walking for a few minutes, and then she reached out and touched my arm, lightly, saying "That was so right to tell him, Sam. Was it about him, or you?"

I looked at the trucks where the boy had disappeared, and I thought for a while. Then I looked back at her. "I guess he reminded me of how I used to think about my dad. It took me a long time to see who he was and what he tried to do for us." I smiled, or tried to. "I guess it was about me, mostly."

She patted me on the shoulder, and it felt like a blessing. "Maybe, but it was just what that sweet little one needed to hear, Sam. Well done."

CHAPTER 35

As the marchers set off again the next morning, I called Bill Page to get an update on plans in Sacramento. He asked me to go off the record, and then said they had been meeting almost non-stop for the last week to try to figure out what they were going to do at the border. He was more pessimistic than I had ever heard him.

"Sam, she really has us. We can't just close the border or the business guys on both sides will scream bloody murder. If we close it for a day or two, she is still there and she can wait us out. We can't get the Mexican government to do anything about stopping them on their side, because she has them completely scared off. You saw what happened when I talked to her—she's not negotiating—not yet, anyway. And we can't just shoot the front ranks of the marchers, unless we want people all over the world to add Tijuana to the list that includes Wounded Knee and ends with My Lai. Every TV station in the whole country is covering this, and they'll go live with helicopters and the whole bloody deal once she gets to the crossing." He shook his head. "All it leaves is tear gas. And I just don't know how you tear gas a million people without having it blow all over the place." He paused, and then went on. "We've got a new problem—we're worried about what the vigilante groups and the militia may do if they get through the border."

Bill was a Republican, but he had served in Vietnam, in much worse spots than I had been in, and he hated violence. He was really worried, and it was the first time I had ever heard any of the Governor's staff say openly that they assumed the March might make it through the border.

Bill said "Hearn has some ugly people in the inner circle, Sam, and they are telling him that his administration rises and falls on this thing. They want him to revert to Pete Wilson's old politics on immigration—blame Mexico for everything and block the border. To his credit, he has resisted it so far, but I don't know if he can hold off much longer."

Then he asked, searching for answers, "How much control does she really have over this crowd? Are they going to stay peaceful? Because the first pictures the media broadcast with any violence at all, it all starts to fall apart."

"I think she has it under control. It is what she is working on day and night." Then I turned it around. "How much control do you think Hearn has over the worst of the militia and his own hard-liners?"

"Maybe less than she does over her side." He anticipated my reaction, and added, "That's scary, I know, but it's the truth."

I thanked Page and then called Washington and Mexico City, trying to get some word on what the feds and the Mexican government were going to do. But neither government was saying anything on or off the record at that point.

Later that same day I called the Border Patrol directly to see what they would say. From my days reporting on migrant issues in the Valley, I had some contacts who would sometimes give me semi-official versions of what the agency was doing. I reached one of them, and he was very guarded, but he told me that they had orders to let the state officials handle everything and to keep the border open as long as they could. They knew official state policy was to "turn the marchers back," but they had no idea how that was going to be enforced. So it was going to be Hearn's show, pure and simple. I asked if he knew where the Pentagon was on the decision, and again, slowly, he said, "Everyone here in D.C. says it's going to be Hearn's show."

Two more weeks went by, hard weeks of hard walking, through Cobarca up to a few miles from the Arizona border at Sonoyta, then continuing west on Highway 2 toward Mexicali and on to Tijuana and the border. As we walked along on this final part of the journey before we came to the border, people seemed tired. The pace was slower, the songs were fewer, and in the evenings, when we stopped and meals were cooked, there was a quieter, more resigned ending to the day, rather than the proud celebration of what had been accomplished that marked days past.

We were still too far from the border for the excitement of the crossing to have infected us, but we had come too far from most of us to want to quit. There were defections, and Maria and her lieutenants almost seemed to encourage them by their unwillingness to bar anyone from leaving. Roberto had told me that they had decided early in the planning that those who wanted to leave would be allowed to do so without any obstacles, out of a fear that the ones who wanted to leave would not be willing to stay at the border if that was what was needed to accomplish the crossing. But the total numbers were still very close to what Maria's team had predicted, as newcomers from the northern states replaced the dropouts.

The landscape had also lost its allure, turning into half-desert, half-scrub brush, a palette of light and dark browns, but not much else. But I was able, in this part of the trip, to indulge another of my strange tastes: I really liked cactus. And this part of Mexico was Cactus Central.

Years ago, I did a radio interview with the world's greatest cactus expert, and what I expected to be a sure snoozer turned out to be fascinating, according to the mail I got after the piece ran. He said that Mexico actually had more than two-thirds of all the known species of cactus in the world—thirty thousand different kinds of cactus. Here, along the road and back up into the hills, it looked as though at least ten thousand different kinds were growing nearby.

There were miles and miles of barrel cactus, as small as a few inches across and as big as several feet. Along the highway and up into the hills we saw saguaro that grew up to fifty feet tall, and dozens of different kinds of prickly pear, which provided a great meal, '*nopalitos*,' tasting like spiced green beans, full of vitamin C. Creosote bushes, called *gobernadora* in Spanish, were everywhere, and were also a source of medicines, billed by some authorities as having analgesic, diuretic, decongestant, expectorant, antiseptic, antimicrobial, and bactericidal properties. Some clusters of *gobernadora* are estimated in excess of 11,000 years of age, which poses a serious challenge to the bristlecone pines of the Eastern Sierra, billed as the world's oldest living things at a mere 4,000 years. I'll let the botanists fight it out, but for me, the cacti were a natural high.

At several places along the route, we walked between rows of tall cactus, cactus sentinels of the road, marking the cultivated cactus plots; cactus barring us from cactus, and reminding us how truly thorny and territorial this land can be. And our walk continued to underscore Maria's amazing achievement in working through all those thorns to build bridges across and above the tribal mindset of much of Mexico, building a sensibility that was about a larger thing than the tribe, achieving here, at least, on this March, what her nation and the world still so greatly lacked.

Back in California, we could see as we monitored the broadcasts and newspaper, the coverage of the March had also shifted its tone. The focus had changed from *whether* a lot of unwanted people would arrive to *when* they would arrive. The length of time it had taken for the March to get from Cholula to the border had tested the attention span of the TV-watching public, but the inexorability of the March was also beginning to sink in. They were there, on TV, every night, and the size of the crowd was still immense. The coverage now featured speculation about what would happen at the Border, some informed, some wildly fantastic, but all heightening the sense of something coming that was not fully under control.

Despite their seeming nonchalance about their weather and geography, Californians who have thought about either for more than a few minutes—or have ever been through an earthquake above the 6.0 line—are used to the fundamental reminders that come their way from time to time with a simple, overpowering message: *you are not in control here.*

At least some Californians have a deep atavistic sense that you have to pay for the sunshine and the oceans and the mountains and all the rest, and parts of the price are these reminders that nature is far less subject to control than the aqueducts and the green lawns and golf courses seem to suggest. These reminders include the stark realities: that water is not guaranteed, that the summer and fall skies will fill with ash from nearby wildfires, and that the earth will shake terrifyingly every now and then.

And now, the earth was shaking with a new reminder, but this time it was not geologic, but demographic.

PART III

▼

IN CALIFORNIA DEL NORTE

CHAPTER 36

At the border, everyone knew that what was about to happen was dangerous. Mobilizing a million people was an extraordinary event in itself, but moving them all through a border crossing that was twenty-four car lanes across, with armed forces on the other side, was asking for a near-miracle. But I was certain, after talking with them during the final days as they crossed northern Baja, that Maria and her team had a strategy that would make it happen.

The border crossing itself is a series of gates with booths where cars and pedestrians could cross through the border control process run by the U.S. Border Patrol. The actual crossing was about 100 yards wide, so no more than 200 marchers could go through at any one time.

The marchers had walked through Tijuana and came to the last half mile on the Paseo de los Heroes that leads up the border crossing itself. As they approached the gates, Maria and her leadership group were in the front of the March. The border crossing had been closed for one hour before they arrived. Apparently the U.S. and Mexican authorities had decided they wanted to handle the March separately without the normal traffic of cars and trucks. They couldn't keep it closed for very long, given the business flows that would start backing up, but they had decided to close it for a few hours to see what would happen and how Maria would respond.

That morning, Roberto gave me an orientation to their planning for the crossing.

"Sam, we don't need to get a million people across to win this round. We need to get the first twenty thousand across, to establish a beachhead, and then the rest of the body can follow. We estimate it'll take about seven or eight minutes to cross that many people. So it is what happens in the first five minutes that will decide it all."

"But how are you going to keep them from gassing you or just blocking the border?"

"We know they won't block the border for more than a few hours, because we have told them every way we can that we will just sit down at the border crossing and wait for them to re-open it. They know and we know how much business crosses that border every hour. They aren't going to shut it down. They have to turn us back or let us in."

It was almost word for word what Elena had said in the meeting with the Governor that I had attended. I didn't tell Roberto that, but his logic looked airtight.

"And the gas—or rubber bullets?"

"We know they will use gas—and we're ready for it." He held his hand up to warn me that it was not something they were going to talk about yet, whether I had "full access" or not. "The other thing we have told them about, in letters and email to the Border Patrol, the Governor, and the CHP, is that the front ranks are going to be mostly American citizens. You know how many American citizens have been part of this from the first—nearly all of them have volunteered to be in the front ranks. So they will not be gassing or firing on so-called 'illegals.' It will be roughly 2,000 of their own citizens, California residents with full U.S. citizenship, who have come to help us."

As the lead group walked toward the gate, I remembered interviewing John Lewis years ago. It was John Lewis who was nearly beaten to death on the bridge at Selma in 1965. There was a mighty rectitude to him that you could feel, which went even beyond the Southern black preacher that he had been. You talked with him for a few minutes and it came to you that you had probably never known another human being who had so fully placed his life on the line for what he believed.

Maria and her followers gave off the same aura. They believed what they were doing was right, and at the same time they knew damn well that it was risky. And they kept walking, toward that army of cops and cameras and police cars, all packed tight together on the other side of the crossing.

Someone in the command structure had the good sense not to bring any dogs with them, but they had everything else—the riot guns, racks of tear gas, and dozens of county sheriffs' buses with bars on them to transport prisoners. It was all very impressive—until you looked away from all the cops and sheriffs and CHP officers and National Guardsmen and saw how incredibly few of them there were, compared to the cresting ocean of humans moving up the Paseo de los Heroes.

The California and Border Patrol authorities must have known that she would get close enough to a million to prepare for it, but they later said that they had assumed that she would lose supporters as they got near the border. They had totally miscalculated the impact of 150,000 residents of Tijuana who were along for the walk and had capped off the million—and then some.

So it was not Selma, it was the force of numbers so big they dwarfed any demonstration in the history of the civil rights movement. There were maybe 200,000 on the Mall in front of the Lincoln Memorial in 1963 when Martin Luther King made his "I Have A Dream" speech. I was there—I had just gotten out of college and had an internship in the State Department. I still remember the feeling of being part of so large an assembly of human beings with the same purpose.

This crowd was at least five times that big.

As they approached within 100 yards of the crossing, she stopped and turned to face the crowd. Someone handed her a portable public address system microphone and said "Remember, my compadres, we have come in peace for justice. Walk with dignity, walk with God, walk with the Virgin. Walk with our proud history of two thousand years. Do not run, do not let them take pictures of you running into their country like little mice."

She was referring to the ads that Pete Wilson used on TV against Kathleen Brown in the 1994 gubernatorial election. They showed a border breakthrough on grainy video, clips of men running through the border checkpoints with a voice over saying *"And still they come…"*

They did as she asked. The marchers began moving slowly toward the gates, heads up, coming on implacably toward the awaiting troops. In the front was the statue of the Virgin, carried on a smaller platform by ten young men. The signs that were carried by several dozen of the marchers had three messages: The ubiquitous "Luke 6:20," "We come in Peace for Justice," and *"Somos Sus Hermanos y Hermanas*—We are Your Brothers and Sisters."

The commanding general of the National Guard troops stood fifty yards into the U.S. side of the border. With his portable PA system, he broadcast a wholly predictable threat: "Stop or we will take action against you. You are violating the laws of the United States, and you are ordered to turn around and refrain from crossing the border illegally."

But the marchers, who, as Roberto had said, included thousands of legal U.S. citizens, continued to walk slowly toward the gates. As they approached the gates and the first wave of Maria and the 200 or so marchers closest to her actually crossed the border, the General brought his right arm down from over his head, and National Guard troops ran up from the rear ranks of the troops and fired the first barrage of tear gas.

The canisters arced up over the border station and came down twenty yards in front of the marchers. Immediately the front ranks pulled our wet handkerchiefs they had been carrying and covered their faces. I looked up and saw the flags on top of the Border Patrol building. They were rippling, blown hard—and blowing due north, toward the U.S. side of the border.

It would have taken all the tear gas in the U.S. Army's arsenals to stop this crowd, and what they had brought that day turned out not to be much help. As the first canisters hit, we began to hear a high-pitched, whining noise coming from behind the front ranks of the marchers. The trucks that had been in the back of the movement, which I had seen an hour before, moving up to about 200 yards from the front of the March, started coming toward us—but they were *backing up* through the crowd, which parted to let them through as if on a single signal.

Later they told me they had practiced this, over and over out in the Sonoran Desert. As the trucks got up to the front of the line, weaving slightly as they drove backward but moving rapidly through the crowds, the canvas draped across the back of each of them was whipped off, and huge fans came into sight. The trucks lined up facing backwards toward the border—and then with a signal from a young man atop the center truck, each fan was turned on and began to blow the tear gas straight back at the U.S. side of the border.

It turned out that she had salvaged the fans from some Hollywood movie that had filmed an "Arabian desert" epic in Sonora in the late 70's. The crew left the fans behind because they were too expensive to ship home after the movie failed in its first three months. Her engineers, a crew who had attended the best tech schools in Mexico, Europe, and the U.S., had hooked them up to the truck engines and a set of high-power mini-generators that somehow multiplied the power so they could blow the hell out of anything within a quarter of a mile of the trucks.

It was nearly over before it began. A northeasterly breeze was blowing in from the sea, which helped a lot. Together with the breeze, the fans blew the tear gas right back in the faces of 15,000 troops, who spent the next half hour backing away from it and throwing up all over their newly issued riot gear and National Guard combat camouflage uniforms.

In the confusion, the waves of marchers began coming through the border station, first with handkerchiefs over their faces and then, after the gas had dissipated, moving on through the gates in the thousands. With the armed troops in total disarray, the Border Patrol had clearly been given instructions to let them through. In the first few moments, the few troops who had gas masks pointed their weapons at the front rank of the marchers, but no one fired. It would have taken firing on the whole crowd to stop them, and no one was ready to give that order.

After it was over, Maria and her inner circle held a press conference. They had camped along the 5 highway, spread out from a few hundred yards inside the border all the way up to National City.

She was not exultant, but clearly proud of the control she had been able to maintain over the crowds after the tear gas and the passage on through the border. She talked about the movement, and the land claims, and how much she hoped that a peaceful resolution of the problem could be achieved.

She was asked by one reporter "Do you expect that all one million of your followers will stay here in California?"

Her answer was destined to be studied carefully by all officials in California for the next several days: "Not one minute longer than it takes to get the justice we came for."

But her answer to the final question was the one that sent shudders through the hearts of the Southern California business leaders and the tourist industry. There was no way of knowing if her answer had been rehearsed or was spontaneous, and she evaded the issue when I asked her later. The lead press guy for the *Orange County Register*, appropriately enough, asked the question.

"Where are you headed next?"

Echoing an old TV commercial, she smiled and answered "Why, we're going to Disneyland."

CHAPTER 37

In the post-mortem—the after-action report, in military lingo—the state military command reconstructed what had happened. The gas and the wind and Maria's surprise were what the TV cameras broadcast. But what didn't happen was more important, and few of the print people, myself included, got all of it.

In my own follow-up reporting on the actual crossing, I wrote that there were three linked events that made a peaceful crossing possible: Maria's ability to keep the marchers non-violent, so that she really could evoke peaceful disobedience; the realization that to close the border was economically impossible; and the decision not to use rubber bullets or any other kind of direct force on the marchers if they tried to cross.

As part of my reporting, I had interviewed some of the Governor's military advisors and the newly appointed commander of the state guard unit, General Rick Richardson, who had been in the front line at the Border. I was trying to figure out what it looked like from their perspective.

"Why didn't they just start shooting?" I asked him.

"Several reasons, Sam. First, they had that statue up in front, and they were carrying all those signs about peace and the scriptures. They *looked* peaceful, not like a mob."

He laughed softly, shaking his head. "We had one Latino captain in the reserve who we interviewed in the after-action report. He just kept saying 'No way am I going to shoot anything at unarmed people who are carrying the Virgin. No way.'"

He went on. "She had broadcast all those images of people walking and praying along the way, the Christmas thing, the worship services, and all that. How were we going to shoot at people who looked and acted that peaceful?"

"Second, we all had orders from the Governor not to use violence if there was no violence from the marchers. They had to start it—and they didn't. She had them under control, as she had said she would."

"Finally," he said, "there were just so many of them. Firing into a crowd like that, we would have killed hundreds—in seconds it would have been the bloodiest incident in this hemisphere involving American troops in more than a century—since Wounded Knee. No one wanted those memories stirred up. So when the gas didn't work, they just came on through, and we melted away. It didn't feel very good, but shooting people would have felt much, much worse. And she was brilliant, having California residents in the front ranks—my troops kept asking if they were really going to have to shoot their neighbors?"

Jim Rose filled in some of the other pieces later on. "The Border Patrol is about one-third Hispanic now, Sam. Some of them are 'I got mine and I worked hard, to hell with these people from Mexico,' but some are just not going to go along with a hard-line policy."

"And you heard us talking about the economics of it in the Governor's office weeks ago. We learned after 9/11 that you can't just close the border. NAFTA works or it doesn't, but it sure won't work if you close the border for even a few weeks." He laughed. "We had half the business guys in the state yelling at us about closing the border and the other half yelling at us to keep it open."

He summed up, "We built those gates at the border to keep bad guys and bad stuff out, one person and one truck at a time. We never even thought about how to handle huge crowds of people without violence or close-downs. Once the Governor decided we weren't going to shoot, there was no serious plan except hoping she would turn around."

It was 140 miles to Los Angeles from the border—110 miles to Disneyland in Anaheim, if that was in fact where she was going. She would be in the middle of several of the biggest of the Spanish land grants in the middle of Orange County. At the rate the marchers had been moving, they were a week or so away.

After passing through the border, the marchers followed the Camino Real— the King's Highway that connected the Spanish missions from the middle of the 18th century on and was still a marked highway in California running parallel to the major interstate highways along the coast. She had made clear to me in our discussions along the way that using El Camino Real was another way of emphasizing the *Californio* history that was at the heart of her claims.

Walking five abreast, they took up 12 feet of the highway. They were always careful, Roberto explained to me, not to block the highway. They had worked out how much space two to five marchers walking side by side would take up, and someone had actually filmed the entire stretch of the 5 from the border to Los Angles County line to see how much space there was on the shoulder. Using El Camino Real meant that they only had to use the interstate at certain points, and could use surface streets to keep most of the marchers from having to risk walking on the 5 at rush hour.

By the time they reached the intersection of the 5 and the 8 near Mission Bay at the end of the first day after the border crossing, the marchers stretched out for eleven miles. The trucks to feed them were ranging out ten miles inland to transfer stations set up and operated by her supporters inside California.

The logistics for all of this had been worked out by the Ivy Leaguers and the UNAMs months before the actual march, relying upon their own networks as well as much more informal village associations from dozens of Southern California cities within fifty miles of the coast. All over Southern California, informal groups of Mexican-Americans were organized into groups defined by the towns and villages their families originally came from, and often returned to for holidays and family celebrations like weddings.

Each of these groups was assigned one day of food coverage and delivery routes, as part of an operation named, predictably, Loaves and Fishes. For months, every day-old bread store in Southern California had been bought out by local village groups, who had used freezers all over the state to store the bread.

As we moved north along the 5, it brought back memories of the first days of the March in the mountains below Mexico City, when we would see only a village or two and very few people in the early days. Here, we were passing along through continuous housing and shopping malls and more housing and commercial office buildings, in an almost unending sea of stucco and concrete and steel. When there was a break, at a lagoon or inlet from the ocean when the 5 ran along the Pacific for a few miles, the respite from all the crowded, developed space was wonderful. And then we would be back inside the built-up areas and it would last for miles and miles more.

Occasionally, we could lift our eyes to the horizon, inland, and see foothills that looked very much like their geological cousins two thousand miles to the south, sloping up from the Pacific just as gracefully, with touches of spring green showing through, despite being virtually covered with houses. But most of the time, the contrast was heavy and continuing.

That night, the day of the border crossing, I asked Roberto to tell me more about Maria. I was trying to do a feature on her for NPR, and wanted to get more material. He was helpful, and as we ended the interview, he said "You should look at her music sometime. Music is very important to her, and she works with music in the background almost all day long."

So when I met with her for the interview we had scheduled that evening, I asked her what she was listening to and what were all the CDs she always had on her table. She handed me five or six of them and looked away, letting the labels answer my question.

They were all requiems—the Mozart, the Verdi, the Brahms, the Fauré, a Mexican mass.

As I looked through the discs, I again had the feeling that this was getting a little too close to home. I had spent a year driving back and forth from LA to
Fresno, covering a grape strike, while my marriage was breaking up. For hour
after hour, I had listened over and over to some of these same recordings, nothing
but requiems. Something I cared about was dying, and this was the only music
that honored it, somehow.

I shook my head at the memory, and said to her, "Great music, but fairly sad,
no?"

She didn't answer for a moment, and then asked me, "Do you know Leonard
Bernstein's Mass?"

I thought for a moment, and then realized why she had asked. "When he
changes it from *dona nobis pacem* to *dona nobis panem*—not give us peace, but
give us bread?"

"Yes, that's the one," she answered.

It was as close as I had ever felt to her, and we were both silent for a long time,
not trusting that we could do better with words than the memory and the meaning of the music.

Walking away, I worried again that I would not be able to do justice to what
she was trying to do. At the same time, I worried that I would try too hard to do
just that, and end up some kind of propagandist. Gerry Swan and the death of
my book deal had started to clarify some of it, but I was still trying to figure out
how to get close enough to write it well—but not so close I would get involved
personally.

CHAPTER 38

I spent some more time with her aides on this visit, and we talked a long time about California and what it meant to Mexicans. I had asked what they thought about the ebb and flow of immigration over the past fifty years.

Isabel Salinas answered first. "You must not think of it like all the other immigration waves. It is so different. They will always speak Spanish—the immigrant experience of coming here, cutting all your ties to Europe, and using only English is over. We can phone home," she laughed, "like ET, for a few dollars now. And we can go home for a few dollars more. There are Spanish TV networks all over the U.S. There wasn't any Russian or Italian or German TV on the Lower East Side of New York a hundred years ago. There are over 500 Spanish language radio stations in the U.S., with revenues of a billion dollars a year. So people can use Spanish all day long and get along fine. And at the same time they can use it to reach out to hundreds of millions of Latin Americans."

Roberto chimed in. "That's what California has missed—you have built-in assets in dealing with the Pacific Rim that go way beyond your container ports and your airports. Your people speak the *languages* of the Pacific Rim. And your only hope to stay at the center of global trade is to get more people who can do that."

Isabel laughed and said, "And Sam, you guys had it all and you threw it away a long time ago. Did you know that the California Constitution and the first laws of the state were written in both English and Spanish? The Legislature created the 'office of translator' to assure new state laws were translated into Spanish. That was in 1850, Sam—*1850*! Imagine what a power California would be today in all of Latin America if you had kept that in place."

One Sunday, after the masses, I sat with Roberto and Isabel and talked about the religious foundations of the March. Isabel was a very powerful voice among the inner circle for the religious part of the movement.

She explained, "It is part of her wanting to use all the weapons she can. She believes in all the legal tools she can get and in all the spiritual tools as well. She once called it 'The Law and the Luke'—she has both the legal case on the land claims and then, underlying that, she is really calling on anybody who has ever read the New Testament to bring it into the 21st century and struggle to figure out what it means to these people."

Isabel added, "But it's not the Church she is talking about—it's the message. Maria stays very far from the organized Church. It is like that joke in your play

Fiddler on the Roof: they ask the Rabbi for a prayer for the Czar, and he answers "May God keep the Czar—far away from us!" Maria loves her religion," she laughed, "I almost said her religions, because she is so deep into the native religions. But she wants to stay very far from the organized Church. The Church was on the wrong side in a hell of a lot of places in our history."

I was losing the thread—or my Anglo sensibility was foundering. "But then who is she, really?"

Roberto started to answer, and then paused. He put his hands behind his head and started again. "You know, when I was at Berkeley, I studied American culture through your movies. I had a terrific professor who thought that a nation revealed more of who it was and who it wanted to be through its movies than any other medium. He said movies happen at the intersection of art and crass commercialism. They are about symbols that sell, but at their best they can also be about using symbols to tell a story that may rearrange the truth, that may tell what we *want* to be true, that may become art somehow and transcend what sells."

He paused, "And the key to it all, I came to think, was John Wayne."

"John Wayne?"

"Yeah. If you study John Wayne movies carefully you get this amazing blend of the two clashing parts of the American character—the lonely cowboy and the leader of the wagon train, the rugged individual and the community on the move. All of American history can be boiled down to those two archetypes. Because if this life in this continent is about the lonely individual, then everybody is on their own, and it really is survival of the fittest. And then these people," he gestured out towards the hills where the marchers were sleeping, "have no place in that kind of Darwinian future. But if it is leaders *and* their communities that matter, then we need to take care of the people in the community who can't take care of themselves. And we need to give them the tools to become whatever they can become."

Hugo Morelia had been listening, and smiled at that point, shaking his head. "I saw those movies. And I couldn't help but notice who was *outside* the wagon train attacking. I think I know who the bad guys were in those movies."

I spoke up. "Now we're getting back into Catholic-Protestant stuff, and I know something about that. You're right, Hugo. From the very first, the Pilgrims' city on the hill was for the Pilgrims only. The Indians were The Other. What matters is where we drew the line, where we put the fences. More than the fences, though." I stood up, knowing I had something to say whether they wanted to listen to it or not.

"Few nations have ever been as inclusive, few nations have ever had as much to share. And the question Maria is calling is how much of it are we willing to share, how much we think we deserve it rather than having it dropped on this 5% of the world by God's grace. It is the question of the 21st century, and it is the question of the future of this nation. Of California, anyway."

Roberto nodded, thinking about what I had said, and then said. "The other part of the John Wayne thing, though, is how it explains Maria and the Governor. It's part of the answer to your asking who she is."

Isabel asked, "What do you mean?"

Roberto said, "All the biographies of John Wayne say that as he got more and more roles that called on him to be the gruff, tough guy, he changed his own persona, which was a pretty nice guy—a guy whose real first name was Marion, for crying out loud! He gradually became what he was acting, until you couldn't tell the difference any more. From what I've seen of campaigns and politics, that's exactly what happens with nearly all politicians and most leaders. They become what their followers believe them to be, what they *need* them to be, whether or not that's who they really were when they started out. And after they do that for a while, you can no longer tell the difference between who they are and who they are acting to be."

Isabel was silent for a while, and then nodded. "I think you are right. It is what she does when she uses the Catholicism as a symbol and at the same time believes in it so deeply. You can no longer tell what is public relations and what is the essential Maria."

I got some of it, but, as Roberto had said in Sinaloa, not all of it. I felt like another layer of a very big onion had peeled off—to reveal more layers underneath.

Isabel had a wicked sense of humor, and it was often directed at the U.S. media. She let me alone, mostly, but sometimes I would get in her range and she would fire away.

One day she was doing a press briefing on the March. Roberto was off at a meeting with Maria and a local group. Isabel got a question from one of the big hair guys from local TV in California. He asked her "Don't you think that the whole point of this thing is irrelevant because of NAFTA?"

She smiled, and asked him "Well, as you know, the trend in exports from the U.S. appears to show a leveling curve in the past three years, but with the emerging Central American expansion, don't you think the flow-through trade will benefit our southern states because of the imbalance in skilled labor in our favor?"

The poor guy was utterly baffled, but struggled on. "But why do you think California should have to bail out the Mexican economy?"

She shot back, "When you're the sixth largest economy in the world, my friend, you don't have to bail anyone out. But if you've got forty or fifty million poor people a few hours away, you might want to think every now and then about how California looks from here." Then she got the smile back. "So near, so delicious, so *ours*." With each word, she became less the world-class economist and more an outrageous tease.

The guy gave up, waving her off with a look that said he knew he was beaten. The rest of the media people who had been listening began to drift away.

I started to laugh, and then saw her looking in my direction. "Sam Leonard, who has been covering our economic planning, is going to explain our views on the global economy and its responsibilities to the marginalized sector of agriculture." As she walked away, she looked over her shoulder at me and made a "gotcha" gesture with her hand.

CHAPTER 39

One expression of the religious side of the March—and how clearly Maria understood its symbolism—came after they had crossed the border. As they passed each of the three missions between the border and Orange County, they had arranged to have a delegation of the senior leaders of the March and a randomly chosen group who would stay at each of the missions.

The first night, Maria and the group that was staying at Mission San Diego left the highway and walked the several blocks up to the Mission, which adjoined Old Town, a collection of "Mexican" restaurants and a few historical sites.

But more than that, Maria's "history team" had, incredibly enough, created a downloadable curriculum module that could be used by every fourth grade teacher in California. In California, fourth grade is the year when California history is taught. Maria's curriculum explained the history of the missions, it showed the route each day of the marchers from mission to mission, and, ever so conveniently, it included the history of the Spanish land grants and the legal disputes over them.

Later, I interviewed some fourth grade teachers in schools along the route and they said it was irresistible as a tool for handling the questions from kids who were seeing the March every night on television and hearing their parents talk about it. It was masterful—the curriculum was downloadable from the satellite and on the Internet and timed exactly to fit with the attention span of a fourth grader. It was just one more example of Maria's team's extraordinary sense of how to get a message across, using their mastery of multiple media to make an impression on the people of California.

As they left San Diego, having passed through the city without incident, after a small contingent stopped at the mission to hold services there, they began to walk along the 5 as it wound past Mission Valley and up through the La Jolla area. At this point, they were walking along the highway most of the time, since fences kept the group from expanding inland or over toward the sea.

Inevitably, the marchers spilled over into the slow lane of the highway on both sides. The Highway Patrol had assigned cruisers to move along the line of march, and with the marchers and the cruisers taking up two lanes, it left only one lane most of the time. Maria had said she was very worried that marchers would be accidentally hit or even driven into deliberately by frustrated drivers, who normally thought nothing of moving along at 75 miles an hour on this stretch of the 5.

But as the March continued, there were very few problems with passing motorists. Most of the drivers seemed to realize that they were part of history and that it was not a normal drive this time. There were some incidents, however— and they were handled swiftly.

About an hour after the head of the March crossed the 8 coming out of San Diego, with Mission Bay on their left, a truck went by the March in the fast lane and paint was thrown at the marchers at the front of the group. The truck sped away, but in a half hour the incident was repeated, this time with garbage.

Later that day, Roberto explained to me what happened next. In a pre-arranged plan, cell phones had been distributed to section leaders every 400 yards along the March. The third time a truck came by, once the marchers saw people in the back of the truck, the license number and description were called ahead and the marchers at the front of the March were alerted. Roberto would not go into the details, but he said, with a laugh, that the truck "had a strange malfunction that led to a rapid flat tire and a very intense discussion with some of the marchers."

Within minutes, the regional captain of the CHP showed up. The incidents were explained to him, he was given the license numbers, and Maria said that there would be no more reprisals against passing cars if there were no more attacks. She also requested that the CHP broadcast the existence of the cell phone system, which they did. And there were no more attacks from passing cars.

At the overpasses, which came every three or four miles, the spectator behavior was even stranger. The overpasses were lined with TV crews and spectators, some standing on top of trucks, RVs, and vans, some with signs. For every sign that read "Go home, wetbacks," there were two or three that read "*Vaya con Dios, Maria*," and "*Andale a* Disneyland."

After watching this for a day, I realized that the March had become part of the OJ phenomenon of California highways. TV coverage of freeway chases had become a staple of Southern California TV viewing since the famous freeway pursuit of O.J. Simpson's Bronco in 1994. People felt that going out to the over-passes to watch a chase, or, in this case, a march of a million people, was a way to be an eyewitnesses to history. So they would load the family up and go out to a vantage point where they could see the chased vehicle and the following dozen or so police and CHP cars and then wait patiently for the whole procession to come by their post. In the late nineties, someone even set up a paging service that paged you when there was a TV pursuit.

But other reactions were not as peaceful. The hate radio broadcasts that had begun several weeks earlier had become incoherent with venom, seeing the border crossing as their worst dreams come horribly true. Their calls for mobilization were filled with vivid images of what they wanted to happen to Maria and the marchers, and the call-in shows were even worse.

But counter-forces were in play here, too. Sermons in Catholic churches from auxiliary bishops, priests, and lay leaders, who had become heavily Latino over the past two decades, were making the point, as one Sunday broadcast put it, that

> *However much we may disagree with those who have come into our country illegally, they have come in peace, they have come with the Cross, they have come with the symbols of our Church, and we must respect their rights as human beings although we may not agree with them coming to our country this way.*

One afternoon three days after we had crossed the border, Roberto came to me and asked me if I wanted to go up with him in one of the media helicopters. "You want to see what this looks like from 2500 feet?"

With some uncertainty, remembering a few too many helicopter rides in Southeast Asia, I said "Sure, as long as I can take some photos."

So we hauled ourselves into a small 2 ½ person chopper—the half seat being the tight back seat where I was jammed in—and quickly lifted up over the March. As we rose, we began to see the full March spread out for the first time, stretching across more than ten miles. We were at that point down below Del Mar, and the March spread out along the 5 all the way up to Encinitas.

It was a stirring sight, with dozen of trucks interspersed among the walking throngs, bright colors among the coats and serapes worn to keep off the morning cold. From a few thousand feet up you could see the movement, a vast, alive organism bristling with points of light and color, moving ever North. Occasionally along the edge of the marchers you could see a tiny, quick flash, as some lookie-loo took a flash photo of the March to show his grandchildren.

The traffic was moving along in a fairly steady flow past the marchers, with the first lane at times slowed because the marchers were close to the edge or fences were herding the marchers back toward the highway when they couldn't expand inland along the right hand side of the 5.

I started shooting as many pictures as I could before my digital batteries gave out. Our pilot had to be careful, because there were more than a dozen other choppers up with us, TV stations, National Guard, and local sheriff's departments from San Diego and Orange Counties, all buzzing along recording what we were seeing: the picture of what a million people looked like, when they all came at once, and when they kept moving north, all at once.

CHAPTER 40

By then, a group of Southern California business heavies, who called themselves simply "the Business Council," had demanded to meet with the Governor. I found out about what had happened at the meeting from a good friend who has been at Occidental in the early sixties when I was there. Mike Humphrey was a political scientist at the University of California's Irvine campus, who had been added to the group, he was later told, because he had done some polling on Southern Californians' attitudes toward immigrants.

The meeting was held in Newport Beach at the plush headquarters of the Coniff Company, the land development behemoth that owned the area now occupied by the City of Coniff and three adjoining towns. James Coniff was a rancher who had purchased three pieces of land in the 1860's and 1870's that became the largest single holding of former land grants in the U.S. It covered 60,000 acres and included parts of seven cities.

As Mike told me the story, it was a heated meeting. The group included corporate types from Coniff, Disney, Rockwell, and a dozen other big companies. Mike knew enough about campaign finance in California to recognize that the twenty people included several who had given Hearn the maximum personal, family, and corporate PAC contributions. Some of them were very shrewd corporate suits, and a few were the kind of third-generation scions of inherited wealth who had far more money than brains.

Ron Bent, the CEO for the Coniff Company, had called the meeting. He was a big Republican contributor, a full-fledged billionaire, and a guy used to getting his way in California politics.

After a few introductory remarks by one of the PR flaks, each participant seated at the huge mahogany table offered his suggestions about what should be done. The ideas ranged from "lock them all up" to "shoot the leaders and the rest will run" to "just leave it to the Marines at Pendleton—they know what to do."

When it got to Mike, he spoke up and said "Why not just give her some land for part of what she wants?"

One of the more self-important suits was some kind of vice-president for community relations, and he was about to have an aneurysm. "Are you serious?! You live here—do you know what that will do to your property values?"

Mike laughed, and answered, "Sure, but do *you* know what it will do to Ron Bent's?"

Mike said the look on the suit's face was worth the ostracism he knew he would get for the next several months as he ate meals at the faculty club at UCI.

At this point, the door opened and the Governor walked in. As if waiting to be assured that he would be meeting with his equals, Ron Bent walked in through a back door to the conference room about thirty seconds after the Governor came in. Pleasantries were exchanged, and then they got down to it.

Bent led off, in an accusing tone, "What are you going to do about this, Governor? We are all disgusted about that fiasco at the border. How are you going to avoid repeating that?"

The Governor was fully in control of himself, obviously used to this kind of high-pressure demand. "We know now how well prepared they are, and how much they are willing and able to use the media if we let them. I do not intend to let this get out of control—there are too many people on their side and ours. We are going to talk to them and make it clear that they will achieve more of their goals by going back across the border than by continuing north. I will be meeting with Maria Chavez tomorrow afternoon. We have also been in touch with the Mexican government and they have assured us that they will cooperate once they cross back. They are only ten miles inside California at this point, and we think we can persuade them that they should turn around."

Bent was nowhere near satisfied. "Governor, let's get down to it. The only people who gave you more money than the people in this room were the damn prison guards union, and we sure as hell know where they stand on all this."

"We do?" the Governor shot back, "I'm not so sure about that, Ron. Are they hot to see 100,000 more people crowding into their hellholes? Think that'll make it quieter inside?"

The Governor went on, "Look, for years we've all been pretending that if we just built the right kind of fence we could keep them all out. As if it wasn't the economy that was the draw. Those damn fences—it's as though FDR's guy had said 'Spend and spend, erect and erect.'" He paused, looking around the room. "And another thing—I'm not so sure all you guys agree with each other on this. My staff has had calls from several of the companies represented in this room begging us to leave the border open, no matter what, because you depend so much on just-in-time product that you make down there. She says she will go back and block the border if she needs to—do you all even agree on what to do about this?"

One of the Disney guys who had been quiet chose that moment to wade into the discussion. "I've had about enough of this talk. Make this go away, Governor—that's why we contribute to people like you."

At that point, Mike said, the Governor finally lost it. The temper we had all heard about blew sky-high. "People like me, huh? Well, how much of the land you own in Orange County are people like *you* ready to give her—or do you want to make martyrs out of 10,000 or so children, you supercilious asshole?"

He stood up. "If making threats is all this meeting is about, we're done here. Call me when you have some ideas about how to respond to this. And make sure the ideas involve your own checkbooks, not just my cops and troops." He shook his head. "I thought you guys were supposed to be marketing and public relations geniuses." Then he walked out.

As Hearn got in the car to head back to his LA offices, he vented on Rose and Page, who later gave me the gist of it.

"Dammit—Lincoln was a Republican—doesn't anybody remember that?!"

Page, who had worked for Tom Kuchel in the U.S. Senate in the days when there were such things as moderate Republicans, spoke up again and said "We've done our best to help them forget it, Governor."

Rose, always thinking a move ahead, said "But what are we going to do when the next million come?"

The Governor looked out the window at the miles of built-up suburbs running into each other, with giant shopping malls in between them. "We are going to get serious about making Mexico work well enough that they won't ever want to come. And we are going to tax the hell out of them when they get here—and pass that word back along every channel of TV that broadcasts over the border. If they can make more money here, we can tax them when they make it. We can also damn well do a better job demanding that our own agribusiness companies and restaurants start collecting our taxes from their cheap workers."

At that point, he got a call on the car phone. It was the Governor of Texas, a fellow Republican, calling to offer him some advice. Rose told me about it, and apparently the Governor loved telling the story himself. He did an amazing imitation of Governor Rush, according to Rose:

"Youall haven't played this one too well over the past ten years or so, mah friend. Ah have to tell you, we appreciate the quadrupling of our bidness with the Mexs that we got out of your darnfool tactics. Pete Wilson alone was worth billions to mah state. But this thing has gone far enough—look at the map and make a deal, Governor. Make a deal."

I had to take Rose's word for it—I'd never seen this comic imitating side of Hearn. Rose said he could have done standup if he had worked at it. But he took the underlying point of the call—Texas *had* made out well because of Wilson's politics.

Later on the trip, on the plane back up to Sacramento, they got a second call. Rose told me about that one, too. Apparently an over-anxious aide had just talked to the feds.

"Governor!" the young aide said excitedly, "We've just heard from the CIA mapping people. They've done a body count from their satellite shots of the March, and they say there's nowhere near a million people. They estimate it's only about 800,000."

Hearn's face looked even more tired than it had a few minutes before. "Gee, that's great. Instead of dealing with a million people who are here illegally, we only have to deal with a little over three-quarters of a million. That should make all those voters a lot happier when they see all those people walking up the 5 blocking traffic on TV tonight."

CHAPTER 41

Back at the March, Roberto called me over. Maria had received a videophone call from the Business Council, which had apparently decided that they didn't trust the Governor's negotiating with her and wanted to establish their own direct link to her.

I walked into her RV just as the call was going through. She began by stating her claims briefly, and then paused for their reaction.

Mike Humphrey, who was still in the meeting, told me they were in the same conference room where they had met with the Governor. Bent spoke up first. "That's extortion, Miss Chavez, and you are in this country now and you are subject to our laws. We are recording this conversation, and we have drawn up papers with witnesses swearing that you are engaged in extortion. We will prosecute if we need to."

She laughed. It was not a little laugh, it was loud—louder than you would think she could laugh if you had seen her. When she stopped she said. "Very good, Mr. Bent. When you send whoever you send to serve me with the papers, we can have an exchange. I will be glad to present him with our claims which will be filed that same day in the World Court." She leaned forward.

"You must realize by now, Mr. Bent, that Mr. Coniff's name will soon go down in history along with Ivan Boesky, Michael Millken, and Jesse James, based on the land grant theft in which your company is historically implicated. We have written up the full history of how the land was taken from the Santiagos and that will be part of the brief. I will be glad to fax you our filing petition and the briefs prepared for us by five attorneys who have practiced before the World Court. They have all told us they will be glad to take this case for us. They are standing by and have told us they can be in The Hague filing papers within twelve hours. I imagine the public relations effect on your company may be substantial."

In the back, one of Bent's drones, a thirtyish woman blurted out involuntarily "Holy shit! She's really going to do it!"

Bent turned and glared at her. Then he wheeled back to the camera and growled "I don't like threats, Miss Chavez."

She smiled again, and said "Then don't make them, Mr. Bent. We were talking about rights, not threats." Then she was silent, folding her hands on her lap, waiting for him to make the next move.

"What is this 10% demand?" Bent said. "Where do you get these numbers from? Our land titles are clear, and you have no rights to any of the land in this county or this state for that matter."

"Your land titles may be clear by your law, Mr. Bent. But in the 1850's, as some of your staff can tell you, all the laws in California covering land ownership were changed to favor the immigrants, who happened at that point to be mostly Anglos. The Land Act of 1851 rigged the system for the Anglos. In the process, over the next twenty years, more than one hundred owners lost their lands. Those are the claims we are prepared to press in the Court."

Bent was fed up with it by this time. He got up from the table and said, "Ms. Chavez, this is getting nowhere. You need to turn around and get these people out of this country, and while you're at it, take the one million illegals who are already here. Then we can talk about your legal claims."

Maria just smiled, again. "But who would clean your houses? Who would care for your children while their mothers work? Who would bus your restaurant tables? Who would tend your gardens? You need to see that movie that came out a few years ago about what would happen in California if all the Mexicans disappeared one day. The state just stopped, Mr. Bent. It stopped." Then she laughed, on a roll, seeing Bent getting ready to have a stroke. "Even your Governor Wilson, who you funded so generously and who got re-elected running against immigrants, had 'illegals' working for him while he was a legislator in San Diego." Then she dropped the humor and stared right at Bent. "And how many illegal workers do you think you have picking strawberries today—right now—on land a few miles from where you are sitting—land that is in your own name?" I knew she had a real number, but I doubted Bent knew it.

Bent waved his hands and said "I give up, Ms. Chavez. You just don't get it." Then he smiled, a self-confident look on his face. "We have a saying in this country, Ms. Chavez—'tell it to the Marines.' You may want to think about that if you come any further north. Goodbye." Then he reached forward and cut the connection.

Looking at the group of us gathered around the TV screen, she shook her head. "Armed force—that is what they think will save them from having to deal with this. Now we will see what the Governor has to say."

Afterward, Roberto gave me the fact sheets that they had put together on the land grants. Somebody had really done a hell of a job. I was no lawyer and couldn't tell if she had a legal case. But she had a fine PR brief.

What they had done was to assemble all of the information that was available on the land grants, from land records that went all the way back to the 17th century. They had marked off each land grant from the King of Spain, and then with overlays, they showed how the land in the three Southern California coastal counties had been divided up between the missions, the land owners after them, and then the Anglo purchasers who came in after California became a state in 1849. Of course, they handed out a PowerPoint version of it on diskette later to all the media people.

But the clincher was two diaries that they had located. The first was a family diary and land record originally owned by the Santiago family that owned the largest parcel of land in Orange County. A media summary told the story: how the Santiagos had been taken to court over and over by Anglos who sued them under U.S. law and then denied their claims because they were granted by Spanish and Mexican authorities, which had no standing in the California courts of the mid-nineteenth century.

When the drought hit in the 1860's and 1870's, the *Californio* owners were forced to sell, because they had no legal standing and they had lost all their cattle and crops by then.

The second diary was just as powerful. It was the daily journal of a Franciscan who told, simply and clearly, the story of what had really happened to the Indians in Orange County. He described in brutal language the rape, virtual slavery, and conversions on penalty of death that had been part of the story of the missions. This brother took the Indians' side so obviously that he was dismissed in disgrace from the order and sent back to Spain, which is where they had found the diary.

Together, the two documents said what dozens of other sources had said for centuries about the underside of California's early history. But these new sources were powerful, and were so well linked to the earlier research that several journalists ended up writing books based on the diaries alone.

Maria was still waging her battle in the court of public opinion, and we would soon see how it was being judged.

I had called Jim Rose in the Governor's office to get his version of the meeting, and he mentioned that Elena was working out of the LA office, handling an assignment from the Governor to check on their links to the local Sheriff's departments. I decided to call her. As I drove up the 5, I prepared an elaborate rationalization about why I needed to interview her on the legal claims that Maria had been hitting so hard.

But the truth was I just wanted to see her again.

CHAPTER 42

She met me at a bizarre landmark along the 5 which was halfway between us—a "snow" covered steak house that had been sprayed with some kind of white sparkly stuff that would have looked like snow if the temperature hadn't been 80 degrees.

We talked about the legal claims for a while, and then she started talking about Maria and what the border crossing meant.

I knew we were getting to a critical point in the conversation, and I was trying to remember her points without making notes, getting the exact language she was using. Unfortunately, just at that moment a long lock of her dark hair came loose from a turquoise catch she wore on the side of her head. It dropped slowly past her face, onto her shoulder. As she kept talking, the lock moved as she gestured, slipping across her shoulder and then dropping to the front of her dress, coming to a rest exactly at breast level. I did everything I could not to follow it, but my eyes had locked onto it with mental Superglue, and the direction of my gaze was unmistakable.

She stopped, and glared at me, then smiled, shaking her head. "Sam, are you listening or just ogling me, you pig?"

"I'm listening, of course. I am not a pig. I am a normal human being of the male persuasion." I was trying to act wrongly accused, but it wasn't selling. So I thought I'd try another tack.

"Elena, tell me the truth. If I were a right wing hack you wouldn't be here, right?"

I was trying to joke her out of whatever was going on. But she was somewhere else.

"Sam, you're so smart and so clueless. It isn't your politics, cutie. You turn me on because I like the way you look, and I like the way you do your job. I disagree with where you come out on some things, but I like how straight you are about it. You know who you are and you don't waste time playing games. I spend the whole day with people who are just falling all over themselves trying to impress the big shots. They don't know what they believe until someone else says it first. Do you have any idea how much BS I listen to all day long?"

I kept trying to kid her out of it. "Henry Kissinger once said brains are the ultimate aphrodisiac. You're saying it's just straight talk?"

"Maybe not Number 1—but it's right up there."

I tried for the high ground. "We can't get involved, Elena. You're a source. You know the rules."

She was furious. "Sam, don't ever assume I'm stupid. You aren't screwing her—but you are damn well involved with her, aren't you?"

"I respect her a lot. Period. Look, Elena, I have covered hundreds of people I respected, and hundreds that were weasly little creeps. Her, I respect. Period."

"Maybe. But from all I can see, she would do anything do pull this thing off. Anything." Then she laughed, a little one this time, not the wall-shaker she usually let go. "Who changed the subject? We were talking about some serious sex."

"Elena, if you want to get me into bed, you've got to remember I'm an old-fashioned guy. If you call it having sex, I'm just not that interested. If you call it making love, now that's a total turn-on to an old guy."

"Sam, you pitiful romantic." She slid over to me in the booth, moved her hand over onto my upper leg, squeezed gently, and whispered, "I want to make love to you so bad I can taste it, Sam." Then she slid right back and smiled. "How's that?"

As soon as I could breathe again, I stammered, "That was pretty good. Thanks."

Then she said she had to get back to LA, and that she wanted to see me again when the March quieted down. I told her I thought it sounded like a great idea.

Driving back, I tried to figure out what was really going on with Elena. But understanding women was a murky scene for me, an area where I had never shown much ability to figure out what was really going on.

But Elena had given me lots of clues. She was, I gradually realized, above all, fiercely *independent.* She believed deeply in the conservative causes she took on, but part of the fuel there, too, was that it made her that much freer to do the opposite of what people expected her to do. It was the old control thing that plays out so often in male-female attempts to connect, a lingering layer of family history that we all struggle with, that some people allow to overwhelm them. We all try to play out a better version of our growing up, drawing on the lives of those we encounter once we're "grown up," trying to make up in the later rounds for what did or didn't happen in the early ones.

And so Elena chose unpredictable causes for a Latina woman and unlikely lovers for a right-winger. And I felt sometimes as though I was just filling a niche, like a new pair of *look-at-me* shoes. But sometimes, it felt like she was trying out something new, something I had or represented, something she needed.

CHAPTER 43

Maria's taunts of the Business Council on the widespread use of undocumented workers had gotten me thinking. I decided to talk directly to the INS to get their view on the marchers. I had a good friend from college, Bill Fairfax, who had been a lifetime federal employee, and was now a high-ranking official in the Immigration and Naturalization Service. So as I drove back down to San Clemente, I called him to talk about the March. Bill was the archetype of the kind of federal bureaucrat who makes the whole government run while politicians are making dumb pronouncements. He was totally professional, had worked in six different federal agencies, and had risen to the top of the Senior Executive Service—the highest ranked civil servants.

Bill had been with the INS for six years and was not reluctant to talk to me as long as I kept it off the record. He was on an inspection tour to San Diego. So I took a break from the March and drove down to San Diego in a car I had rented once we crossed the border. We met for lunch in a little Vietnamese place in Mid-City.

Bill began talking as soon as he learned what I was up to, as though he had been waiting to tell the story from his side. "We have five million illegal immigrants that we know about—and some estimates say the real number could even be double that. Three of the five million came across the Mexican border, and the other two million are people who came in legally on student and other visas and just stayed here. We don't have the staff to go after them, so we just wait until they try to leave and come back and then we catch them. Sometimes."

"This is still the easiest country on the planet to get into illegally. We don't have a national ID card, and the things we use for ID are ridiculously easy to forge. We raided a shop in LA last year that had 200,000 Social Security cards all made up. They sell for $40 to $75 each, and any guy with a state of the art computer and a decent printer can set up a production line in a closet somewhere. Until we can persuade Congress to use the technology that's already there for fingerprint or retina ID, we are at the mercy of the forgers' technology. Congress won't give us anything that might upset somebody somewhere in the private sector, so a lot slips by us."

I asked him "How do you feel about the March personally, off the record?"

He paused for a long time, and then said. "I hope she succeeds. I spend my Sunday mornings and part of my week trying to figure out how some of the scripture she is quoting relates to my work. It doesn't always, but sometimes it makes me wonder. Those people have walked across some of the most desolate land in this hemisphere to get to the border. When you see people as poor as they are try-ing to get into this country, you have to stack that up against a federal budget that still has over $150 billion a year in federal spending for corporate welfare."

He looked disgusted. "That's payments we make directly to huge American corporations to increase the size of their profits. I've worked on the budgets of six agencies—and some of what I have seen makes me want to puke."

He stopped, shaking his head. "I think the morality of what she is trying to do is stronger than the morality of saying that we should just ignore one hundred million people who live next door. I've seen those signs she has them hold up: Luke 6:20. She picked the right verse."

He went on. "The walk north has been going on for more than a century. For millennia, really, since the original walk south from the Bering Strait. They came south, then some of them go back north. In the last century, the pattern is so clear: we invite them north, then we send them back south."

"After the Revolution in Mexico in 1910, hundreds of thousands of Mexicans came north, and the Border Patrol only asked them to show their hands as they came across the border. If you had all the fingers on both hands, it meant you could work, and you were allowed to cross. Then the Depression hit, and thou-sands were sent back to Mexico. World War II reversed the flow again, when Cal-ifornia agribusiness needed workers, and then in the 1950's with Operation Wetback, they were sent home again. The issue became hot again when the reces-sion hit California with defense cutbacks in the early 1990s, and the hiring of thousands of new Border Patrol officers was the response."

He sighed, looking out at the highway. "So it's as much our fault she's com-ing, the way our economy works, as it is theirs. More, really. Our immigration policy is really just a residual of our war policy—we either bring 'em in because they were on our side and they lost, or—and here is where the Mexicans come in—we bring 'em in because we need somebody to work here while our guys are off fighting. That's how it worked in WWI, and that's how it worked in WWII."

He went on. "A few years ago, Peter Drucker said that to try to prevent immi-gration is to try to prevent the law of gravity. The gravity of population runs mostly North in this Hemisphere now, and it will for the next century at least. Sam," he was tapping the table with his fist now, gently, but repeatedly, "there have always been these two rivers of people moving north and then south, mostly south for the last ten thousand years, but sometimes north, and then for the last hundred years both north and south." He shook his head, looking out the win-dow of the restaurant. "When you try to dam up a river, you'd better have lots of cement and lots of land for it to back up into, or you are going to get a flood."

He went on. "They have a million people, and they show up great on TV from a helicopter. But some years, well over a million people have crossed illegally in less than twelve months. What she has done is so simple—and so powerful. She is showing Americans what a million people looks like *all at once.* Look, there have been marches in Washington that came close to that, that filled the mall and spilled way over into the streets. But they were there for a day and then they all got on buses and trains and planes and went home. These people are just walking, and that is the power of what she has done. It is not a demonstration—it is a *manifestation* of what a million people looks like. And they are only 1 per cent of Mexico. That's her message. We are here, she's saying, and we're from a place that is very near. Stop ignoring us and stop using us only for your own ends."

As I drove away from our lunch, I wondered what would happen if one of the networks just let Bill Fairfax and the Governor and Maria talk it out for an hour or two. Three articulate people, full of knowledge—not just information—but knowledge about the forces that led to the March. Would anybody listen? Or would they all be watching talk shows that turn into screaming matches—or cartoons made for adults?

CHAPTER 44

I was walking along with the core group somewhere north of Carlsbad. It was a cool day, looking like rain but not yet there. Suddenly I heard somebody from the direction of the highway yelling "If you people don't get rid of that reporter, we're gonna lock all of you up!"

I looked over, knowing that I was going to see a black and white CHP cruiser—and that's what it was. My brother Kevin had been with the CHP in Ventura County for twenty years. The only way to handle him was with an equal amount of invective, so I let fly, once I made sure it was him.

"Look, compadres—a real live California chippie. Hey, mister, are you a real TV star?" The marchers around me were dumbfounded that I was yelling back at this guy, and when he pulled his cruiser over to the edge of the road, they started to back away. One of them said to me in a voice he hoped wouldn't carry "Señor, shut up—you are going to make him mad!"

But when Kevin jumped out of the cruiser and walked over, all 6'2" of him, and gave me a massive bear hug—risking the vertebrae I had wrecked in high school football—people calmed down and kept walking around us, looking back to try to figure out what was going on. "*Mi hermano,*" I said to some of them who were nearby. They looked like they wanted to comment on my choice of brothers, but nobody said anything.

"You turkey," Kevin hollered at me as he stood back. "I might have known you'd be out in the middle of this. What the hell are you doing?"

"My job, just like you." Kevin and I had long ago worked out how to talk about politics. Neither of us ever took the other seriously. He was a life member of the NRA, had never voted anything but Republican, and worshipped Ronald Reagan.

"Get in, I'll give you a ride up to the front of this mess." My Highlander was being used to carry kids that morning, so I got in.

As we drove up the highway, I said, "What are you doing this far out of your territory?"

He frowned, "This Mexican broad has got the CHP mobilized all the way up to Santa Barbara, man. She really has us going. Once she got through the border, it got hairy." Then he looked over at me with a serious expression. "This could get ugly, Sam. We're picking up some heavy, bad stuff."

"Like what?"

"Let me tell you something we've picked up. Don't tell anybody you got it from me, OK?" I agreed, and he went on. "You know I've been assigned to monitor the militia groups up in our area, right? About a week ago, we began to hear rumors that they were headed down here to put a little welcoming party together if she got across the border. We lost track of them at that point, but they are supposed to be down here trying to hook up with some of the local bad guys." He looked over at me again. "Stay low if they start something, OK?"

I said I would and asked him what the CHP take on the March was.

"I'll tell you one thing, she has these people under control. We have maybe a dozen complaints from the locals all the way down to the border since they crossed. If this was some biker group, we'd have gotten thousands of calls by now. This sure is a hell of a lot of people, but they aren't acting like a mob. Thank God—we'd get wiped out pretty fast if they got upset about something." He pounded the steering wheel once, hard. "How the hell do you stop a million people, man?"

"What do you think is going to happen at Pendleton?"

"Who knows? Once those asshole politicians in Sacramento decide what to do about this, it's anybody's guess. They think they can stop them but the General has been running around giving everybody orders." He frowned. "But a whole lot of us agree that we don't work for him."

I told him about seeing Cousin Pill and he laughed. "Good old Cousin Pill, always waiting to see what way the wind is blowing before he makes up his mind."

Then he got serious. "If you don't hear from me for a while, don't worry about it. I've got a new assignment and if I can ever tell you about it, you might end up with a hell of a story."

I pressed him to tell me more but he clammed up, and wouldn't say another word. He started talking about his kids and my daughter and how she was doing at USC, and that was all I was going to get from him.

But later, after the March was over, he filled me in. It *was* a hell of a story.

He had volunteered to go undercover on an assignment to scout the militia groups that had been organizing a counter-strike aimed at the March. He had some wild tattoos from his Navy days, and all it took for him to look very redneck was to shave his head. He had done some undercover work on bikers and meth labs in the Valley and had been responsible for breaking up a huge network of labs outside Fresno in the foothills. He was smart, and he could get people to talk to him. So he was good at undercover work, and they used him that way when they could. And he ended up with a story as good as he had promised—but even hotter than I had expected.

By that time we had gotten to the front of the March. He let me out and I thanked him and said I'd see him after it was all over—and told him to take care. We were on different planets politically, but I loved the guy and trusted his humanity. Underneath the macho cop surface, he was a terrific human being. He had raised four of the finest kids I had ever known, with a mixture of hard and soft parenting that worked. If it were left to Kevin, law enforcement in California would be a whole lot better than the sad collection of political showhorses and abusive bullies who ran the police departments and sheriff's offices in a lot of places. He was my brother, and of course I was biased, but he was the best of California law enforcement, and at its best, it was pretty damned good.

CHAPTER 45

Everyone knew that the Pendleton part of the trip was going to be different, but no one knew exactly how. The Camp Pendleton military base is perhaps the finest piece of real estate in the nation that is still 100% controlled by the Defense Department. It consists of 125,000 acres of prime beachfront and open land sloping up into the low hills that begin about two miles in from the Pacific Ocean. Pendleton had been a Marine training base for over a half century, providing miles of beaches and hillsides for amphibious landings and helicopter maneuvers. It still had 50,000 troops stationed on the base.

But the heart of the matter was the fact that there was only one way to get from San Diego to Los Angeles—along U.S. Interstate Highway 5, which runs along the western edge of the military base at the edge of the Pacific for eleven miles. To get where she was going, Maria and the marchers absolutely had to go through Pendleton, unless they wanted to make a 100 mile detour inland.

This geography made the commander of Pendleton the military professional on point, unless the Pentagon or the White House decided to take it away from him. The commanding general was named Albert Walker, and my friends on the Pentagon beat said he was a fairly predictable, by-the-book guy with the appropriate tours of duty in the Gulf War, Panama, Iraq, and riding desks in Washington.

As soon as the Business Council meeting in Newport was over, the Governor continued south to meet with General Walker at Pendleton. As Jim Rose later told me, the meeting between the Governor and the General had not gone well. General Walker felt that the state authorities had been too lenient at the border and that it was time for the federal government to end the crisis.

As the meeting began, the General said "Governor, we are prepared for this. We're not going to screw around with any goddamn fans or tear gas. We're doing what the Israelis and the Brits in Northern Ireland did—we're going to use rubber bullets this time that will knock them flat on their asses. These people are getting ready to trespass on U.S. Marine Corps territory, and we're going to kick hell out of them and send them back where they came from."

The Governor looked irritated. "You may want to check your history, General. The insurgents in Ireland and Israel manufactured martyrs out of the kids and women who got killed with those fancy rubber bullets, and both governments ended up giving away more than they ever thought they would because of it."

The General responded, "This is not about public relations, Governor. This is about persuading that mob to turn around and go home. We're ready to do it and I have the orders to do it."

"We'll see about your orders after this meeting, General. This is still California, the last time I checked." He shook his head at the General's obtuseness. "You know, if you're not careful, you are going to end up with a picture out of this deal. Remember that guy in Tien An Men Square facing the tank in 1988? He lost that day—they took him out of the Square. But all we remember is the picture of him standing up to the tank. That picture told the world more about China's government in 1988 than dozens of books before or after."

He went on. "General, these people may or may not be on the right side. *We* may be on the right side. But the pictures will make it seem as if you and your troops are on the wrong side, unless you are very, very careful not to fall into their trap."

The General said, "There is no way we are going to let media take pictures like that. We learned in the Gulf War and Iraq that we could let them see what we wanted them to see. None of this Vietnam crap with them wandering all over the theater talking to anybody they wanted."

"Oh for God's sake, General," the Governor fired back, "do you really think you can keep the press from talking to any one of a million or so people? Or from renting a helicopter with a telephoto lens to shoot whatever they want?"

The General's response was immediate. "We don't allow anybody's helicopters to fly over this base. If they try that, they'll be forced down within five seconds of coming into our air space."

At this point the Governor clearly thought Walker was hopeless, and looked over at Jim Rose. Rose was the press guy, but he was that great rarity and asset—a complete truth-teller. Apparently the look was a signal to Rose, who laughed and said, "That's quite a novel thought, General; in addition to firing on unarmed civilians you also plan to fire on the media. That should do a lot for your coverage."

The General was flustered by this. He was the kind of hard-nosed military type who could handle a lot, but who had no idea what to do when somebody outside his chain of command laughed at him and made him look dumb. "That's not what I meant. We tell the air controllers not to let them up in the first place."

The Governor shook his head and said "General, I don't think you're hearing us. The whole world is tuned into what we are doing here, and we can't just throw a cover over the base and remove a million people surgically—or any other way. I would recommend very strongly that you set up a secure fence and hold it without any other action until we have had a chance to talk further to Maria Chavez."

Hearn added, "One more thing, General. We have some unconfirmed reports of militia groups from the surrounding area preparing some kind of action against the marchers. I am formally requesting that you give us a detachment to join the California Highway Patrol helicopters that are up in the hills now trying to find these vicious bastards before they do something that would escalate this way out of your control and mine."

"You have it, Governor," said Walker. "But if the marchers come across our line we are going to take action to protect this base."

Rose said they left at that point and caught a flight back up to Sacramento. Neither the Governor nor any of his staff were feeling very hopeful about what would happen next.

Later that day, I was back at the head of the March, just outside Oceanside. The March had stopped a half mile short of the section of the highway that ran closest to the Pendleton gates.

As I came over to where Maria was standing, she motioned me to step back off the highway.

"Sam, come here." She had the strangest look on her face, like a teenager with a secret she was dying to tell someone. "See that third TV truck?"

By now there were more than fifteen TV trucks and refitted RVs following the March, with satellite dishes and antennas bristling off their roofs. Some of them were bus-sized, with full mini-studios inside. The one she had pointed to was a nondescript dirty red one with the letters BCC Studios on the side.

"Yeah."

"I'm going to tell you something that has to be completely off the record, OK?"

"Deal."

"It's not a TV truck. It's an FBI listening post that is taping all our cell calls."

I was amazed. "How did you know?"

"Sam, we have friends everywhere." She smiled, almost laughing. Clearly she had some contact inside the Justice Department who had tipped her to the taping.

"Now here comes the fun part." She motioned to José and handed him a second phone. She whispered. "Do not answer, just say 'Yes, Maria.'"

Then she dialed his phone. Standing twenty feet away, his phone rang and he keyed it in.

"José, Maria here," she said.

"Yes, Maria?"

"José, it is time to make the move to the beach that we talked about. You need to take the main branch of the March over to the beach front and start walking along the shore. We are going to bring most of the marchers up that way as we had planned."

"Yes, Maria."

"Move as quickly as you can. I want the main body of the March on the beach by 2 pm."

"All right, Maria," he responded.

She hung up. She turned to me and said, "It is not only fun, it may make it safer for us." She explained that whatever body of the troops were diverted to the beach would reduce the pressure at the road where they had always intended to go through the fence anyway. The beach was a mile away from the main fence on the 5 and it would be a serious diversion. She had planned for this, and the FBI intercept was simply her way of executing the plan.

But she couldn't have been more wrong.

CHAPTER 46

At first the fake worked. Within minutes, you could see helicopters banking away from the March and hovering over at the beach area. Trucks of marines and National Guard troops could be seen moving toward the beach along the internal access roads inside the base.

But the confrontation was unavoidable. It was swift and tragic. I was with the rest of the press core on the marchers' side of the clash. As the first wave of the marchers came up to the southernmost, fenced border of the base, just north of the town of Oceanside, the Marines blocked them. Car traffic on the 5 was still being allowed through, but the marchers were being held away from the highway by the fences.

But the Marines couldn't cover the whole area, because their ranks had been thinned out by the fake. Once the marchers' wirecutters came out and the fence had been cut on the flank of the Marines, they did what any good soldier does when flanked: they retreated while firing.

They fired rubber bullets, as the General had promised. The front rows of the marchers were all men, and you could see the impact on the first wave of them, staggered as the rounds hit them. Several went down, which was when the worst of it happened. As they fell, the groups behind them all dropped to the ground, ducking by reflex when they heard the firing. But a group of children had been moving toward the rear once the firing began, shepherded by their caretakers, and they didn't see the rest of the crowd drop until too late.

The first rounds hit the children nearest the front of the marchers. Fifteen children went down, most of them struck somewhere in the body. But three girls—two sisters and a cousin—were lying lifeless, hit in the head by bullets fired a few inches higher than the others or ricocheting up off their targets.

By the time the children and adults who had been injured were all picked up out of the press of thousands of people, the whole group had edged back away from the southern fence. Meanwhile, the Marine troops had reformed and been reinforced by the state National Guard units who had been on reserve in the rear. For the moment, the face-to-face confrontation was over.

The wounded marchers had been moved back to one of the mobile infirmaries that had been part of the truck brigade along the March. Maria and her entourage, who had been off to the side to make the diversion look real, were just arriving as I got back to the area where they were treating the children and the others.

The three girls had been laid out on stretchers and no one had yet had a chance to cover them. The youngest couldn't have been older than four, and the other two were maybe six and seven.

Maria walked slowly over to the stretchers. Except for the medics who were working on the wounded, everyone stopped and silently watched her.

She placed her hands on each of them, slowly, as though she were blind and wanted to see what had happened to them through her fingers. She touched their eyes, and she held her hands, one on top of the other, on each child's chest for more than a minute, and then lifted her hands off and went to the next, and the next.

And then, Maria went over to the last girl, and knelt down. The medics were still working on her, and Maria watched them for a second, and then reached over and put her hands on top of the medic's as he tried to resuscitate her. Maria closed her eyes, and her lips moved. The medic, pushing gently on the child's chest, looked up and saw Maria was there, nodded once, and kept working, bending over and giving her mouth to mouth, then back to her chest. There was no sound, aside from the faint sobbing of one of the mothers of the other girls.

Then the child jerked, opened her eyes, and looked straight at Maria. Maria looked back at her, then reached forward and smoothed her brow, softly saying "*Sí, sí,* it is not yet your time, little one, *querida.*" The child whimpered for a second and then stopped, breathing steadily now, and closed her eyes. The medic said "She will be all right, the bullet hit her in the stomach and knocked the wind out of her. She will be fine."

But that, of course, was not how the story was told around a hundred campfires that night. If the legend of Maria could possibly have been enlarged, it had happened. Maria had "brought the little one back to life," and since that is what they wanted to believe, that is how the story was told.

But the other two little girls were gone, and Maria could see that. She straightened, and the tears were now obvious. She spoke as if to all who were standing there, but with her head angled up to the sky, "I am no miracle worker, and I can't bring them back to life. I am just a scared granddaughter of peasants, and I don't know any longer if this is the right thing." She looked up at the late afternoon sun, stricken and now weeping uncontrollably. "I knew we would lose people, but why did it have to be these little ones, these innocents? Why them!?"

I looked up from the highway to get my bearings, a journalist's instinct to fix the location. The exit sign off the 5 was a quarter of a mile away. It was for a street called Los Christianitos, named after the first Indian children in that area who had been baptized by Father Serra. Los Christianitos—the Little Christians.

As Maria turned to walk away to their truck with her closest aides, I got a cell call. It was the LA office of the Governor calling to say that the Governor had issued a press release saying that he wanted to meet with Maria together with the General to express his regrets and to ask her again to stop the March and return to Mexico.

CHAPTER 47

Predictably, she refused to meet with the General in private. The Governor had been delayed in Sacramento by fog and couldn't get into the Orange County airport until that afternoon. So she went ahead and met the next morning with the General without the Governor. The whole press contingent was there at the fence when she arrived. The Marines had set up a field table and a few chairs on both sides. Walker sat at the head of the table, looking fierce.

She spoke immediately after sitting down, clearly enunciating her words into the microphone that had been set up. "This march will not end until we have been given what we came for. We will not turn back until we have a reason to go home with the justice we came for. The violence we saw today did not have to happen and was not provoked. But it will not stop us."

The General, nearly shouting, said "When you cross our borders and come into our military bases with a million people, I call that a provocation. You cut our fences. And you may not know much about American history, but we respond when people threaten us like that."

I had been standing next to Bernie Williams, a local TV guy I had known for years who was covering the March for an LA station. I turned to him and muttered "Uh-oh. I think the General is about to get a history lesson."

She leaned forward and lowered her voice. By now I recognized that is what she did when she was really angry. "General, if you would like to talk about bravery and history we will oblige you. Have you ever heard of General Vallejo who fought on the Union side in the Civil War with two battalions of California soldiers? Or the two Spanish speaking *Californios* who were awarded the Congressional Medal of Honor for their deeds in the Civil War? Do you know *any* of this? This is your history—and mine. Don't you know any of it?!"

She went on. "There are warriors here in our group, General, and there are proud descendants of warriors. There are Aztecs and Toltecs, Mixtecs and Purépecha—descendants of brave warriors, some never conquered by the Spanish, and some who did terrible, cruel things to their enemies. And in case you are thinking of them as savages, all of them came from a nation that abolished slavery fifty years before yours did, General. But they would *never* have used modern weapons against children as you just did. Yesterday we did not come as warriors. We came in peace, and now the whole world sees how you answered our peaceful march."

Then she stood up and pointed at him, with a terrible look on her face. "You lost yesterday, General, more than you will probably ever know. The shame of it will be on your unit for all time. You killed children today, General—is that what your country stands for? Is that what you want this base to be remembered for?"

She had tongue lashed him in front of his own command, and in front of the media, and he was furious. But he hadn't completely lost control. All he said, looking her straight in the eyes, was "You brought them here, lady, not me. If you're not taking them home, we're done talking." Then he turned and walked stiffly out of the tent.

Later, the Governor's staff told me what happened next. The Governor and Walker had a shouting match on the phone, and the General had threatened to ask for federal troops as reinforcement. The Governor, who had worked very hard to keep the feds out of the whole thing, said that he would not accept additional federal troops, and demanded that the General not fire on the marchers again if they tried to pass through the fence a second time.

Once it became clear that the marchers were going to cross the border in force, the Governor had finally made some kind of deal with the White House that they would stay out of it except for the Pendleton part of the trip. It was a California show, mostly, and the Governor knew it. He said he would rather take the heat for something he did than take the heat for something some jerk in Washington decided to do. So he made clear to the White House that if they got into it heavily, he would blame their interference if anything went wrong.

The White House wanted to stay out of it. As Page had told me, with Hispanic voters in key states all over the country, and having made a sizable difference in several of them in the 2000 elections, they wanted nothing to do with any more confrontations with several hundred thousand Mexicans. And they knew Hearn was exposed on the issue and wanted him to take all the flak for it. So they were more than happy to let him.

Hearn's own staff said he believed he could negotiate it. He knew that any more violence on either side would make the whole thing uncontrollable. So having the marines stand down was the only choice, while he continued to try to negotiate.

As we walked away from the tent where they had met, I talked for a while with Bernie. He was a solid reporter—for a TV guy, that is—and was pumping me for information from inside the March. He could not get over her quoting history to the General.

"Is there anything she hasn't read?" he asked me.

"I think she has checkers," I answered, half-seriously.

"Checkers?"

"Yeah—like big magazines that have staff who do nothing but check facts before they print them. I think she has some students back there somewhere in the crowd with laptops and Internet satellite hookups who check this stuff for her."

Bernie shook his head. "Peasants with computers—now we *are* doomed."

Of course that was exactly what she had, plus a twenty-four hour satellite hookup to the library in UNAM in Mexico City and about twenty students sitting there waiting to answer any query her brain trust came up with along the way. Bernie's phrase was closer to the mark than he realized. But the story we all missed at the time was what Maria's technology tools said about the capacity of mass movements in the 21st century to use the mass media in a way which was totally ahistorical.

CHAPTER 48

I was tired of sleeping in my SUV or by the side of the road. So I crashed in a Best Western in San Juan Capistrano, which was conveniently right off the 5. It was a decent top-floor room with a skylight. After checking in and making sure that the coffeemaker had coffee, I sat on the edge of the bed and checked voice mail on my cell phone. There were a lot of messages from media people, and one that came with a small shock. It was Elena.

"I need to talk with you. Please call me." No emotional overlay, no drama, just a simple declarative statement. With a please in front of it, for Elena, it sounded almost like begging.

It was enough to make me return her call immediately. As I dialed, I thought that we were going to go somewhere or we weren't, and maybe it was time in the middle of this massive Event that was going on to get clear about at least one personal thing.

She answered, and said simply. "Thank you, Sam. Can I come see you? Where are you?" I told her. She was in LA in the Governor's field office and said she would be there in an hour or so. I gave her the room number and lay down on the bed. I tried to get a short nap but kept waking up with light-sleep dreams of what could have happened at the border. I heard what I thought were automatic weapons and then I woke up, realizing she was knocking at the door.

As I opened it I said, trying to keep it light, "You really did make it in an hour. Flying low?"

She was wearing a business suit, a striped thing with lapels that still made it very clear that she was female. She laughed and said "Those CHP stickers and the Governor's office license plates do wonders for speed cops." Then she got serious and said "Sit down, Sam."

I sat on the small couch and she sat down in the armchair next to it.

She began, "This started to be about my talking to you for the Governor, and then it got all mixed up with what…what I am feeling for you. And whatever is right or wrong about this March, those little girls didn't deserve to die. And I am just so sad about that. And I wanted to be with you."

The tough guy act was gone, and she was just a very strong woman telling me about a very strong emotion. It was troubling, and yet it was wonderful, the games were gone, she was laying it right out there, daring and wanting me to respond.

"Elena, how are we going to do this?"

"Do you want to?" she asked.

And for once, I answered from my heart, letting the calculation of costs and benefits drift away as I watched her wait for an answer. "Oh, yes, Elena. I do."

I was sitting on the couch, with my legs resting on the table in front of me. She walked over, unfastened and stepped out of her skirt, and slowly swung her leg, gracefully, in a nearly balletic move, over my outstretched legs, and then sat down, not on my lap, but on my thighs, easing her bottom up against my knees. Then she leaned forward and touched her fingertips to my shoulders, at the very top of the point of my shoulders. She began stroking my skin, skimming her fingers along my chest and stomach, lifting her chin and slowly tilting back her head until her long neck was stretched and her face lifted to the starlit skylight. She was humming softly, and then, as I reached forward and began unbuttoning her blouse, she exhaled with a long sigh, whispering "Ahh, yes, ahh."

Her eyes were closed and her breathing became audible, sighing in and out as I moved my hands across the smooth, light brown surface of her skin. Then slowly, she slid down my legs to my middle and matched the movement of my hands with hers, stroking my neck, my chest, and lower.

The rest of our clothes seemed to slide off, and I carried her to the bed. Then, slowly moving, moving rhythmically, then with no rhythm at all, we sought each others' mouths, bodies, and souls. Atop me, she gently rode, rosy-copper points of her full breasts swung slowly from side to side in Creation's sweetest arc, then less slowly, then not so slow, not slow, not slow at all. Involuntary sounds from both of us exploded in the room, a faint memory that I was in a thin-walled motel room flashed by, then, thankfully, it became very still. Breathing together, breathing hard, but slowing now, slower and resting.

As marvelous as our bodies were together, and I will never forget it, the memory that lingers longest today is that as we finished the first time—there were more, that same night and into the morning—we both breathed the words "thank you" at the same time. It was a benediction, better than coming together, it was being grateful together for a moment when we had made a full connection with each other, walls down, games over, we had found it, and had, for a time, become one.

In the morning, she was up after less than an hour of sleep, looking great, though a bit rumpled. Seeing me watch her from the bed, she explained, "I can stop at my sister's in Downey—I have clothes there." She walked back over to the bed, kissed me softly, and said, just before heading out the door, "This is not over, Mister."

I hoped not.

CHAPTER 49

I drove back down the 5 to cover Maria's meeting with the Governor. This time they met face to face. The meeting was held in the open, in a state park just north of Pendleton, which gave the Governor's people the ability to save face by saying she had come to a state facility for the meeting. I had been permitted by Maria's press people to cover it from their side. The Governor had asked for a press conference after the meeting, but I could tell as he walked into the picnic table area where the meeting was to be held and saw me that he was surprised that she had allowed me to cover the whole session.

They greeted each other, warily but on her side with more warmth than you would expect for the representative of a state that had just authorized the use of armed force against her group. She said "Hello, Governor. Thank you for coming to meet with us."

He said "Thank you. I want to express my deep regrets at the violence that happened earlier. I hope there will be no repetition of it. For our part we are prepared to guarantee the safety of all your followers as they return to the border."

She flared for a moment, and then calmed herself with an obvious effort. "I hope you can also guarantee our safety as we proceed with our mission, Governor."

"You know I can't do that. You are simply too big a group for such a guarantee to be effective. Many Californians are understandably concerned that you and your followers are disrupting their lives."

"No less than ours have been for decades, Governor, by the economic disruption which your state has caused to our country."

Hearn smiled grimly, preparing his counter-attack. "Actually, Ms. Chavez, I have been doing a little history reading, too. I'm not sure any of us here have clean hands. Let's talk about that for a minute. You are trying to claim lands held by *Californios*—Mexicans who were here before we became a state. You must know that the *Californios* were given those lands that originally belonged to the missions. The missions took them from the Indians who lived there when the Spanish came. The Mexican government took them from the Church and gave them to the *Californios*."

He paused, seeing that she was listening and would let him finish. "And like all landowners, they were really interested in increasing their own landholdings. Some of them made out like—if you'll pardon the expression—bandits. These landowners also went after the Indians who were attached to the missions and tried to get the authority to control them as their own virtual slaves." He paused, this time for effect. "Are these the ancestors whose rights you are seeking to exercise?"

"Very good, Governor. We certainly have had our fair share of thieves and exploiters. But yours are the reason we are here. We do not intend to change the subject."

Hearn pressed on. "Miss Chavez, do you have any idea what this state spends to care for illegal immigrants? In our jails alone, we have more than 20,000 prisoners who are undocumented. They cost us more than $350 million annually. The total we spend is over $2.5 billion a year."

"Then send them back, Governor. If they break your laws, they have no right to be in California. But the people who have come with me have broken none of your laws. They are here seeking justice, not the opportunity to steal."

The Governor then seemed to shift his whole attitude, as if he knew he was getting nowhere and needed to go at the problem through a different route. In a much more reflective tone, he said, "Miss Chavez, help me understand. Californians need to understand Mexico better. Tell me how to explain a nation that includes deep reverence toward a virgin and a fierce pride in a set of bloodthirsty ancestors whose rituals included cutting the heart out of living victims."

Maria looked angry for a moment, but then her tone seemed to soften, as if she recognized that he was genuinely trying to comprehend what no elected official in his nation had ever confronted. "Don't think we are so unique, or that you are. All people—all nations—have two sides. One of the best books ever written about Japan is called The Chrysanthemum and the Sword. It explains how a nation can revere flowers and violence."

She was using her hands now as she talked, softly pounding one fist into the other palm. "Your own history includes lynchings and the civil rights movement, Hiroshima and the Marshall Plan. Most cultures have these two sides—your mythmaker Lucas calls it 'the dark side' and 'the force.'" Those extremes are as old as the human race."

Hearn was still looking puzzled. "But what is it about Mexico that leads this many people to come here with these demands?"

She smiled sadly. "How much time do you have, Governor?" She went on. "There are all kinds of Mexicans here, and some of them wouldn't even call themselves Mexicans. There are more than 100 indigenous peoples in Mexico today, even though the government wants *norteamericanos* to believe that everyone is either a *criollo* businessman or an illiterate Mixtec peasant."

She sighed. "Sometimes you *norteamericanos* are so clueless. Did you know that in 1993, after NAFTA passed, *Newsweek* predicted that Mexico would turn into a 'U.S. sunbelt state?' Some kind of Arizona South, I guess." She shook her head. "That is not very likely. We are different economically, socially, and cultur- ally. We have class and ethnic differences you can barely imagine. But Governor, the nub of it is that we are just stuck with each other geographically." She smiled again. "And you are even more stuck with us demographically, because there are 25 million Mexicans living in your country and 8 million of them are in this state. But California is different, it is not stuck with all that Puritan constipation. It is the one place in this country that could so easily become a part of the rest of the world, if you would just look around and see *where* you are and *who* you are becoming!"

She went on, trying to make him see, trying to explain it to herself at the same time, it seemed. "In some ways, Governor, we are naive, idealistic, full of illu- sions. We are asking for justice when we have nothing to bargain with except our bodies and our being here, now. But part of what we do has to be pragmatic and brutally realistic, calculated to the last meal and the last mile. So we are naive and we are realistic, maybe even callous in what we are trying to do. But we have thought about this for a long time, and this is the only way we can see any hope of justice. Maybe we are naive, but we have hopes for justice from enough of you in California to make it worth the walk."

"But Miss Chavez, it's not just about what is happening here—it's also where they came from. If the governments in your sender areas—I read Mexican news- papers too, now—were less corrupt and more open to private investment, half or more of these people would have jobs at home. But who is going to invest where crooks run the state government and private business isn't welcome if it speaks with an American accent, even if the jobs pay five times more than workers in Mexico get today?

She looked at him for a long time, and then nodded. "You have said nothing that is wrong, but you have also said nothing that answers these people who are here, now."

He tried another tack. "What do you expect from Mexican-Americans and others who are already here?"

She paused for a moment, looking up the 5 at the foothills behind the Coniff Ranch land. "Somebody told me the other day that the mascot at Coniff High School is the Vaqueros. All those rich little boys and girls, driving their BMWs and pretending they are *vaqueros* who had to live off the land at its roughest."

Now she had let the mask of amity slip, and what came through was the anger she felt at the UCLA part of her life, when she was an outsider. But she was partly wrong, and the Governor saw it—and he let her have it.

"Yeah, but some of those Vaqueros are probably direct descendants of the Santiagos and the Sepulvedas, and they drive Chevies and beat-up old VWs. And some of them came from Vietnam or Iran or Taiwan because their parents or grandparents picked the wrong side—our side. And they work hard and they study hard and they go to our state colleges and they become professionals. And we foot a lot of the bill. And some of the rest of them are filling their trucks up with food and bringing it down the 5 to your million friends. You're wrong to dismiss all of them as enemies—just as their parents are wrong if they dismiss all of you. It's not that simple, Maria."

She flashed a look at him that was pure rage, for only a moment, and then she let it go, almost perceptibly, letting it drift away.

"Maybe. Maybe I am too harsh on them. But they have so much, even the ones who are Santiagos and Sepulvedas, if they are living here. And we have so little. That is why I get so angry. They will bring us food for a week or so, but they would never dream of eating less for the rest of their lives, or giving up a hamburger, or buying their clothes from companies that don't exploit children, or turning up the temperature a few degrees on their air conditioning so the rest of us can breathe in twenty years."

"I think you may be wrong about that." He looked at her, then smiled. "You know, we are both really in the teaching business, whatever else they call us. There is a great John Kennedy line from the Wisconsin primary in 1960. Teddy White quoted it in the first Making of the President books, the one that was the best of all. Kennedy had had a really good day and knew he got through to some of the audience and he said something like 'You can get through to them one by one. But how do you make *all of them* see it?'"

He looked at her, seeing that she was still listening. "That is your problem, Maria—how do you make all of those kids and their parents see it?"

"I think that is your problem too, Governor." She paused and looked at him with a steady gaze, determined to try to make *him* see it, one last time. "Governor, one final piece of history. You remember Stalin's question when someone warned him that the Catholic Church would oppose something he was going to do. Stalin said 'How many legions has the Pope?'" She paused, letting her anger show but keeping it in check so she could finish the story. "You're a historian, Governor. You know that a Roman legion had about 5,000 men. That means we've got about two hundred legions out there right now. They are unarmed, they are not here to make war, they are here to make justice. But they are *here*! And that is where they will stay, until they receive commitments that what they have done for the past three months was worth the walk."

"Governor, you tell me if the power of military conquest or the power of citizens is going to be the most important force in the 21st century." She got up and started walking, gesturing to hit her main points, looking more like a college professor than I had ever seen her. "Was it military conquest that determined what happened to the Berlin Wall? To the Soviet Union? To Solidarity in Poland? To the Russians in Afghanistan or your country in Vietnam?"

She went on. "It was the *people* bomb every time, not nukes, and not those pathetic suicide bombers, but the power of millions of people who decided they were done with one kind of government—tyranny—and that they wanted another. Your Jonathan Schell has written about it better than anyone else, in his book *The Unconquerable World*."

Hearn answered, looking not too thrilled to be the lectured instead of the lecturer. "I grant your point about population trumping military conquest in some of those, but that's not how it played out in Iraq. And more important, there's a third force—the power of global markets has been greater than either military or citizen power. That's what Eastern Europe was after, and that's what people want to be free to work for everywhere."

She shook her head as if batting his argument away like a fly. "Global markets are just people voting with their dollars. And some of them will buy junk to keep the junkmakers in business, and some of them will buy better food so their kids will be healthier. But the people power is going to finally bring down global monopolies the way it brought down the Berlin Wall. You know why you can't keep us out—it is because some of those monopolies would dry up if you shut the border for longer than a few days. And so our people power balances their enormous wealth and the combination of junk and useful things they make and sell."

They had gotten nowhere on the fate of the marchers, but watching them, I thought they had still made progress. What they needed most was some element of trust in each other, some sense that the other would stand up to the cross-pressures each was facing and make a deal that could stick. By talking about the larger problems instead of how to get the marchers turned around, the Governor had gambled that he could get to know Maria better. By responding in kind, Maria had gambled that she could get some of what she wanted by using the Governor as an intermediary.

The talks had helped, at least a little. But they wrapped it up by saying that each wanted to talk to their advisors and that they would talk to each other the day after.

At the end, the Governor took her aside as he shook her hand and said something so softly none of us could hear it. She looked at him for a long time, and then said "All right. Until I hear from you."

CHAPTER 50

Later that day at a staff meeting, Maria explained what the Governor had said. He had asked her to stop the March for a day while he explored alternative offers he promised to bring back to her.

Judith Izquerido was furious. I remembered her attack and her history. She was almost shouting. "How dare they tell us to stop, when we have come this far?"

Maria answered her, softly, with a steely look. "I told the Governor we would stop until I heard how his negotiations are going. He is trying to get something real for us."

Judith was almost incoherent with her rage. "And you believe him?! How can you believe him? You are not Maria the virgin. What a fraud! You are Malinche, who sold us out to Cortés!"

There are few worse insults to a Mexican Indian woman, and Maria fell back as if physically struck.

At that, José stepped forward and put his block-like body between them. "You must leave now, Judith," he said. "Go now."

"Gladly. I cannot stand the stink of the lies and betrayal here. Get out of my way." She pushed him aside, glared once more at Maria, and ran off to get into one of the staff cars. José moved to stop her and Maria held up her hand, saying "No, let her go, we will get the car back. It doesn't matter."

Roberto later told me that Judith had tried to take some of the more hot-headed captains with her, having stirred them up with stories of Maria's "compromises." A handful of the captains left with Judith, but Maria's constituency work held strong, and the great majority of her command structure stayed intact. If there was going to be an internal revolt against Maria, it would not be Judith who led it.

But the Governor couldn't deliver that quickly. She talked with his staff and the fallback deal was made. They would proceed up the highway past Pendleton to San Clemente, leaving the base area and would then stop in San Clemente for another day. She had refused to stay on the base one minute longer than necessary, Roberto told me.

The next day, the General allowed them to pass through the fence without incident. Marines were lined up at the gate, but not in battle gear. The March passed through and stayed very carefully on the 5, not spilling over into Pendleton proper on the other side of the base's fence that lined the highway.

After walking on the 5 for a little over two hours, they came to the hated Border Patrol checkpoint, still inside the boundaries of Camp Pendleton. Dozens of immigrants had been killed in this strip over the past twenty years. This was where the Border Patrol stopped cars looking for illegals, and knowing that, hundreds of illegals had jumped out of cars along here, seeing the checkpoint looming ahead. Several of them had been hit and killed by cars slowing for the checkpoint. It had gotten so bad that there was a sign in silhouette of a man, woman, and child running, making clear that pedestrian traffic was prohibited but also warning drivers.

Maria had talked for a long time at the morning masses the day before, impressing upon the marchers that they were to take no action against the hated Border Patrol, *la migra* of countless tragic stories of arrest, imprisonment, beatings, and death. "They have only been doing their job, sad as it is, and we must give them no ammunition to use against us. We must turn the other cheek, brothers and sisters, as hard as it is, and walk through the checkpoint as we did the border, with our heads held high."

And that is what they did. The Patrol had pulled its officers off of the checkpoint, and their cars were lined up along the side of the road where their control station buildings were located. Hundreds of them in the hated brown uniforms stood there, glaring at the marchers. Every now and then one would step forward and make an obscene gesture or spit, but most of them stood silent, watching the marchers as they took five hours to cross the checkpoint. Clearly they had their orders too.

After another half mile from the checkpoint, the front of the March had come to San Onofre—a narrow strip of land that ran from the shore up about two or three hundred yards into the foothills. It was the point on the trip where the hills were closer to the highway than at any other spot on the route they had chosen. After that stretch, the nuclear plant at San Onofre came into view and then San Clemente loomed up ahead and the highway swung inland with the sea out of sight. The nuclear plant was only a few hundred yards from the highway, its two circular holding tank containers in full view.

There had been negotiations about the nuclear plant from the moment the March had crossed into California, since it was such an obvious flash point. The top officials at the Energy Department in Washington had almost melted down themselves at the thought of one million uncontrollable people walking within a few yards of the plant, and Maria had pledged early on that the Marchers had no designs on the plant and would respect military barriers there.

Again, Marine and National Guard troops were lined up between the plant and the 5, which were separated by only a few hundred yards at that point. The marchers moved on, and there were no incidents. Then the March stopped and camp was set up just outside the boundaries of Pendleton.

CHAPTER 51

I had settled into my tent and was making notes, when Roberto stuck his head inside. "Something has happened, she wants to see you."

As we were walking toward her tent, he spoke softly to me so no one could hear. "She wants to see you to explain, so that it doesn't come out as some kind of scandal. It is about her children."

"Her children?" I was floored.

Motioning for me to speak quietly, he said while walking "She had the twins—a boy and a girl, Angelina and Esteban—when she was at UCLA. Their father is a Latino from Villa Park whose family is very wealthy, and he kept the kids. That is what it is all about."

I entered the tent and saw her standing by her desk. She had been crying, and she made no attempt at all to hide it. Tears ran down her face. "They are trying to make me turn around by using my own babies against me. They are threatening that I will never see them again."

I had never seen her like this. She was completely in collapse, could barely hold herself up. She slumped into a chair. She sobbed for a minute or two, then made a visible effort to stop, holding herself as tightly as her arms would allow. Gradually, I saw the control coming back.

She motioned for me to sit down. "I want to tell you the whole story, and then you can write whatever you want. I have never tried to hide them, but," she closed her eyes and slumped forward for a moment, then re-opened them, "but I have not been able to be with them. Their father wanted it that way."

"Tell me about it," I said.

And so she did. They had become lovers at UCLA in her junior year, and when she told him she was pregnant, he pulled away from her, as she put it, "like I was a hot rock." His family then came into it, and his father met with her several times over the last month of the pregnancy to negotiate the transfer of the twins to his family. She agreed because she was certain she had no future with Eduardo, and she had already begun to plan to return to Mexico to finish her degree at UNAM and begin the anthropology work with the native groups.

"So you see I am no Santa Maria." She said in a very small voice. "I had my babies out of wedlock and then I left them to come back to Mexico. I have seen them four times in the last fifteen years—they are fifteen this month. I cry every time I think of them for more than a few seconds, so I try not to think about them. It is the hardest thing I must do. It is why the music—" but she couldn't finish the sentence and lowered her head into her hands again, weeping.

"But why did you leave them?"

She sighed, tossing her hands up in the air in a gesture of hopelessness. "Eduardo and his family are very much of the old school, the way of life that many upper-class Mexicans aspire to. They are *criollos*—or they think they are—and *indios* are lower class to them, almost outcasts. Eduardo could never get over the fact that I had so much *indio* blood and that I talked about it all the time and wanted to go back and work with them. But by the time we figured out how high that wall was, I was pregnant."

She went on, frowning, "Eduardo's phrase—which I will never forget—was that he would never allow his son to be raised 'in a stinking Indian village in Mexico.' He doesn't know what to make of Angelina, and I am not sure how she is turning out. But Esteban is lost to me already. He is his father's son, hating *indios* and all that goes with it. It is the same thing we face in Mexico, every day, this terrible gap between the upper class and the *indios*. But here," she paused, starting to sob, "here it is my son who hates us."

She had written Eduardo repeatedly and asked to be able to see the children on a regular basis. On her other visits, she had simply shown up at their house and refused to leave until they allowed her to see the children. He had not even answered her letters until that morning, when he sent her a letter by a messenger.

Eduardo's father, who had a large construction company, had pressured Eduardo to call Maria to a meeting. The quid pro quo was she could continue to see the twins if she would back off and take the marchers home, drop the land grant claims and settle for some cash for job development in Mexico. Once she agreed, Eduardo's father would tell the Business Council that they had made an arrangement with the Mexican government to force the marchers to come home in return for the new jobs. "They want to avoid all visible contact with us."

She shook her head sadly. "Eduardo and his father want so much to be part of the oligarchy here—they would do anything to get invited to those homes in Brentwood and Newport."

"Are you going to go?"

"I would do almost anything to see my children regularly," she said sadly.

"Even change the goals of this march?"

She smiled through her tears. "Always, always the hard questions, *mi amigo*. No, I will not do that. But I will meet with them and see what they want. At worst, I see my children again."

As I walked away, I realized that it was Sinaloa all over again, but in a far more personal way. What was newsworthy about Maria's children, and what was just her own sad history, unrelated to what she was trying to do? And again, I knew I would have to decide what to write and what to set aside.

CHAPTER 52

Later that day I got a call from my daughter, who was more than a little worried that I was in the middle of all of the violence and wanted to talk with me. Elisabeth said she was driving down from USC and wanted to meet with me for breakfast in San Clemente.

I've been a good father, much better than the husband I was. And one of the rules that made it work was she wouldn't ask me for a lot, but when she did, or when she wanted to see me, I did everything I could, wherever I was, to get there. So I got in the Highlander and headed north on the 5 again.

Elisabeth was a business major at USC, with her mother's acute sense of selling and enough offhand charm to shine in any role she took on. She had never cared much about the stuff I did—politics and journalism were just what I did, they were not of much direct interest to her. But she saw through people like a laser. Sometimes I counted on her to cut through the BS and give me an honest reaction to whatever I was working on at the moment.

We met at a Denny's restaurant. It was a family joke—when she was growing up, I had her convinced for a long time that eating at Denny's was the best thing in the world. Later, when she figured out that it wasn't really the height of upscale, she forced me to take her to some really expensive places as "makeup calls," as they say in baseball. But recently, we had gotten retro about it and ended up usually going back to Denny's when we met.

Having a meal with her was always a kick for me. It was like sitting with a circus troupe—something was always happening. She would check out the waiters, check out the menu, check out the people in the next booth over—and then when she stopped and riveted her attention on you, it was spellbinding—she made you feel like the whole world was waiting to hear what you had to say. Coming from a kid I really liked, it felt terrific.

After we had ordered and exchanged family gossip, she asked me, "What is this all about, Dad? Is she nuts or what?"

"She is not nuts. She is absolutely sincere about her goals, and people see that. But she also understands the power of media and knows how politics works both in her country and here. She reminds me—this is crazy—but she reminds me of your grandmother. You remember how your grandmother would get an idea and then there was no budging her on it, no matter what? She is just like that. She just *knows* she is right and she can convince people of it."

"Is she going to get what she wants?"

"She is going to get some of it. I don't know if she has an end game worked out, or if she waits for divine inspiration, or just improvises beautifully. But she is not going away empty-handed from this."

"You seem like you really like her."

"I more than like her—I respect a lot of what she is doing. But I have also seen her manipulate people and the media to get what she thinks is right. She has thought a lot about what she is doing and she just believes that it is the only way to break through the attitudes here and in Mexico. She cares totally about working class Mexicans and the Indian cultures that she knows so much about. But I sometimes think there is nothing that she won't do to get what she has set up as the goal of this whole thing. She is not going back without getting a lot of something."

"I hear some terrible stuff on the radio—is she in danger?"

"Anyone who wants to change things and decides to walk through two of the most conservative counties in this country is in danger. Now that they have crossed the border, they have to get through a hundred miles full of right wing gun nuts, militia members, patriotic bikers, ex-marines, real marines, skinheads, and wall-to-wall Republicans. Some of the decent Republicans, for sure, but also some of the I've-got-mine-and-to-hell-with everyone-else Republicans, people hanging onto the middle class by the skin of their teeth and frightened to death that someone is going to take it away. There are a lot of people out there who think she is a threat."

"What about you—are you safe? Why are you doing this?"

I had thought a lot about both questions, and I still wasn't sure I could explain it, even to somebody who knew me as well as my daughter. "I think I'm OK—shooting a reporter is a crummy way to get your ideas across in this country. And I guess I'm doing this because it's a hell of a story, and because she has let me in to see it up close. I think I know a lot about California and Mexico, and I want to try to tell the story as clearly as I can."

I could tell she wasn't completely sold, but she knew me well enough to know that I was going to go ahead and cover it. "Take care, Daddy—I need your checkbook around for graduate school." This was our tough-guy way of talking to each other, and the translation was *I am worried about you and I want you to be careful.*

As I drove back to the marchers' camp, I thought about her questions and how I had answered them. I added it up and realized that the subtext was that I was not yet convinced that it was that safe, and I wasn't at all sure what was going to happen if it wasn't.

CHAPTER 53

Maria had asked me to come along for the visit with her children. Whether I was along as a reporter or as a friend wasn't clear, but I agreed. We drove up to a private home in the Orange Hills behind the city of Valencia.

She was quiet all of the way, worried and frowning, lost in herself in a way I had never seen before. The only smile on the trip came when we passed a hastily painted sign on an overpass. It read *"Vaya con Dios, Maria!"* The slogan had become a battle cry for the pro-marcher segment of California's population, and we were to see it many times in the next few days.

The car pulled up to a very large house set on the peak of one of the foothills. In one of the countless ironies of life in California, it was a Spanish colonial style mansion.

As we got out of the car, she leaned for a moment on José. For the first time, she looked tired, and I could tell that this visit was taking a lot out of her. But then the door of this very large house opened and out came a beautiful young woman who could only be her daughter, who ran forward and hugged her. "Mama, Mama, thank you for coming. I am so glad to see you, oh, I have worried about you, Mama."

Maria was crying, José was crying—he of the rock-hard countenance, I was crying—my Irish genes, no doubt. As we walked inside, Maria and her daughter, walking side by side with their arms around each other, were talking a million miles a minute to each other, lost in each other.

I was not part of the meeting inside. Perhaps Maria had finally decided she needed to get out of the fishbowl for a few minutes and be a person, a mother, without observers. She went into an inside room with Angelina, and José and I walked out a patio door to wander around the grounds of the estate.

"What do you think is going to happen?" I asked him.

"It is going to be very sad. Eduardo wants her to agree to leave California and says if she does, he will let her see the kids regularly. But her son doesn't even want to see her. The girl is different. There is a lot of Maria there. One day she will be all right, I think. But she is not going to leave all this"—he gestured at the grounds and the mansion—"to come walk along the highway with us. She is not ready. And anyway Maria will tell Eduardo 'No way, we are not ready to go home yet.' And it will end sadly."

We spent an hour or so just sitting among the roses in the garden. Then one of the staff from the house came out and beckoned us to return. We walked back to the house, and in a few minutes the inner door to the living room opened and Maria and Angelina came out. They were both crying.

As Maria and Angelina walked to the car, tears flowing down both their faces, I heard Angelina saying to her mother "I see what you are trying to do, Mama, and I love you for it. I am so proud to be your daughter. It is not something I can do, but I am so proud of you for trying."

We got in the car, and Maria quickly rolled down the window to see Angelina, who stood next to the car. She reached in and embraced her mother, then stood back and said, with a defiant look on her face, "*Vaya con Dios*, Mama."

The drive back was heart-breaking. Maria completely broke down as we drove away, sobbing uncontrollably. She said little, but kept repeating "He was only with me for five minutes." Apparently her son had come in, said a few words to her, and then refused to speak.

After ten minutes or so, she got herself under control, and I felt I could ask her the question I had to ask.

"Why did you ask me along on this part of the trip?"

"Because one day you are going to write a book, and I want it to be the truth—all of the truth. But not now—not until they are grown and can make their own choices about me."

By the rules of journalism, she had said those two words—*not now*—too late to be binding on me. I could write what I had just seen, and its full history going back seventeen years, if I wanted. Maria had not asked me for any conditions on my going with her to see her kids, and I had not agreed to any.

But by the rules of any kind of human decency, the story was spiked, as the oldtimers used to say—stuck on a *don't use* spike because it didn't fit today's paper or someone decided it wasn't a story we were going to use. And it wasn't a story I was going to use. It was about Maria, not about the March, and I could tell the difference.

CHAPTER 54

It was very early the next morning that it happened. We were at the new camp, beside the 5 at San Clemente, just north of the nuclear plant and near some foothills that sloped back up from the highway. Only the head of the group was there, the first thousand or so of the marchers. The main body of the marchers were still scattered back along the 5, partly inside and partly out of Pendleton.

We had gotten some reports that local groups opposed to the March were starting to line the main highway and that there could be trouble that went well beyond a few punctured tires and cans of paint.

She was speaking to the small group around her as the Mass broke up. I had wanted to interview her about what she was going to do next, and had passed the word through Roberto that I would see her after the Mass. As she finished and the group began moving away from her, she turned to move back toward the body of the marchers. Seeing her moving away from me, and afraid I would miss the chance to talk with her, I called out "Maria, over here!"

She heard me, and turned quickly toward me. Just then we all heard a loud crack, and then three more. She dropped without saying a word, and the whole right side of her dress was instantly covered with blood. Roberto was also hit, in the leg from what I could see.

Eight of her aides quickly linked arms, forming a shield, and turned outward, as though they had practiced the act. I pushed through the crowd, and then joined them, trying to keep the crowd back. The doctor who traveled with the lead group, Dr. Luis Ortega, rushed up and checked her and then said to José, "Call immediately for a county Medevac, and ask that she be taken to Doctor's Hospital in Citrus City—they will take her there, I know."

José shouted "We cannot trust her to their hospitals—they will try to get her again if they have not killed her now."

Ortega shook his head furiously. "Listen, I know the doctors there. She and I planned this in advance. We picked hospitals for each of the days of the March. Now make the call, quickly, we are going to lose her!"

We stood around for a few minutes, watching Ortega work on her and Roberto. Then, as the Medevac chopper arrived and quickly loaded her in and took off, I jumped into a van that Isabel had commandeered to drive some of the core staff up to the hospital. As we drove, I replayed the incident. I realized that I may have shifted the shooter's angle when she turned as I called to her. I hoped so, and said the first real prayers I had offered in a long time.

José told me, as the ambulance sped away up the 5 toward Citrus City, that as she was being lifted into the back of the ambulance, she had reached out and grabbed his arm, and told him urgently "Tell them no violence, there must be no violence, no revenge. Stay here until you hear from me." As they were shutting the doors, her final phrase was "No violence, please—no violence, tell them for me."

And so the word was passed, and hundreds of meetings were held around the campfires that night, and the marchers talked it out, and her words were repeated. And they honored her by sitting quietly with their sorrow and their fears, instead of raging out into the night and tearing apart suburban Southern California, as might have happened in another time and another place, with another leader. But here, they kept her peace.

It was another of the big things that didn't happen—the rage at her attempted assassination was not transformed into riots that would have ended the March's peaceful message.

PART IV

▼

GOING HOME

CHAPTER 55

Jim Rose told me what happened back in the Governor's office once he heard. He was beyond angry—he was white-hot determined that it was the last incident.

He called General Walker at Pendleton ninety minutes after the shooting. Rose said Hearn was practically screaming into the phone.

"General, these people operated from your base. We have proof of that—the media have pictures of her being shot, we have one video shot of the hills showing a puff of smoke, and the CHP labs have already analyzed it. They say that shot had to come from your base." He was boiling angry, Page said, furious in a way he had never seen Hearn before. "So what are you going to do about it, General?—because I am ready to charge the Defense Department with dereliction of duty in my next press conference. First you shoot kids and then you let assassins onto your base. I will put whatever you want in writing but I want your people to take them out and I want it now. And I want no repetitions. Will you do it?"

Walker was more controlled, and knew he had to respond. "Calm down, Governor. We have our choppers in the air. I talked to the Corps Commander and the Joint Chiefs this morning after the shots were fired, and they have all talked to the White House. Everyone agrees we've got to avoid any more threats to peaceful demonstrators. I have moved two regiments of marines to line their march. I already have four strike units in the air over the hills behind San Clemente—we will have the militia units neutralized within the hour. We have had our spotters up since the attempt on her life and know exactly where they are. I will call you back when they are in our hands."

He paused, "We will do it right this time, Governor. Those bastards operated from our base and I am going to find out how it happened. You are going to remember more about what we do today than what happened at the gate at Oceanside. No one else is getting hurt on this base unless they are genuine bad guys."

Back in the car as they drove to the airport in Sacramento, Hearn told Page and Rose, "This is over now—now we have to protect them. We are not going to have assassins operating in California. I lost my options the minute that nut pulled the trigger. The doctors told us a few minutes ago that she will survive, and that means that she is in control now. My job is damage control and I am going to do one hell of a job of damage control from now on."

Rose asked him who he thought was behind it.

The Governor answered, as they drive to the airport in Sacramento. "None of the top guys who oppose her would stoop to this, but they have a way of making it happen as old as Becket and Henry in the 12th Century. Some corporation president or rightwing nut says 'I sure wish somebody would take care of this for me.' And somebody thinks they are going to be promoted because they are going to be more ruthless and tougher than the next guy, and so they hire a triggerman and it takes off from there. But the top ones never spoil themselves with this kind of work. They are far above it, far too elegant for it. They mostly hire smart people to work for them, but every now and then they need to hire a dumb one to do something like this and be available to take the rap."

As we learned later, the Governor was right about the motivation—but dead wrong about where the plot started. It had been his own remark, and the actions of his own staff, that had set the assassination attempt in motion.

Back at the March, they told me it had turned into the most amazing sight of the whole amazing journey. Starting at 8 am, less than an hour after she had been shot, the marines started coming out of the Oceanside barracks and loading into trucks heading up the 5. Every hundred yards they dropped off two fully armed marines. At first the marchers were terrified, thinking they had been pursued from Pendleton, but then they realized that as the marines jumped out of the trucks, they were turning toward the hills and away from the marchers, watching for any hostile threat. It helped that about half of the marines spoke Spanish— they must have done one hell of a job of screening files for languages since the girls had been killed.

Within thirty minutes, there were eleven miles of locked and loaded marines, strung out along the highway, on the eastern edge of one million people. There was a Marine every 50 yards for 11 miles—a total of seventeen thousand of them.

It looked like something out of a surreal John Ford movie, updated to the 21st century: the cavalry riding to the rescue. Only it was Marines in trucks, instead of the army on horses—and they were protecting a crowd that was probably half Indians from domestic terrorists with sniper rifles.

Out on the highway, most of the locals who opposed the March melted away once they figured out who the Marines were protecting and who they were aiming at. But out of sight of the deployment, a group of skinheads who had been blocking the road at the head of the March was getting bolder. I heard this story later from one of the March captains who was at the front of the line.

The skinheads had moved down the highway toward the marchers early that morning. The leader, a pimply-faced, pear-shaped six-footer who probably weighed 280, was screaming obscenities at the marchers. Just then, the first of the

Marine trucks pulled up to the head of the marchers' column and four Marines jumped out of the back in full battle gear.

The skinhead leader yelled "Hey look, it's the Marines come to kick some beaner butt. Hey guys, let's rock and roll."

As the four Marines jogged up to the front of the column, they spread out five feet apart from each other, facing the skinheads, with their M-16s at port arms. The lance corporal who was in charge barked at the skinheads, "People, stand back away from this group of marchers. That is an order. Stand back immediately."

The skinheads looked dumbfounded at being ordered to back off. "Who are you to tell us to lay off these miserable Mexs, buddy?"

The Marine answered "I am Lance Corporal José Martinez, mister, and you are about to get my foot planted on your face unless you take fifty steps to the rear NOW!"

Before the skinheads could move, the four Marines reached down to their belts, pulled up their bayonets, and snapped them on their weapons in one smooth movement. The one on the left started shouting as he started taking short slide steps toward the skins with his rifle extended fully out in front of him, "And I am Private Richie Alvarez and you are going to back off, scumbags." The one on his right yelled out, taking the same short steps toward the skins, who were now falling over themselves running backwards, "And I am Private Eddie Molina and you are going to leave these people alone *forever*."

The last marine, who was about 6'3", blond, and as Anglo-looking as George Washington, hollered "And I am Private James Patrick, and these guys are my buddies, and I hope to God you assholes give me an excuse to kick your sorry, sloppy butts from here to Denver. Move!!"

By now the skins were running full out down the highway, looking back over their shoulders at the horrible apparition that had suddenly confronted them: U.S. Marines hell-bent on perforating them some new orifices.

CHAPTER 56

Back up in the hills, they caught all of the militia, after a brief fire fight. The militia guys had split up on three escape routes, and the leader of one unit, a guy named Lutkin, decided to fight it out with the Marine chopper team. He got off several rounds at one of the choppers, but the Marine after-report indicated that the cross fire from the .50 calibers on the two choppers had completely cut the guy in half. The General had demanded that they try to take the militia members alive to find out who was behind it, and although the militia people were pretty well shot up, only Lutkin was killed.

Later the interrogation revealed that Lutkin and one other guy, named Shaw, were the triggermen. The guys closest to the shooting thought that Shaw had actually fired the shot that hit Maria, but they weren't sure. Shaw had taken several rounds in both legs and wouldn't be walking again without a lot of plastic and wire. He gave up the names of his backers immediately—no tough guy shield stuff for him. It was not difficult to track the calls and meetings from Lutkin and the other leaders of the militia units back to the Governor's aide.

Several careers ended abruptly, including the nearly the entire top echelon of the National Guard brass. The Governor's military liaison who had first carried the message from the staff meetings in December was indicted on conspiracy charges, tried, and found guilty. Luckily for him, it was decided that there was no prison in California that was safe for him, and he was sent to federal prison for ten years.

The connection to the Governor was obvious, but he handled it well by turning his guy in the minute he got the report from the state police investigation and the FBI. The way the California papers played it, it came across as a rogue operation that Hearn completely disavowed. But if Hearn hadn't made the moves he made in the next few days, it might have started to look very bad for him.

It was not a story I wanted to write, but within a week after the shooting, I had the details. I had it from my brother, who surfaced after his undercover assignment. He hadn't gotten all the way into Lutkin's hit squad, but he had talked to two guys in the militia who knew of Hearn's conversation with the military liaison officer in the room.

Kevin told me he wasn't going to tell anyone else about the link to the Governor's remark. His words were "This story is never getting out through me, man. It's up to you. But he started this thing. He said he wanted her taken out. It may not have been what he meant, but he said it."

On something like this, my brother had the sense of morality of an Inquisition judge. He doesn't do a lot of grays—the world is naturally black and white for him. But on going public with it, it was my call. He would let me go with the story and risk his career, or drop it.

As if reading my mind, he said "And don't worry about my job, man. I put my papers in three months ago—I'm out of here by the end of the year. There is nothing they can do to me."

The other stories about the militia had all missed the connection with Hearn's remark, and the staff guys who were arrested weren't talking about that either. But I had it, and I knew the background. It was a careless remark by a usually careful politician. But like a small stone rolling down a rocky slope, it started many other, more dangerous shifts in the substrata of California's most militant haters.

They actually found a journal written by one of Lutkin's lieutenants, a former Green Beret who had never wanted the war to end—any of them. It was a pretty ugly little document, full of racist slurs and xenophobic attacks on the marchers and all Mexicans.

But it also revealed the tangled economic underside of the anti-marcher sentiment at its most vitriolic, a strange mixture of resentment at seeing Mexicans working and an admission that the jobs they were doing were "beneath" American workers. The crop-picking, lawn-mowing, and pet-bathing jobs that legal and illegal immigrants took were the bottom rung of the California economy, a rung that most workers were glad to skip over on their way up—even if their own move was going to end at the next rung up.

I had long believed that there should be Departments of White Trash Studies at California universities, given the importance of that remarkable and sizable segment of society. If they wanted to call it "Anglo lower-income studies," or some other euphemism, fine. But anyone remotely familiar with the demographics of methamphetamine production or child abuse or alcoholism or crime in trailer parks could contribute to "white trashology," and it would be a very fertile field.

So now I had another story that was hot, and no clear idea of what to do with it. Maria had kept the story of her kids completely out of the media, and I had decided my accompanying her was off the record, whether she wanted it to be or not. So deciding what to do with either or both of them brought me right back to where I had been before Sinaloa—trying to figure out what to use and why.

The first day Maria made me the offer to go inside, she said it was because I would tell the truth. And now, five months later, my greatest value to her—and to Hearn—was my resolve not to tell the whole truth. It had come to this: I had been allowed so far inside this story that I had learned more than I could handle as a reporter, and I had to decide whether I was a reporter or a human being.

So I called my confessor.

My confessor, as I had called him for decades, had been a full-fledged priest when he had finally left the Church. Francis Sampson was one of those guys with a strong moral center who never wanted to leave the Church and at the same time knew in his heart that he wanted to be married. Once he met the right woman, the Church went ahead in its brutally single-minded way and proceeded to take the decision out of his hands entirely. But Frank had refused to sign the final agreement that they try to force you to sign when you leave. He wanted to be a priest and he wanted to be a husband and the Church thought, with all the institutional blindness it could summon, that you had to choose. This conveniently ignored the fact that the first Pope, Saint Peter, had been married, along with lots of the other ones. But the hierarchy never let little facts like history or overpopulation or modern science stand in the way of its power drive.

So Frank and I had many talks over the years, sometimes about the Church, sometimes just work-talk. He had taught at Boston University for a long time, and was one of the nation's top experts on the criminal justice system. As we had gotten to know each other, I found him to be the most accepting person I had ever known, able to talk out personal stuff, including some mistakes I had made over the years, in a way that was absolving, whether or not he said "the words." So he was my confessor.

He listened, and he asked me how much I remembered about sins of omission and sins of commission, and listened some more, and then asked if I was ready to decide. I said not yet but that it had helped a lot to talk to him, as it always did. Because of his own history, Frank had a comfort level with choices that most people never acquire. Sometimes he had a sense of what I wanted to do before I wanted to do it.

But I still wanted to bounce the decision off one more person. Elena also had some of Frank's self-assurance with choices, but I wasn't sure Elena was the right place to get advice. We still disagreed about almost everything about the March, and yet I wanted to talk with her. So I called her.

CHAPTER 57

When I finally caught up with Elena, I told her the whole story about the kids. I had decided not to tell her what I had heard about Hearn—it was too close to her job, and we were already crossing the line with what we were doing.

For her, she was quiet—letting me tell the story to the finish without interrupting. I ended by saying "I trust you with this, Elena. I am telling you because it happened and I care about it and I care about you."

"So that's it—you're not going to use it, even if she recovers?"

"I can't. It's personal with her, and it has nothing to do with the March."

"Oh Sam, you are pathetic." She sighed, with what I thought was affection, in contrast to her belittling words. "It is the only thing you could do, wasn't it? You are who you are, you poor liberal dupe, and she has you in the palm of her hand."

She was insulting me in the worst way, and I wanted none of it. I mumbled something and got ready to hang up.

"No Sam, wait, I don't mean you are wrong." Her tone was more sad than angry now. "We are just too far apart. We are who we are, and this damn California-Mexico thing will always be there."

"Are you going to tell anyone? I trusted you."

She was silent for a long time. "No, Sam, I won't use it. It's your story. And I guess it's her story, too." She laughed, not happily. "I know how bad those macho bastards can be about Indian blood—I got some of that along the way, too." Then she was quiet again. "Ah, Sam, I just thought we could make it—I thought the politics wouldn't be as strong as it is. If it isn't this, it will be something else, won't it?"

It was my chance to argue with her, to tell her we would be OK, to tell her what we had was stronger than the other stuff. But I didn't believe it. I knew enough about who she was and who I was to know our differences would come up over and over. Politics matters, and it can become personal, and it can poison people's loves and lives. It takes trust away, and when trust is gone, both love and politics get badly ruined. So I said nothing, and then, after a while, she said goodbye.

CHAPTER 58

It turned out that Maria had some aces up her sleeve, which she began to play as soon as she came out of the anesthesia from the operation.

She had been shot once through the ribs, but the round had miraculously tumbled away from her body instead of into it. The Medevac crew and Ortega had stopped the loss of blood immediately, and she was out of danger. But she would be in the hospital for at least a week.

Roberto had been shot in the lower left thigh, but not straight on, a glancing impact, that was stitched up and healing well within days. He was using a cane, but otherwise irrepressible and as active as ever.

So Maria began framing her response to the Governor, knowing her bargaining power had increased. First, she had prepared a letter to the Governor with a copy to Disney threatening to occupy Disneyland—which would have affected gate receipts for months or even years. The letter simply said that there were many children with the March who wanted to visit the Park, but the threat was clear. This quickly cooled off the Mouse People's enthusiasm for harsh action against the March. Mike Humphrey at UCI heard that they left the Business Coalition high and dry, once they figured out that she could really do it.

Second, I learned later that Maria had also gotten word to Hearn indirectly that she was prepared to go back to the border to block it—which would have struck at both U.S. and Mexico trade revenues in ways that were intolerable to business people on both sides who had ready access to both governments.

Third, as soon as she regained consciousness, she gave Roberto a pre-arranged signal that sent her financial people into feverish activity. Early in the March, I had realized that there was a "financial RV" in which Isabel ran the money side of the March. In this RV, which had its own satellite system that monitored every major market in the world, daily cash draws from the main accounts of the March in Mexico City were carried out through electronic transfers to the banks in the major cities along the route. The financial team also managed the cash from this RV, moving money around the world with a 24-hour arbitrage operation.

The signal from Maria relayed through Roberto triggered a set of phone calls from Isabel and her crew to the twenty most important financial backers of the March, asking them for immediate cash. Within twelve hours, they had more than ten million in hand. What this guaranteed was that the March had the capacity to stay in Orange County for more than three months.

Finally, Maria played her last geographic card. She gave instructions that the March should move up fifteen miles to what she called a "semi-permanent encampment." She picked some of the most accessible land between San Diego and Los Angeles—the sites of the former El Toro and Tustin Air Bases, which were about seven miles apart—all within the city limits of Coniff.

The Navy had turned the sites over to the County, but it had been debating for years what to do with them, and the sites were still mostly empty. They made great campgrounds. In a final piece of irony, the largest part of the marchers settled into a site adjacent to the Tustin base that had been used as an encampment before—it was the site of the international Boy Scout Jamboree held in what were open fields in Orange County in the 1950's. They settled into this site along what had come to be called Jamboree Boulevard.

With all these pieces in place, Maria had done all she could to up the ante. Then it became a question of who was going to respond.

What happened next taught all of us something about California. No one knew how much support Maria and the marchers had while they were on the move, even with the food supplies and all the other help they had gotten. But from the moment the news flash went out about her getting shot, the whole picture began to change.

A friend who covered religious news told me some of it, since he had been in the group covering the confrontation between Cardinal Rivera and the Business Council. Apparently the Business Council had been holding a strategy meeting about the March every morning at the headquarters of the Coniff Company, with some in attendance and some on videophones.

As the meeting began on the morning of the shooting, the Cardinal walked in and basically invited himself to the meeting. He had alerted the press that covered him and they all marched into the meeting with him, to the great distress of the Coniff PR people.

"It's time to resolve this thing, Ron," the cardinal said briskly to Bent. "What are you going to do?"

Bent responded, "Can't you see that we have our hands tied, Your Eminence? This has gotten out of control now, just as we said it would."

"I agree it's out of control, but I think it may be your side that has lost it. What I see out there every day when the sun comes up is hundreds of thousands of people at altars praying to your God and mine, under the same cross we both revere. Now tell me, Ron, why is that a bad thing for California?"

Sputtering, Bent said "Now wait a minute, Cardinal. They started this by invading. We just want them to go home and leave us alone."

"You want them to go home and stop threatening your profits, Ron, and that just isn't what this is about. Not any more. Your hands aren't clean on this thing and neither are ours. And we're going to do something about it, whatever you say." He proceeded to chew Bent out so badly that Bent finally walked out of the meeting.

What had happened, as the Governor's staff explained to me later, was that the attempt on Maria's life had finally mobilized the latent support she had from the four groups that supported her in California—the Mexican-Americans, the evangelicals, the Catholic church, and the California Indians—both the rich ones and the other ones. These four groups had all been helping with food, but they hadn't yet come down on Maria's side. Many of them still hoped she would go home. But now they had become an intense minority ready to work for her demands, and it was more than any elected official could resist—it represented 30% of the voting public in California.

Page summed it up in one of my after-interviews. "She mobilized a basic truth of modern politics: you don't always need 51% to win. You need an intense minority of voters who care more about an issue than the majority. And she had that intense minority, energized when she got shot. She won, not by winning, but by coming close enough to convert a critical mass of Californians. People who had started out hoping she would succeed finally became willing to do something themselves so that she *could* succeed."

So it became loss-cutting time for everybody. As bad as the precedent was for giving in to the Marchers—even though the final settlement was a lot less than Maria had sought—the political and economic effects of waiting for the next crisis, hoping it would stay non-violent, were just too great a risk for Hearn and his backers to accept. Maria's final moves were powerful ones, but she wouldn't have gotten as much as she finally did if her shooting hadn't set in motion another set of forces that made it easier for Hearn to lead the negotiations in a positive direction.

Her supporters ranged from some very wealthy philanthropists who had stayed out of the March until they saw how it was going to go, to some very poor workers in California who knew exactly what they had at stake in Maria's success.

A friend of mine told me a wonderful story about walking into his office late one night after the March had crossed the border and seeing a cleaning woman leaning on her supply cart, holding a vacuum cleaner she had turned off, and watching a TV set that she had turned on in one of the offices. He told me, "She had tears running down her face, watching Maria and her people crossing the border. She kept saying, '*Mira, caminan con sus frentes en alto*—Look, their heads are held high.'"

CHAPTER 59

We were all waiting to see what happened when Maria got well enough to talk with the Governor. The marchers had settled in at the Tustin and El Toro sites, and they were being left alone for the time being.

So I invited Roberto and Isabel to come with me to the mall, as I again tried to get some sense of what the typical Southern Californian thought about the March. I thought their perspective on the interviews would be helpful.

It turned out to be a bad idea.

As we walked through the mall, seeing it through their eyes was even more painful than I had expected. Of course, both of them had traveled the world and had doubtless shopped in Harrod's and at Sak's Fifth Avenue and Nieman Marcus. They were not innocents just off the farm. But they had spent the last six months of their lives surrounded by families with very little, and the contrast was immense.

We walked slowly past the fronts of the stores, facing into the interior of the mall, huge palm trees growing under the skylights. The post-Christmas, post-New Year's sales were still on, and it was crowded. I went into a music store to buy some more tapes for my audio recorder, and came out to see the two of them staring into the windows of a toy store across the walkway. They were looking at an elaborate three-dimensional electronic train that filled the entire window. It was marvelous, reminding me of the three-foot circle of tracks and trains I had once had as a child.

The price was $8,000.

"Eight thousand for a toy." Isabel was shaking her head. "It's what we pay for a car. Who buys this?"

"The people who live in tract homes that cost a million and a half," I answered.

"Tract homes—you meant they build them all at once and they are all the same?"

"They are mostly the same—they have three or four different models."

"What a country." She wasn't angry; she knew enough about the U.S. economy to understand what fueled a retail center like this one. But she was feeling the contrast, too—we all were, and we all wanted out at the same time.

As we walked out to the car, Roberto asked me, "Sam, you grew up here, how do you feel about it?"

"I feel sad, sometimes, and the rest of the time I don't see it or think about it. I feel sad when I think about how many people in our culture define themselves by the labels on their cars and in their clothes."

Isabel replied, "What power—what unbelievable economic power." She laughed. "And I know damn well that nearly everyone camping over at El Toro, once they got over the shock of it, would love walking through those stores, and covet half of what they saw. That's sad, too."

As they were walking back to the car, I fell a step behind them to look for my car, and noticed that Roberto and Isabel were holding hands. Not wanting to disturb the moment, I waited until later to ask Roberto about it. He tried to play it lightly.

"Soon I'm going to be as old as you, Sam. Maybe it's time to settle down."

I hoped so, but I worried about it. Isabel was so strong, and I wondered if she would eventually toss Roberto aside for a more powerful connection. But I kept quiet.

As we came up to the car, I saw one of my least favorite sights and began cursing softly under my breath. Roberto heard me and said, "What are you so ticked off about now?"

I pointed to a shopping cart taking up the space next to our car. "I taught my daughter as she was growing up that there were really only two kinds of people: those that take their shopping carts back and those who just leave them in a parking space, blocking the next car. I believe that with a large grant I could prove that some kind of fundamental selfishness index could be developed and refined, just by sitting in a supermarket parking lot for an afternoon and watching who returns carts and who doesn't. It is such a unique act of egotism to leave your shopping cart in a parking space, rather than walk a few steps and put it where it goes."

Isabel laughed and said, "Poor Sam, you get upset by so much, and there is so little you can do about it."

She got that right.

CHAPTER 60

The Governor came to visit Maria in the hospital the day after the shooting. No one was in the room except José Robles, Roberto, and Jim Rose. I heard most of the details later that night from Jim and Roberto, since both sides wanted the full story to get out.

The Governor began. "I am glad to hear that you will recover. I hope you have heard about the action taken by General Walker and our own state troops yesterday. We do not want any more bloodshed. I am here to tell you we will negotiate seriously about your demands. I cannot commit the owners of the land, but I can commit to you that I will do everything in my power"—he paused—"including risking whether I can ever get re-elected to this job, to make sure that we respond to your followers with enough to justify their going home." He stopped and looked at her for a long time, then added, "But they must go home. Most of them must go home."

He went on. "I don't know if it's good politics or good humanity. But more people *are* going to get hurt on both sides, and it will be my fault no matter what I say or do. So I would rather take the flak for making a deal than take the flak for hanging tough and have more kids' deaths on my conscience."

She sank back into the pillows, showing how tense she had been before he finished what he had come to say. She responded, "Thank you, Governor." Then she smiled at him, and said, "Do you suppose this means I won't get to see the Matterhorn?"

The tension was broken, and the Governor even chuckled. "Miss Chavez, if it will help resolve this crisis, I will ride down that damn water slide with you myself."

Then, the guys inside the room told me, they began the first serious negotiating involving non-Anglos and Spanish land grants in California in over a century and a half. It took three days, and she was only able to talk for an hour at a time. But they carved out a deal which turned out to be a lot less than she wanted and a whole lot more than anybody in California officialdom ever thought they would have to give up.

From the very first, Hearn had insisted that she commit to leading "most" of the marchers back to the border, and she agreed, once the core of her other demands was met. So eventually would Hearn win, too—they went home, most of them. The pictures he needed were 900,000 people crossing the border going south, and that's what he finally got. The settlement was too complicated for most people to follow—they knew that some of the marchers were staying here, but that they are going to be spread out. As Hearn said more than once in the negotiations, "It's a big state, after all."

None of it was yet legally binding. But Hearn had committed to pressure the Coniff Company and the other landowners in Orange County to give her enough land for a new community of 100,000. He agreed to seek state legislation that would give Coniff partial tax relief for the land. In addition, the state would set up a jointly administered trust that would invest in economic development to create jobs, both for the residents of the new community and for the marchers who returned to Mexico, who would be resettled in three new economic development zones. The marchers who stayed to settle the new community would be those with U.S. resident status—Maria claimed that over 10% already did—and a lottery would be held if more than the hundred thousand wanted to stay.

The Coniff Company would be reimbursed by other land owners, including the state, for claimed land that would not become part of the new community. Hearn agreed to set up a commission to examine her claims, and Maria agreed that the value of the new land and the trust would be negotiated based on the percentage of each claim that could be substantiated—strong claims would get 100% of the amount she was claiming, the weakest ones would get only 10%, and so on. The Commission would include three appointees of the Governor and three appointees from statewide religious groups, and a two-thirds vote would be required for action.

The total value of the land and the trust over twenty years was estimated at $15 billion to $20 billion. In 2002, total U.S. direct investment in Mexico was only $25 billion in total, so the new funding was a lot of money. Hearn made clear that he was also going to use the 55-member California delegation in Congress to press for a portion of the aid to be made up from grants and loans from U.S. foreign aid.

As she had predicted, the Mexican stock market soared when word was released about the direct investment, and the World Bank team went home reasonably happy about Mexico's future prospects. That forced the Mexican government into reluctant support, and the leadership began trying to take credit for the settlement as if they had supported Maria all along. No one was fooled, but it meant that they would be forced to help with resettlement in the new economic zones that were being set up. The three new zones were to be created in Baja California, outside Guaymas, and further south in Michoacán.

In a master stroke that had been worked out by a team of Maria's economics advisors, all marchers and their families would then get shares in a cooperative venture that would cover a portion of the profits anticipated from all three sites.

A few weeks later, I heard Maria arguing for this scheme in a videodebate one morning with Robert Novak: "Now they have all become capitalists, Mr. Novak—isn't that what you want peasants to become? Isn't that the eternal promise of capitalism?"

A major part of the deal was a hole card that Maria had waited to play until the last day of the negotiations. Through her international philanthropic connections, she had been monitoring research by Israeli scientists on new techniques of desalinization. A major breakthrough had happened a few months before which had not yet been released to the public, which assured major new supplies of converted seawater that could be used for crops and industrial plants in the new economic development zones.

She had secured private grants from several major foundations to use the new desalinization techniques in each of the three zones. In a further economic coup, she had been granted the patents for use of the techniques in North America. Apparently there were two former classmates of hers in the Israeli Cabinet who were delighted to tweak the U.S. foreign policy establishment by taking this independent action.

On the last day of the negotiations, Maria played another card. I was allowed into this one, since Maria was feeling much better and had asked for me to come in. Hearn began the talks.

"All right, you said there was one big issue remaining. We're ready to talk about it, whatever it is. Where should we start?"

Maria smiled and motioned to Roberto. "Let me have the book, Roberto." He handed her a well-worn book.

At the sight of it, Hearn frowned and then started laughing, shaking his head. "You're not going to quote me against myself, are you?"

She had marked a passage in what was in fact the Governor's own book, his second history on the California governors of the late 20th century. "No one has said it better, Governor," Maria said

And then she read the quote she had marked.

> *None of these governors had ever sought to use one of the biggest economic tools at their disposal—the multi-billion dollar pension funds of the state. While governed by a separate board, the pension funds belonged to both the state's workers and its taxpayers. But no governor ever tried to use them for the good of the taxpayers—or any of the other citizens of the state except the workers.*

Hearn shook his head. "So this is about state investments? Is that where you are going?"

Maria answered, "That is part of it. Peter Drucker called it 'pension-fund socialism' long ago. I would *never* use the s-word," she was smiling broadly at this point, "but any time you have nearly 200 billion dollars of state money sitting somewhere, the question of where it is invested is both an economic and a political question—as you said in your book, Governor. We believe that these funds could be used to support housing for lower-income workers which would be paid for by their rent, the contributions of the growers, and those who buy their products. For a penny a tomato more, Governor, those funds could easily get at least the 7% return they now average."

Hearn smiled at her audacity. "We'll look at your numbers—that is the only commitment I can make now. That board is independent, but I know you've done your homework—you know I control several votes on that board. I could probably get a majority if I wanted to trade for some things people want. Some people would call it a smelly political deal, though."

Maria quickly responded. "We know some legislators and editorial writers who will call it leadership, Governor."

What Maria wanted was a second new community to be built in the Central Valley, outside Fresno, for migrant families and seniors among them. As the Governor had said, it was going to be up to the board of CalPERS, the mammoth, multibillion dollar pension fund that handled state employees and teachers' retirement money in California. It was the largest public sector real estate investor in the world, with a total of nearly $200 billion in investments, as Maria had noted. Although the Governor had agreed to start trying to move the votes, as they wrapped up the negotiations, the Valley site was still up in the air.

CHAPTER 61

After the main face-to-face negotiations had been concluded, Maria agreed to meet with me at the hospital to fill in some of the details. As I entered her room, I was surprised to see how good she looked, and I said so.

"Apparently being shot agrees with me, Sam. It seems to have helped, doesn't it?" And then she turned sadder, adding, "I only wish it could have happened before the gates at Pendleton, so the little ones would still be here."

I asked her to talk about the settlement from her side, and she went on for a long time, alternately serious and then lightening up as she told some of the more ironic pieces of the story.

"One of the hardest parts of the negotiations was between the Governor and the Coniff people," she explained, "once we made clear that the new community was going to be economically and racially integrated. The funny thing is that Coniff has done this better than almost anyplace in America in their planned communities, but they have been terrified to advertise it." She laughed. "They have been afraid the right wingers will call it social engineering—which of course is exactly what it is. They have been doing it for decades on their own land."

"I heard you got some ocean views," I teased her.

"You bet we did. They were going to give us the worst land they had, back up in the foothills where the cactus is thickest. But we had an old map from an old *Californio* manuscript talking about how close the sea is to the land. We ended up with some of the hundred-acre plots they were saving right next to Pelican Hill, where you can see Catalina almost every day. We will lease the land and sell the houses—isn't that how you do it here?"

She had gotten up out of bed and was looking out the window at the hospital parking lot, which opened out onto the Pacific Coast Highway. I knew she was looking at the hundreds of luxury boats in Newport Harbor. "You know, Sam, the Governor was right when he challenged me in our first meeting about the California land claims. This land," she motioned to the hills behind her and out to the Pacific, "has been stolen so many times it is hard to keep count. The people who walked here over the Bering Strait fifteen thousand years ago got here first, but that is only part of the claim—who lived here first. Then came what you call California Indians, then Spain, then the missions and the Church, then Mexico, then the *Californios*, then the California ranchers and then the developers. And now it is owned by development companies and the state and some—"she laughed, "even by the people who live in the houses on top of the land."

She shook her head and smiled sadly. "But in the end it is all so simple if we just remember that the land is God's and it is only ours for a little while by his grace."

"Hard way to run an economy, though," I said.

"Yes, it is."

"You have to admit, Maria, the Church mattered in this. You may not like the organized church, but the Cardinal came through on the right side in this one."

She nodded. "I agree, Sam. We needed them and they were a part of it. They are capable of so much good, Sam. It is not wrong to try to organize the doing of good—but it is all the rest of what they do—all the control games they play with women and the hierarchy. But you know that as well as I do, don't you?" She was smiling the sad smile, and it brought back, thankfully only for a moment, all the ache of leaving the Church.

"Yes, I do." Then I asked her, "How was the Governor to negotiate with?"

She looked over my shoulder and smiled. "Ask him." Hearn had come into the room for what would prove to be their final visit. I offered to leave, but both of them said I could stay.

By this time, I could see that they had developed a real respect for each other. It was careful respect, founded on more than talk, on hard negotiations and what Hearn had been able to deliver. But there was genuine liking, too, of the kind that adversaries sometimes develop when they have fought through a conflict with each other and emerged with something both sides needed.

The Governor, after asking how she was feeling, said "How are the preparations for the return going? You know that a lot of people are asking me how we can be sure they're going back. What should I tell them?"

Maria smiled, "The harder part will be getting some of them to stay. Do you think they would rather live here than where they know the land and the people? Do you think we want to stay here? It is about our families, not about your precious state, Governor."

She went on, "Of course we have terrible smog in Mexico City. But do you know what color the sky is in the mountains of the Sierra Maestra? It is not the dirty gray of what your newspapers call 'the Southland'"—she said the word almost pityingly—"in the winter smog. It is a blue you will never see in your life in this state, unless you are miles offshore and you are looking toward Asia. Why on earth would you think that people would want to come live under a dirty gray sky like this one if they did not have to do it to feed their families?"

She went on. "Let me tell you about some research done right here in universities in this county, Governor. They did surveys comparing Mexican families that had been in California for four generations with those that had only come within the last five or ten years. In every case—in *every* case—the ones who had been here *longest* had bigger problems with their children than those who had just come up. More drugs, more violence, more teen pregnancy, more suicide."

She paused, and the tone in her voice became sadder. "That is what your country does to my people. We know this is what happens—it is not a mystery. We do not need more studies to document it—you can see it in a hundred of our villages after you have been there an hour. The ones who have been Up North are the problems. And many, many of us do not want to be here one minute longer than we need to be here. It has been that way for more than a hundred years."

She stopped then, trying to find the words to make him see. Then she smiled. "The old saying may be exactly wrong, you know—we may be *much* further from the United States than from God."

Shaking his head at her passion, the Governor said "You know our history better than most of us do."

"It is history from the bottom, Governor. History as the people live it, not as the winners tell the story after."

Hearn nodded. Then he got a mock-irritated look "You pulled one on me with that desalinization stuff, didn't you."

José Robles was in the room by then, and she motioned to him. "Show them the poster, José." He pulled out a poster which I had seen all over Israel. It was divided into two halves—a desert on one side and gardens on the other—only the point is it is *all* in the desert, and the gardens are on the side with water. "They have been working at this for half a century, Governor, and they have finally made the breakthrough. We will make the desert grow, just as they have. Water and information are the only commodities that really matter in the 21st century—and that is as true of California as it is of Mexico."

The Governor briefed her on the progress with the state legislation on the trust they were setting up. "I have had some trouble with the cavedwellers on the 50-50 split of the trustees, but I told them you had insisted, and I pointed out that there were still a lot of people camped out there and their districts were not that far way. I also heard this morning that the CalPERS votes are looking good for the Valley site. I may have to appoint a few lightweight egomaniacs to state commissions to firm up two of the votes, but that goes with the job. How are your own investment plans going?"

"We have lined up forty major investors from several countries, Israelis, Taiwanese, Japanese, Europeans, and even some moderate Iranians." I remembered Roberto telling me about the networks of rich foreign students she had begun to cultivate at UCLA, and I assumed the data bases had been at work again.

"I am going to have an interesting time explaining Iranians with bases a few hundred miles from our borders," the Governor commented with a frown.

"Not bases, Governor, factories and agribusineses producing jobs. Your businessmen have been telling us for years what a good thing it is to have factories on our side of the border. Under the right conditions, we agree. But why should American investors be the only ones who put money into such businesses? And with NAFTA, those businesses would be an easy drive from one of the biggest markets in the world."

She smiled, less beatifically this time and more slyly. "Isn't that what it means to have a global economy?"

"Will you let UN inspectors in to make sure that they are only producing peaceful products?"

"I certainly would, but you will need to take that up with the Government in Mexico City." She turned serious. "I am trusting your promises, Governor, but I cannot trust theirs—and you should not, either."

"Why do you think my promises are worth trusting?"

She answered quickly. "I think they are worth more than those of the people around you. I would not have believed most of them if *they* had made the promises. But I have studied you for a long time—you were an important part of this."

"You thought I would bend?" He was nearly angry again, as much as he had come to respect her.

"I thought you were *just*. I was mostly right." Then she looked at him with the hard look again. "By now you know that if we must, we will come back." She said it quietly, controlled, looking him straight in the eyes.

"I know. And you know it may be harder to control what started to happen here."

"Governor, no matter what we do, there is no other border on the planet that has so many wealthy people living so near to so many have-nots. The 21st century will be about the people of the South using their bodies to seek justice—sometimes peacefully, sometimes with brutal force. Their bodies are all that they have, and so they will use them to get food for their children."

I spoke up, recalling one of our conversations along the March. "*Dona nobis panem.*"

Maria answered, "Yes—*panem* or rice and beans—something to feed their children. So Governor, know that the big causes of it all have not changed. We have bought some time, and we have shown that justice is possible. But there will be many on both sides of the border who will want a different outcome. So we may need to come back."

Trying to soften the hard words, she smiled the best of her smiles, 200 watts worth, and said "Remember, you never got to show me the Matterhorn."

As the Governor began to get up to leave, I asked her "What are you going to call the new town here in Orange County?"

She smiled. "We are not sure what we will call it. The names that people have been talking about are Sepulveda or Santiago or Pio Pico or Nahua or Aztlan or Murrieta—after the honest cowboy your land grant thieves hung as an outlaw. Many of our group lean toward Murrieta, however. However it seems there is already a town over on the other side of those mountains," she gestured to the southeast, "named Murrieta already. We were surprised that you would name a town after an outlaw—perhaps he was more than that."

She was really going now, full of laughter that had not yet spilled over but threatened. It was remarkable to see this side of her—the near-laughter, the teasing, really, that showed both how angry she still was and how right she thought she was, but that she could laugh at all of us and not just scream at us.

The Governor asked her, "What do you do next? Where will you go?"

She was quiet for a moment, then answered, "I have to go back with them. I cannot stay here. I want to see my children again"—they had clearly talked about it privately while they were negotiating in the hospital, "and then we will head back."

She was now in a more reflective mood. "In a way, Governor, we leaders lost. If we are doing our job right, we always lose something because we have to make a deal. It is the people who came with us, those of the land, the least of us, who will go on and maybe make something of this. They will win, and that is enough. It is more than enough. It makes it worth the walk."

She turned to me. "Remember the plaque in the Plaza in Mexico City, Sam? 'It was neither a triumph nor a defeat.' Same here, but maybe—just maybe—the beginning of a new bond between California and Mexico that will in the long run be good for us both."

The Governor spoke up. "Maria, can I ask you something? Have you learned anything from all of this that you didn't know before—or was it all clear when you started out?" It was the Governor as historian again, not elected pol, wanting to get the factors right.

Maria looked serious, taking the question as it was intended. "The main thing I guess I know better than before is that the motives change and people change sides, sometimes. Bad guys can be the good guys, sometimes. So don't ever write anybody off forever. That is what diplomacy is about, as I read it." Looking at me, she added, "And in a very different way, that is part of what Christianity is about, too."

Trying to understand what she was saying, I mused, "I used to have this refrain with my daughter when we would watch movies. I would say 'but he turned out to be a good guy in the end.' So she wouldn't always be scared of the villains. Like the woodsman in Snow White who took her out to the forest and then let her go. Not everybody turns out to be a good guy, but you want kids to believe that some of them can."

Nodding, she said "And some of them *can*, Sam. The picture of what the marines did after I was shot is as important to telling this story as the picture of the little ones who were killed."

She went on. "You have a great journalist in this country, Dan Schorr, and I heard a broadcast of his the other day. He said the one thing that is hardest to sell to the American people is ambiguity. And he was right. But that is what we are selling finally, and I think maybe we sold some of it here."

Hearn smiled, and said "Well, I'm not sure who was selling and who was buying. But ambiguity we have, and on most days I think it beats those cold polar extremes that the left and right wing jerks try to serve up. Ambiguity—I'll take some of that."

"With hot sauce?" she teased him.

"Red, not green," he answered with a smile.

CHAPTER 62

I last saw Maria at her temporary camp in a big vacant field off the 405 freeway just north of the intersection of the 5 and the 405 freeways in Lake Forest. She had agreed to a wrapup interview between finishing her negotiations with the Coniff Company representatives and preparing for the first wave of marchers to return home.

Before I met with her I wandered around the camp doing a few interviews with marchers. I found a group of young men I had interviewed on the way up who were part of a church group from Jalisco. They were still marveling at what they had seen in Southern California.

"Do you see how these people live, Señor Leonard? Their houses are all the same two colors, that funny greeny brown or a brownish green. And many of the houses are the same size and shape, too. They are all in rows, with no trees, not like a proper village where some of the houses are over here and some are over there. My cousin works for a gardening company and they go in and mow the lawns and cut the bushes and trim the flowers, and get paid for it, because the people who live there do not want to do that kind of work. It is so strange, the way they live."

Another continued, "And someone told me that the average house here in this area costs 2 and a half million pesos! Imagine—2 and a half million pesos—and that is only the average. Some must cost much more than that."

The first young man went on. "And they have to use their cars to get anywhere. They can't just walk to the village to get their food at the store. They have to drive in these big cars and park and walk into the store and then carry all this food out. One car like that takes more gas than five of our cars. Their cars are like buses!"

Another spoke up. "And did you notice they all have these *Mexican* names for these big cars? Durango and Montana and Sierra and names like that! One is even called *Aztec*!"

I asked them if they thought the long walk had been worth what they had gotten. The first young man quickly answered.

"Oh yes, we showed that we were not afraid, we showed them that we are nearer than they want to think about and that we must be treated with justice. It was definitely worth the walk—but I am glad I will not be part of the group that is staying here. I am ready to go home."

I went on further into the camp and did other interviews that morning. One of the interviews was especially memorable and ran on most of the NPR broadcasts that week. I had met the father of one of the little girls who was killed at the Pendleton gate and I located him again and asked if he was willing to give me an interview. He agreed, and I began by telling him how sorry I was about his loss and then asking him what his own plans were.

"I will be returning with my wife and other two children to our village in Oaxaca, where we will bury Lupita. Then I hope to get a job at the factory Maria will be building in Michoacán."

Apologizing for the question, I asked him the obvious. "And do you think this was worth the death of your daughter?"

The sadness in his eyes made me wish I had let my decency overcome my journalistic instinct. But he nodded and said "I have thought about that many times, Señor Leonard. We will always grieve for her—she was the happiest of our children. Nothing can replace her, ever. But my wife and I have agreed that Lupita was sacrificed for a big enough thing. It was a very powerful thing that happened when she was killed, it showed people here that we were peaceful and that we were trying to find a better life for our children, just as they are."

He looked back toward the south, where it had happened. "Do you remember the name of the road where it happened, Señor? Los Christanitos? It is a memory to the little ones who were baptized there hundreds of years ago, I know. But we also think of it now as a memory to Lupita and the other little girl who was killed there. Las Christianitas, they were, Las Dos Christianitas. And they gave their lives so that many more could have their needs better understood." He paused and looked at me hopefully. "Don't you think that is how they will be remembered?"

All I could say was "It is how they should be remembered. I will do what I can to tell their story, Señor. Thank you for talking to me."

I found my way to Maria's RV, and she motioned me inside. I told her who I had been interviewing and she fell silent. Then she said "It will never be enough, I think. We could work our whole lives, we could get hundreds of thousands of new jobs—and it would never be enough. All we can do is honor her and remember her and watch over her family the best that we can."

I asked her how soon they would be leaving.

"Roberto and Hugo and Isabel will stay here to begin the construction planning for the new town. I will go with the first wave of 100,000—we have agreed that the groups will move back into Mexico in waves of 100,000, leaving a week apart. The State will feed the rest while they remain here. We even offered to pick some of their winter crops to pay for the food—"she smiled, "but the irony of doing what thousands of these people do every year and doing it as part of the deal seemed to escape the Governor's negotiating team."

"How is the deal going down with the marchers?"

"Better than I expected. The fact of it is—" she frowned and looked away, "they trust me—probably more than they should trust anyone. I am worried about that part. I've got to work harder at letting our Council become more visible so it is not all personalized in me."

She turned to some of the papers on her desk, and pulled one out. "This is the latest working estimate of what we got. It is far more jobs than we originally thought. It is up to 450,000 jobs over the next five years in all three locations, and if the Valley site for the second new town comes through, we'll go over a half million. That's almost as many workers as we have on the March."

Wanting to tell her what I thought, but trying not to cross over the line again, I said "So you won."

She shook her head. "We didn't need to win, Sam, we needed to show up. Once I read a quote from Woody Allen or somebody, who said 90% of life is showing up. That's all we did."

I laughed. "Yeah, but Woody Allen never mentioned the million people."

Then she put the paper down and sat in her chair, pulling it over so it almost touched mine. "Sam, I want to say something to you."

Trying to deflect her serious tone, I said "We're still on the record, right?"

She shook her head. "This is personal, not journalism or history. I know you think that sometimes I made compromises that went over the line. We had to do what we did, and you have to write what you want to write. Write whatever you want about me, but please, I am asking you now what I have never asked you for in your coverage—do not write anything that would make these people" she gestured to the camp outside "feel bad about what they have done."

"You know I can't make that promise, Maria," I answered, but went on. "You also know that I have great respect for what they did. I will keep writing about that as long as the story needs to be told. You said it when we first met—they came in peace for justice. The real story was that it stayed peaceful on your side, and that you got some of the justice. That is how I will write it."

"That is good enough, Sam. Thank you. And thank you for being my friend on the March and letting me talk to you at the end of those many days and for letting me get mad at you sometimes."

I admired her greatly, I felt manipulated by her, but at the same time, the quiet evening wind-downs we had together had built a bond between us that was more than friendship or admiration.

"Sam, you know, in another life, we could have been wonderful together." Her eyes filled with tears, and for a moment I got a glimpse of how much she may have wanted a normal life, walking quietly on the smaller stage of family and friends.

"We have been wonderful together, Maria. I have loved being with you and the time you have given me."

"Thank you, Sam. But you know what I meant."

I did, and the possibility of what might have been brought an ache.

She changed the subject, talking for a moment about the return, and then said, sadly, "I will miss you, Sam." And then she got a look on her face that was almost mischievous. "You know our sources are very good, Sam. So what is this I hear about you and a right wing Latina on the Governor's staff?"

I told her it was over, and I guess she could tell I felt lousy about it.

"I hope you find someone, Sam—you deserve someone." Then she stepped forward and hugged me, "*Gracias para todo, mi amigo. Vaya con Dios.*"

"*Vaya con Dios*, Maria." And I walked out as quickly as I could, given my tears. One thing more the woman had given me: I cried without shame at the thought of not seeing her again.

CHAPTER 63

I arranged a wrapup interview with Hearn about three weeks after the last of the marchers had crossed the border heading south. The planning for the new town was going well, with Isabel Salinas, Hugo, and Roberto in charge, and the Governor had gotten all but a few pieces of his package through the legislature. The feds were balking at some of the foreign aid pieces of the deal, but Hearn had kept most of the California congressional delegation in line and they were holding out on some votes the federal administration wanted, so it looked like the final pieces would fall in place.

As we sat talking later that afternoon in his office in the Capitol, I could see that the Governor was very reflective this time, clearly wanting to muse about what it all meant. He sat low in the softer chair over by the fireplace, looking out the window at the State Capitol grounds.

"Sam, what if this *is* just the first of these things—what she calls 'the people of the South walking North?' What if 2 million people from the Sahel decide to go to France, rowing inflatables they buy with Libyan oil money? What if China sends 5 or 10 million people into North and South Korea on their way to Japan?"

He shook his head. "Maybe we are the first ones to have to deal with it, and maybe we did it right. Or maybe none of this matters and some hardliners will just decide that's what the neutron bomb was invented for—take out the people and leave the property."

I decided I had an opinion at that point. "The hard line just won't work, Governor. The numbers just won't work. Set aside the morality of it, if you can. It doesn't make sense in any other way, either. The raw power it would take to hold the line, and the terror that would build up as a backlash, would make the 20th century look like Sunday School."

He looked at me, hard. "You're right—but only if there is a 21st century standard of morality that comes anywhere near the best of the last two thousand years. But if it isn't there and we go back to the last days of Rome—I don't know. I just don't know."

"Sam, I've done a lot of thinking about this. What we can't escape is that the numbers are so obvious. I wonder why there isn't a congressional committee tearing its few remaining hairs out every day of the year, frantic about it. It's simple: there are 300 million or so of us and 4 billion or so of them, those who have so little. And most of them know what we have—and what they don't."

I asked him, "So it's not Maria's question—how do you stop a million people? It's how do you stop 4 billion?"

He continued, his voice intense and strained. "All they need to do is start walking. And when they get here, we need to remember those little girls at the gates at Pendleton. How much do we want to multiply them by? And then, finally, we will have to decide what kind of a country we really are." He shook his head, frowning. "It could be tougher than anything we have done since Valley Forge and the Civil War—it may come that close to ending whatever we have been—and whatever we could still become."

He looked out the window at the Capitol grounds. "And maybe Maria has done us an immense favor by showing us early on what's going to happen. Maybe she has given us the wakeup call we needed."

He went on. "You know, she would probably never admit it, but she was like Gandhi in another way. He went up against a more humane nation than most colonial powers. If she had been up against the Russians or the Iraqis under Saddam or the Turks—or even the average Latin American government—it would have been a lot tougher. Most of them would have had a very simple answer to her question 'how do you stop a million people?' It would have been 'you mow down the first thousand with automatic weapons, and the rest get the message.'"

"Governor, are you saying it helps to have Anglo-Saxons on the other side?"

"Something like that."

I couldn't let it stand, not because I disagreed, but because the counterpoint was so obvious. "I can think of about two million North and South Vietnamese who would disagree with that point. Maria used to talk about that a lot. She said it was so ironic, we believed in *annihilation*—the Pilgrim way, the cowboy way—while Mexico was all about *assimilation*—the melting pot that *our* politicians always talked about. She said the Anglo-Saxon way was to kill whoever got in the way, while the Spaniards preferred to sleep with them."

He smiled. "Maybe. But this was a peaceful march, Sam. If that is what we are facing—they are going to win something each time. It will be much harder to resist them as long as we are a media democracy. You can't kill unarmed demonstrators live on CNN and then pretend to be a moral superpower."

Then he looked at me as if he wanted to make sure I got the point as a journalist. "The other thing I think a lot about is that it wasn't just her population blackmail, as some of her detractors still call it. It was also those bond raters sitting in Mexico City and those scientists in Israel. And Cardinal Rivera getting into it and my having the extra votes on the CalPERS board. It took more than a million bodies crossing our border to put this together. She knew where a lot of the pieces were, but she needed help putting them together."

I agreed, but thought he was missing some pieces. "It was also what didn't happen, Governor. The March never turned into an angry mob after she was shot, and your troops never used heavy weapons against them."

He nodded, then he chuckled. "But she really had the angles figured out. This thing started to get settled when she got shot, but in a way it was preordained once the bond raters scheduled their trip to Mexico City."

"I'm an historian, Sam. She kept telling me that, and she made me think harder about some of it. The two original sins of this country were slavery and the genocide we aimed at the first Americans. I don't think a great country gets three chances to screw itself up. And immigration—who we decide to let into this country—is turning into the third chapter. We've got to get it better than we did the first two."

He shook his head, frowning. "You can't be this wealthy while they"—he gestured south—"are that poor. You just can't expect to keep all those people out forever. Most of us have so much, and most of them have so little, and they are so close. They get our TV, they know how we live. And there are a hundred million of them, with twenty million of them within two hours of the border."

"It's not about which of them we let in. It's about what we do to make it less necessary for them to try to get in. Our economy is the vacuum they try to fill; their own still can't hold enough of them. We need a richer Mexico, Sam, and one that's a hell of a lot fairer, while they're at it."

He went on. "They may throw me out of here next time, they may decide this worked out fine. The polls are all over the place. But she had a solid group of voters with her at the end, and it was the right thing to do." He smiled, putting his hands behind his head and leaning back.

"There may be a new kind of political leadership in this country, Sam. When we are spending a billion dollars a day on military power and a few million on roads and water and schools for the rest of the world, sooner or later somebody is going to turn that into a political issue that works. It's what Roosevelt had to do when most Americans wanted to stay out of World War II. It's getting ahead of public opinion and reshaping it—transforming it and not just being blown around by it. Joe Nye at Harvard calls it "soft power," and he and a lot of other smart guys think it matters more to our future than the hard kind. It's what I might try to do next after I finish this job. And maybe we learned enough from Maria to convince some more people that it's a job worth doing."

Seeing he had wrapped up, I thanked him for the final interview and turned to leave.

"What are you going to do now, Sam?" he asked.

"I don't know. Get away from it for a while and head into the Sierras. I saw so much of their mountains, I want to see ours for a while."

He smiled. "Yeah. Good idea." Then he got what would have been called a twinkle in his eye if he had been thirty years younger. "You know, they say their mountains *are* our mountains—the Sierras just roll on down and become their Sierras. Geologically, it all runs together, doesn't it."

"Sure does, Governor." I gave him the last word. Politicians love it—and historians demand it.

CHAPTER 64

I finished talking with Sophia and fell silent. We had closed the restaurant in Oakland and moved across the street to a coffee shop.

"So that's the story."

"That's the part I saw or heard about."

"And what is she doing now?"

"They say she may run for Governor of Michoacán, but I don't think so. It would confine her too much. In the last three years, she has raised more than $10 billion in investment and over $150 million in private foundation funds for projects in the three new regions. She goes to New York and the big foundations pull out their checkbooks the minute she walks in the room." I laughed. "Liberal guilt is such a wonderful thing when it comes attached to large piles of old money, don't you think? She really has people listening when she talks about Gandhi versus Bin Laden."

"What about her kids?"

"That's the sad part. I heard from Roberto a few weeks ago. Eduardo refused to let her see either one of them. But José had gotten a call from her daughter, who had snuck off to a mall with some of her friends. She was asking if she could meet Maria somewhere. So maybe she will be able to see her, at least. And someday she may be tough enough and free enough to go see what life with Maria would be like, out of the cocoon of Orange County."

She smiled. "And how do you *feel* about all of it now, Sam?"

I laughed. It was code—she had been at me for decades, asking me to talk about my feelings when all I knew how to talk about was what I had written about other people's actions and what I *thought* about it.

"I'm not sure. I guess I *feel* that it made a big difference to California. And"—seeing her getting ready to object because I was doing journalism instead of emotion—"I *feel* that I let myself get into the story too far."

"That's why she picked you, Sam."

"I know. But how do you deserve that and still do your job?"

"You don't. You've forgotten the seminary part of yourself, Sam. It's called grace—you don't deserve it. You just get it."

"Maybe. The stories I wrote got me a Pulitzer, and I'm not ashamed of that. I worked hard, it was a long haul, and I let the voices of the people on the March and in California tell a big part of the story. It took hard work to get all of those voices."

I paused, thinking about it. "But the stories I didn't write made me a better human being. And I've come to think that was as important as the Prize. I'm at peace with that—with what I chose. I know Maria and the Governor letting me inside was a big part of what I was able to do. But I don't think the stories I passed up were what it was all about."

"Sherlock Holmes, huh?"

I laughed. We had a running joke in college about what didn't happen between us, and once she put it in terms of the famous Sherlock Holmes story about the dog that didn't bark. Not barking was the clue to the case. It got to be a shorthand way of referring to things that didn't happen—and how they were sometimes the most important things of all.

"Yeah—Sherlock Holmes." I went on. "Sophia, what I didn't write was probably the most important part of my story of the March. What I didn't write were acts of omission. In the Church, we used to talk about sins of omission and sins of commission. And the things left undone were sometimes as bad as the bad things people actually did."

I took her hand, wanting her to understand. "But here, maybe, what I left out was what I did *best*. It's hard to admit for a writer—you want what you put *in* to matter, and you dig for it and pry it loose and set it down in your own story. And you don't want what you left out to matter more than what you put in. But not writing about what the Governor had set in motion without knowing it, and not writing about Maria's kids, were acts of omission. They had both made mistakes, and for me to tell the whole truth, I had to tell about their mistakes. But then I made myself judge, and judged that they meant no harm—that the harm done was ultimately not their fault."

"And?" Sophia could tell that there was more.

"And if I had written about their mistakes, the outcome could have been different. Either Hearn or Maria could have lost control, and by that time I believed they were the only ones who could make this work out without a lot more bloodshed."

"So you got in the story, you decided what you were going to tell and not tell, because you were afraid if you wrote it all, worse things would happen."

"Yes."

"Then you acted on your feelings, you hung-up, repressed guy—and you also did the right thing."

Maybe Sophia was right. But either way, what happened and what didn't happen would be argued about for a long time in California. Though it might be a shorter time—if Maria came back.

Afterword

Careful viewers of the classic film "The Magnificent Seven," part of which was filmed near where the March began, will recognize my debt to the film's writers and adapters at a few points. I have slightly altered the geography of Southern California for dramatic purposes.

There are many books about Mexico that have helped make up my curriculum for learning about this extraordinary nation whose destiny is an inevitable part of ours. Notable among them are *Days of Obligation*, by Richard Rodriguez, *Strangers Among Us*, by Roberto Suro, *Friends or Strangers*, by George Borjas, *The History of Alta California*, by Antonio Maria Osio, *Shadowed Lives*, by Leo Chavez, *The Mexican Shock*, by Jorge Castañeda, *Californios*, by Jo Mora, *The Crystal Frontier*, by Carlos Fuentes, and the incomparable *The Labyrinth of Solitude*, by Octavio Paz. I am also grateful to the Chilean poet Pablo Neruda, whose poem, "The Potter" is the source of the title and the phrase "together we are complete, like a single river."

The novels of two Californians with giant footsteps who went on ahead, Frank Norris and Upton Sinclair, gave me hope that themes of California and justice could be combined in fiction a century after they wrote.

I want to thank the remarkable San Antonio based singing group San Antonio Vocal Arts Ensemble (SAVAE), whose recordings of Nahuatl songs and songs to the Virgin of Guadalupe often formed the background music to my writing. Linda Ronstadt's *Canciones* albums and Johann Sebastian Bach helped, too.

Sid Gardner
May 2004
Irvine, California

0-595-31544-5